MARY, THE BOOKKEEPER'S DAUGHTER

CRYSTAL CREEK MONTANA SERIES

MARTHA LINDSAY

MARTHALINDSAY.COM

To my loving parents, Nonja and Tuan, who taught me to appreciate the diversity of life and to never judge a book by its cover.

CHAPTER 1

Philadelphia, Pennsylvania — May 1882.

Closing the heavy oak door behind her, Mary's mother Sarah Schulman rushed across the parquet floor to her daughter. The noise from the door latch closing resonated throughout the chamber. Startled, Rachel Conroy stopped checking the hairpins in Mary's hair. Mary's body tensed as a chill swept over her. She could see her mother's eyes tearing as she came to a stop in front of her.

"I am so sorry, dear. Robert's cousin Harley just told your father and I that Robert is not coming," her mother blurted out, wiping away the tear on her cheek.

"Wh — what do you mean he's not coming?" Mary asked, her voice trembling as she spoke. "WHY? Has there been an accident? Is he hurt? What has happened to him?" she implored, barely able to get the words out of her mouth.

Robert Cornell was not the most punctual of people. Nor, come to think of it, was he the most thoughtful. However, this was their wedding day! Mary's throat tightened. An uncomfortable feeling settled within her. *I saw him yesterday. He said nothing that would lead me to believe he was changing his mind about getting married.... Was there something I missed?*

Distraught, a wave of nausea began to overtake Mary. She leaned forward. Within a moment Mary's mind went blank. Exhaling, she paused finding it hard to get in the next breath. Panic gripped her. Unable to breath, her eyes began to well up. Trying to hold back the tears, Mary looked up to see the ceiling spinning. She slumped to the floor in a crumpled heap of white satin and lace. The room went dark.

Waking up to a pungent odor, Mary opened her eyes. She drew back to see a blurry vision of her mother holding a vial of smelling salts. She took a deep breath and recognized her corset had been loosened.

"Oh, thank goodness. She is finally waking up," whispered Rachel.

A hot pain shot from the back of Mary's head, she cringed and blinked again. "What happened?"

A frown appeared on her mother's face. "You fainted. How are you feeling, dear? You gave us quite a fright."

Mary saw the worry lines on her mother's forehead. Gradually the room came into focus. "I NEVER faint," she announced. But the throbbing in her head suggested otherwise. Mary winced. "Why is Robert not coming?"

Sarah and Rachel helped Mary into the nearby chair.

Mary reached up to feel her head. A low moan slipped through her lips. She looked to her mother for any kind of an answer.

Tears glistened in Mrs. Schulman's eyes. She grasped her daughter's hand and whispered, "No one here knows why, or at least they are not saying. I am so sorry, my dear," her mother wiped away more tears.

Mary was stunned. *They said he is not coming. But, why? Why? How could he do this to me?* Her mind struggled searching for possible answers. Tears streamed down her cheeks.

Anxious yet patient, she had waited in the anteroom for over two hours. Enough time to become aware of every sound. Earlier the church had been almost quiet with only the low murmur of voices and music softly playing in the background.

Now, she could hear the guests talking loudly, their words echoing through the half-open door. Rachel stepped closer to Mary's side and rubbed the small of her back. As thoughtful as the gesture was, it did not dissolve the large dark pit in her stomach. *All those guests – what am I to do?* Taking a hankie from the sleeve of her dress, Mary wiped away the tears. She tried to slow the spinning of her mind by studying the embroidery of her wedding dress, as if the answer could be found there. It did not help.

Distress clouded her mother's face. Looking into Mary's eyes, "Your father and I will ask everyone to please leave the church. This way, we can avoid any initial questions," her mother said reassuringly.

Sarah released her daughter's hands and hurried towards the door. Pushing her hair away from her face, her mother composed herself before exiting. Mary's chest tightened. With her mother gone, she couldn't control the sobs.

Rachel pulled a chair up close to Mary and putting her arms around her. She whispered, "I'm sure he is safe. Perhaps, he is just nervous? You should go back home and rest. We will know more tomorrow."

Shivering, Mary felt the tall ceiling closing in on her. The room became smaller and much colder. "But he said he was looking forward to today." She brushed away her salty tears. "Do you think the wedding was too big? I know he preferred a smaller affair."

Rachel reached out and held Mary's hands in her own. "Only he knows for certain. We need to look forward, not back. Tomorrow will be a new day. Let's get you ready to leave."

Mary stepped out into the aisle. The pews were now empty of wedding guests. The sun had slipped down behind the large stained-glass window. Only the Reverend remained, and he was putting out the candle lights.

Watching the Reverend put out the last candle, Mary felt her future die with the flame. Walking past the flowers decorating the end of the pews, their fragrance was no longer sweet. Rachel gave a light tug to Mary's arm and ushered her forward.

Outside the church, Mary stopped to hug her dear friend good-bye. Rachel and her family solemnly stepped forward and gave Mary a kiss on the cheek.

Hurrying down the steps to the waiting hack on the street, Mary tried very hard not to make eye contact with the few remaining guests lingering outside the church. She entered her family's carriage, and a wave of embarrassment engulfed her. With a face that looked ten years older, her father reached over and patted her hand offering an apologetic smile. Mary nodded and turned to look out the window opposite the church. *How pathetic I must look, a bride in a wedding dress leaving the church without a groom.* Mary felt her silent tears begin to trickle down her cheeks.

Everyone rode back home in silence. All throughout the ride, Mary tried to slump down in her seat hoping to become invisible. Finally reaching the house, she rushed upstairs to her room and slammed the door shut.

Once inside her bedroom, she looked down at her dress. *I have to get out of this horrid dress.* It was meant to commemorate her happiest of days. Now it only reminded her of Robert. She sobbed again.

A little while later, a light knock sounded at her bedroom door. Mary lifted her head from the pillow, "Yes?"

Opening the door, her mother quietly walked in the room. "Can I bring you some supper, dear?"

Her mother's smile was a comfort, but Mary's stomach was still churning. "No Mama. I just want to be alone for now." Mary hoped the words did not disclose the depth of her anguish. "Has any word come from Robert, yet?"

"No dear, not yet. I'm sure there will be some word, perhaps in the morning?" her mother uttered softly.

Mary's shoulders slumped. She didn't reply.

"I will be downstairs if you want to talk." Her mother gently closed the bedroom door. Mary heard her footsteps trail off down the hallway and descend the stairs.

Like bees in a hive, Mary's thoughts buzzed around in her head. Her mind went over her most recent days with Robert. *What was it I missed? Was it something I did? Or didn't do? Why is this happening?* Answers eluded her, and she could only think of more questions.

Making preparations for bed, she tried to erase her despair. Her father had always told her, 'there's always tomorrow.' She could only learn the truth after talking to Robert.

THE SMELLS OF BACON AND COFFEE IN THE HALLWAY ALERTED Mary that she was not the first one up. Rounding the corner into the kitchen, she heard her mother's voice.

"What would you like for breakfast? You must eat something, dear. You ate less than a mouse yesterday."

Mary sighed. "Just some toast and tea would be fine, thank you." She was feeling exasperated with having to wait for an answer as to why Robert had not shown up at their wedding. And foolishly she hoped he would have shown up on her doorstep earlier. A nagging feeling of dread filled her.

She walked over to the table and picked up the teapot. "Mother, I am so sorry about yesterday. It was so humiliating for everyone — not to mention the wasted expense of the wedding breakfast. I had no idea Robert was not ready for the wedding." Her voice strained while her eyes glistened as she spoke.

"Don't worry about a thing, my dear. We will be just fine. None of this is your fault. The responsibility lies with Robert. You did nothing wrong, and I don't want to hear any further talk about it. You are a wonderful young lady, and he would be the luckiest man to have you as his wife. If he's too daft to see that, then he doesn't deserve you." Taking the sizzling bacon out of the frying pan, she continued. "I truly thought those Cornels' raised a brighter son than that."

"Mother, why haven't I heard something by now? Robert owes me an explanation!" Mary's voice changed to an angry tone with each word becoming more distinct than the last. "Should I send word to him that we NEED to talk?" Mary paused and poured her tea into a cup.

Her mother placed the plate with the bacon and toast on the table beside an assortment of blueberry scones and other goodies. Coming to a full stop, she turned to face her. "Let him make the first move; it is best you wait till then. This mess is of his making."

She is correct. I should wait. Mary looked down at her teacup on the table. The old saying – 'patience is a virtue' was wearing very thin for her. Reaching over to the plate of toast, she took a slice. Nibbling, she thought of how to bide her time. Considering her present mood, she knew it was best to go to her bedroom. Lumbering forward, she could hear her grandmother's voice, 'Now, Mary, a proper lady must be patient.' *Well, I have been patient -- two years patient! And, look what it got me?* Every time Robert had told her he needed to make more money so that he could afford to buy her the best house, she had been patient. She was sick of being patient. She just wanted to go somewhere and scream, but there was nowhere to go. And even if she could find a place, it would be just her luck for someone to see her, thus, adding more fuel to the gossip fire. Last but not least, it would not be a lady-like. She let out a long sigh. Knowing she had to do some-thing, she considered attempting to read or doing needlepoint. However, for the moment, she settled for keeping her cup of tea and plate of toast steady as she mounted the stairs.

A LITTLE AFTER TEN THE SAME MORNING, A SOFT KNOCK WAS heard on Mary's door.

"Mary, it's me."

She knew that voice anywhere. Rushing over to the door, she jerked it open and hugged Rachel. "I am so glad to see you. I still haven't heard anything from Robert. Mother says I should wait until I hear from him. What do you think?"

Rachel took Mary's hand and led her over towards the bed. Speaking in a tender voice, she began, "Mary, you best sit down. I have some news for you."

Hearing Rachel's tone of voice, Mary caught her breath, and her eyes widened.

"Mary, slow down. I have news about Robert."

She sat down. *Finally — news.* Seeing the concern on Rachel's face, Mary frowned.

"He cannot see you," said Rachel. She quickly wiped her forehead and continued. "Be — because he has already married Edith Townsend!"

"HE WHAT?!" Unable to slow her words down, Mary questioned. "Mma…MARRIED? Why would he want to marry her? We have been planning our wedding for years!" She stood up and paced in a small circle. "I know her father has that huge racing stable. And, Robert is always hanging around there. Edith isn't even pretty. She's so, so, frivolous. Just stares at people with her tiny eyes and that large beak of a nose. Why did he do this to me?" *Why did he lead me on for so long? Yes, I feel petty saying that about her about her, but he was mine!*

Concerned, Rachel continued in a low voice, "Apparently he likes the pony races and some creditors caught up with him and threatened to do him bodily harm unless he paid up. And, we all know Edith has money from her grandmother and will someday have her father's too."

Shocked, Mary realized she was never to marry Robert. She paused sensing her anger was growing. "Oh, I see. So, he must have been around Edith enough to have her readily accept him AND — be convincing enough for her to permit him to find a preacher straight away! " her voice rose with each word said. She took a deep breath. Feeling light headed, she stopped walking and sank slowly on her bed. All at once, she broke down and cried as her whole body shook with betrayal and heartbreak.

Quickly, Rachel sat next to her and enclosed Mary in a tight hug. They were both shedding tears.

Several minutes later, Rachel stood and whispered, "dear one, you need someone who will be true to you. Please, let us not talk or even think about that worthless scoundrel anymore."

Now, Mary knew there was nothing she could do to resolve the situation. She wiped her eyes and sat up. "You are right. Having a gambler in the family is no way to live." She rose and walked over to the window. Gazing out, she pronounced, "The truth of it all is he said he wanted to marry me but he never once said he loved me — as he meant it. That should have told me something like this would happen."

"Like I said — a worthless scoundrel! And he deserves what he gets with Edith. She can be so spiteful," Rachel staunchly stated.

Looking at her friend, Mary saw that a mischievous smile and a glimmer in her eyes soon appeared. *You are the very best and most loyal friend.* Wiping away her tears, she replied. "So, I count myself lucky." It would take more than one brave statement to rid her mind of Robert, but she would not let yesterday's events over-whelm her again.

Desperately wishing to change the subject, Mary asked, "Rachel, tell me about your coming trip. I want to hear all the details."

"Well, as I told you earlier, I am going to the Turner Bridal Agency in Cincinnati. They are THE best. An agency sounds like the only way to go. On the other side of the coin, if you answered one of those ads in the newspaper about a man wanting a bride, you might end up going all the way out West. And, when you get there, the man may be smelly, with no money or no place to live. Maybe even no teeth." Rachel giggled. "Can you imagine the pickle you would be in? Then what? And, how would you get home? So, with this agency's superior standards, the men need to provide letters of reference to Mrs. Turner. One letter needs to be from the local minister. In this way, she has some assurance that the applicant is a man of good character. He will have property and good standing in his community."

"But you will be so far from family," Mary said.

Rachel mused. "I have thought about this, and I keep coming to the same conclusion. There isn't anyone here that I am excited about marrying. I want my life to be full of adventure — wholesome adventure, not all the time but at least sometimes. I don't think I was meant to stay in Philadelphia. Yes, I will miss my family and my sisters, and of course, you. However, I want a better life than I could have here."

"It sounds like a promising adventure," Mary contributed.

Rachel leaned towards Mary. "From all I have read, it HAS to be better than here. Think of the wide-open spaces, the beautiful mountains, and the clear blue sky. Out West, the towns have room to grow, and the houses have space for gardens. And if I am on a ranch or farm, there will be room for my children to play and there will be horses. In addition, the family will own the house and land. Not like here, where it takes years to become a landowner." She paused. "I have been thinking; perhaps you should join me. Just think, out West you would have a fresh start. No one would have to know about Robert and you. And maybe, we can tell Mrs. Turner that we want to end up in the same town. We will be able to visit, and our children can play together."

"Well, it would be a fresh start. Nevertheless, I would be so far from Jenny, Mother, and Father. I do not think I am as adventurous as you are."

Taking Mary's hand, Rachel smiled and gently squeezed it. "I have to leave to finish my last-minute packing. But I do think it would be wonderful if you joined me at the agency. I believe you are much more adventuresome than you let on. And it would help you in your current predicament. So, just promise me that you will give it some thought. I'd hate for you to stay here and be miserable."

"I will think about it," said Mary.

Both ladies stood to say their farewells.

Rachel opened her reticule and took out a small piece of paper. She handed it to Mary and gave her a long hug.

Leaning back, she committed to memory the image of her best friend and placed a brave smile on her face. *I wish I were more like you.*

Whispering, Rachel asked, "Just please consider it, I know this is the right path for me, and it might be for you, too. I will write as often as I can."

Mary felt her heart warm. "I could never ask for a better friend. Have a safe trip, and I will write to you often as well." Tears welled in both of their eyes. Walking out of the room, Rachel smiled and closed the door behind her.

Mary sat down at her desk and read the advertisement.

The Turner Bridal Agency in Cincinnati, Ohio is seeking honorable young women interested in finding happiness in marriage to a man in the Western Frontier.

We only entertain requests from men of good character, with property and means to support a wife and a family. We require of them references from both the local business community and the local minister. These references provide great assurance that the men requesting wives from us meet our highest standards. Applicants to this agency must be honorable young ladies, not more than 29 years of age, never married, and with references of their own. Interested parties may mail a letter of application along with two references, one of which must be

*from your local minister. Please mail to Mrs. Turner at the
address below.*

<u>*The Turner Bridal Agency*</u>
<u>*137 Myrtle Street*</u>
<u>*Cincinnati, Ohio*</u>

Mary felt better about Rachel's prospects as she read through
the advertisement. It sounded like a well-thought-out way to
approach becoming a mail-order-bride. *Rachel, I doubt I'm brave
enough. I'll just have to make the best of my current situation.*

IT WAS EARLY AFTERNOON, AND MARY HAD CONFIDED IN HER
mother what Rachel had told her about Robert marrying Edith
Townsend. Her mother had been appalled and tried to be comforting. However, the last person Mary wanted to talk about was
Robert.

Later, Mary wandered into the kitchen. She was looking for
something to do. Her mother was baking.

"Do you need any help? I could go to the store for you," Mary
offered.

"Yes, do you want to take Jenny down to the corner to get a
box of cornmeal for me? She is good at diverting any unwanted
thoughts concerning Robert. Besides, the fresh air will do you
good."

In spite of Jenny being a cheery sort, Mary didn't feel like
company. "I think I'd like to go to the store by myself." She looked
at her mother for understanding.

Sarah closed her eyes for a moment and then opened them to
smile at her eldest daughter. Then she walked over to Mary and
clasped her hands. "I understand, my dear. I just thought Jenny's
chattering might possibly cheer you up." Taking a step back, her
mother reached up with her fingertips and brought Mary's head up.
She kissed her on the cheek.

Mary headed out the back door. Once outside she rubbed her arms. The air was cold and damp. Glancing towards the sky, she hoped for a sign of some divine guidance. It was then she noticed the dark gray afternoon clouds gathering. It would probably rain soon. Continuing her walk down the street, she observed Nina Peron and Lilly Thompson had entered the store ahead of her. *Oh no, just who I didn't want to see. Hopefully, they'll ignore me, as usual.*

Coming through the entry door of Sander's Mercantile, Mary soon found the aisle containing the cornmeal. A little way away, Mary saw Nina and Lilly. They were talking and had not yet noticed her. *I hope they'll be quick about their purchase.* Arriving where the cornmeal was stocked, Mary bent down and picked up the bag from the bottom shelf. As she stood up, her eyes made contact with Nina's. Instantly Nina looked away. As Nina whispered to Lilly, they both glanced towards her.

Mary's heart pounded with the realization that she was the subject of their conversation. Feeling as though she were standing in the middle of a frozen lake, she knew there was no fast exit. She slowly inhaled and reminded herself she had done nothing wrong. *The nerve of them! I don't even get the benefit of the doubt.* The two busy bees continued their conversation to one another in low voice tones. Periodically, they gave Mary an occasional furtive glance. As they concluded their transaction with the store owner, Mary approached the counter. With a smile on her face, Mary approached them. "Good afternoon ladies." No one replied. Instead, the two gossip-mongers scurried out the door. Now more annoyed than hurt, Mary knew she should not have been surprised. *Humph! Those two left as quickly as the north wind and didn't spare a word or look back. Some friends they are!*

As she left the store and headed back home, she saw Nina and Lilly across the street. And now they were talking with another of their friends, Patricia. The three ladies continued talking in secretive tones. Despite feeling hurt, Mary lifted her shoulders and continued to walk home. *Why do I want to stay here and put up with those kinds of people? They are no friends of mine!*

Finally reaching the front garden of her house, she decided that perhaps, she could become more adventurous.

THE SITUATION HAD ALREADY GOTTEN MUCH WORSE THAN SHE HAD expected. It had been less than three days, and she was already the object of neighborhood gossip. She had waited two years for Robert to propose and in just a short time, all her dreams had vanished! *I have always dreamed of having my own family ... of having a life like my parents.*

Mary sat down at her small desk. Thoughts of Rachel went through her mind as she fingered the pen Rachel had given her. She had always been such a good source of comfort – and the pen was a reminder to stay in touch. Her eyes grew misty. Straightening her shoulders, Mary pondered ... she wanted to be married with a family of her own. Staying here, she would always have a stigma attached to her name, through no fault of her own. She bit her lower lip. *Now, wait a minute.* She took out the advertisement that Rachel had left with her and looked at the piece of paper with more interest. It looked intriguing. *The question is — will I be jumping from the frying pan and into the fire? She thought about her recent days.* She knew how detailed Rachel was about everything she attempted to do. *If she thinks this will be an ideal answer to my problem, I'm going to try it.* So, she carefully re-read the newspaper clipping.

Admittedly, at first Rachel's idea had taken Mary by surprise. It was only a few months ago, her best friend had first shared her plans to become a mail-order bride. There was no doubt Rachel was convinced this was the correct path for her. However, following Rachel in this course was a big decision to make. Smiling to herself, Mary began to daydream about the prospects of life in the West.... *My own family with a house, a garden, and children to read to. It'll be a fresh start, away from the whispers and definitely away from those nasty looks.*

Mary decided it was time to talk with her father. Descending the stairs, she found him downstairs hunched over a set of green account books in his study. As he often did, he had brought work home. Dietrich Schulman looked up as Mary entered the study. "Father, can we talk for a minute?"

"Certainly, I always have time for you. I suppose you want to talk about what happened at the church?" He got up and walked over to close the door behind her. Motioning for her to sit in the leather armchair opposite his desk, he sat down in his chair.

"Father, did mother tell you why Robert didn't come?"

He dropped his head and gave a heavy sigh. His tired brown eyes had the look of lost sleep. "Yes dear, she did. And I cannot tell you how sorry I am. It is best you found out about Robert's transgressions before it was too late. You must look forward, not back. From today on out, you must try your best not to be concerned about him or let his deeds ruin your life or your disposition." He shifted in his chair and continued leaning forward across the desk. "Your mother also told me that Rachel had a suggestion for you."

"She did? I didn't know Rachel had told Mother." She took a deep breath and searched her father face. "What do you think of Rachel's plans?" she inquired.

Pausing for a moment, he said, "the important thing dear, is what do you think about it?"

"It is a bold step, and it would mean such a big change. I know I can't stay here. I don't know if going out West will make me any happier. I would be so far away from you, Mother and Jenny. How can I know I would get someone better?"

"Nothing is a certainty, as you well know. Now dearest, how about an answer to my question?" And, he patiently waited for her response.

Mary considered the fact that her father clearly wasn't going to tell her what to do. But she hadn't expected that of him. The answer was obvious. Mary decided now was the time to make a decision. It was time to follow Rachel. "Father, I would like your blessing to become a mail order bride."

With a look of approval, he said, "you know you have my approval, whatever you decide. You can always take the first steps down the path and if you change your mind, remember you can always return home. Although we will miss you terribly, I understand how you feel. We want the best for you, and we will always be here for you."

Rushing around the desk to hug her father, she tried to choke back her tears. "Thank you, Father, somehow things always become clearer after I talk with you."

"What else are fathers for?" he responded with a laugh. He stood up and kissed her on the cheek and gave her a big hug. Stepping back, he opened the small right-hand drawer of the desk. He pulled out a small leather bag and placed it into her hand. "Mary, please take this. Inside you will find five double eagle twenty dollar gold coins. This money should help you in your new life. I know you will use it wisely. Remember, my daughter, you are dearly loved and are always welcome to return home."

Mary stood frozen in time remembering her father at this moment. Tears of a grateful and loving daughter trickled down her face. *I would be lucky if my future husband would be anything like you.* Her father gave her fond embrace and stepped back to see he was a little misty-eyed himself.

"Well, what are you waiting for? I think you have something important to tell your mother."

CHAPTER 2

CRYSTAL CREEK, MONTANA — JUNE 1882

CHARLES HAD JUST FINISHED HIS EARLY MORNING CHORES, AND IT was time to head in for breakfast. Running a hand through his thick wavy blond hair, he raised his deep blue eyes to the sky. He was a tall man with a physical frame that supported the life of a hard-working farmer. After looking at the clouds above, he judged the weather to be agreeable. One always appreciated a warm pleasant day while working outdoors in Montana.

His gait was slow as he walked back to the house. A disturbing dream from two nights prior was plaguing his waking thoughts. In this dream, he was an older man living alone on the farm. There was no sign of his daughter or anyone he knew in this dream. Thus today, he realized why the occasional idea of marrying again had crept back into his mind. The biggest stumbling block was … he was not the least bit interested in anyone in town! When he thought about his childhood friend, Owen Nelson, and his wife Daniela, his heart filled with a deep sense of longing. Owen was a lucky man for certain. Oh, Charles had no regrets as he had married his childhood sweetheart, Josephine. However, Charles' situation differed from Owen. Josephine held no real desire to be the wife of a farmer. She had always hoped they would sell the farm and move into town. Charles sighed, again. It had been two years and four months since his wife and father had died in the diphtheria epidemic. The epidemic had taken a terrible toll on everyone in the Valley.

He sighed and then stepped up onto the front porch. There were chores left to finish this day. Opening the front door, he entered and walked into the kitchen.

"Mom, Lizzie, remember we are going to the Nelsons for dinner today."

Helen, his mother, turned from the stove where she had been warming the ham for breakfast. "Yes Charles, I will also bring a jar of apple butter as our thank-you gift." She tucked a few stray wisps of gray-blonde into the bun she wore on the back of her neck. She was of small stature and often had a tired look on her face. After all, she had been a farmer's wife for many a year.

Charles leaned over to where his daughter, Elizabeth stood in the kitchen. "Lizzie, can you be a big girl and get dressed before we need to leave? All by yourself?"

The little blonde and blue-eyed girl shifted from one leg to the other. "Yes, Papa. I can. I'll be a big help." Continuing to look up to her father, she gave him a big smile – less two of her front teeth.

Lizzie was the shining star in Charles's life. Gazing at her, he noted she always made such an endearing picture. She was a sweet and good girl. He knew she would enjoy a little more time with him. However, there were always so many farms chores to do each day.

Dinner with the Nelsons would be a welcomed change for everyone. Owen Nelson was a few years older than Charles and had done fairly well for himself. His wife, Daniela was as sweet as they came. She worked hard cooking her Italian meals and fussing over Owen and their children.

Glancing around the kitchen, Charles saw his mother struggling to finish serving the breakfast. Strolling over to the table, he stopped and watched Lizzie putting the knives and forks alongside the napkins. On finishing, she quietly sat down. Recognizing he spent so little time talking to his daughter, he thought a few words of praise were in order. "Lizzie, I see you helped Grandma by setting the table. What a good job you have done." Lizzie nodded her head but continued to be quiet. He gave her a quick wink. Everyone knew Grandma was a little grouchy in the mornings.

Not surprising Charles heard his mother mumble, "It will be nice when she is a little older and could be a bit more help with the chores."

Yes, his mother was grumpy, most likely because she missed his father. Lately, there were more complaints about the little things. He knew his mother loved his daughter. It was true – his mother had her plate full accomplishing her tasks and watching after Lizzie for most of the day. Realistically, how much help could a seven-year-old girl be? More to the point, he didn't want Lizzie to feel poorly about it. Charles gazed at his daughter while she sat twiddling her thumbs in her lap. He recognized his little girl was often sitting in this boring position. *Lizzie is lonely, too. No one to play or even quibble with. It would be nice if she had a brother or sister but what she really needs is a mother. I need a helpmate.* He also knew he didn't want to be that old man on the front porch, in a rocking chair all by himself. It was time to talk to his best friend, Owen.

Turning, Charles walked over to help his mother finish putting the eggs, ham, and flapjacks on their plates. He brought two plates over to the table one for Lizzie and one for himself. Following him over was Helen with her plate and a warmed jar of maple syrup. She slowly sank into her chair.

With everyone seated, Charles expressed his appreciation. "Thank you, Mom, and, as usual breakfast looks great!" He gave Lizzie another wink. After cleaning his plate, Charles got up and walked over to place it in the sink. And, with a kiss to Lizzie's forehead and a wink to his mother, he left the house to finish his chores before dinnertime.

HAVING FINISHED HIS LATE MORNING CHORES WITH NEWFOUND energy, Charles went into the house to wash up. Tonight was dinner with the Nelsons. He put on his Sunday clothes and checked his appearance in the small bedroom mirror. Before stepping outside to begin the preparations for travel, he called to his mother." If you can get Lizzie ready, I'll have the buckboard hitched in a few minutes."

"We will be ready, just as soon as I can get all the tangles out of your daughter's hair." His mother's answer was sharp. Exiting the house, he wondered if his mother's impatience resulted from being tired or she just wanted to finish Lizzie's hair. *Poor Lizzie.*

Entering the barn, he was greeted by a friendly neigh from Buddy. The hitching went smoothly as it usually did with the mild-mannered old horse. *I wish Mom were as patient as you are, Buddy.* Standing with the horse and wagon, he turned to look towards the house. He saw his mother and Lizzie approaching. His little girl was carefully holding the jar of apple butter. *Ah, yes, the thank-you gift.* When they arrived at the wagon, he helped his mother climb onto the bench. Once seated, Helen gestured for Charles to give her the jar of apple butter. Charles shrugged and smiled at Lizzie, took the jar and gave it to his Mom to safeguard. Then he lifted his daughter up to sit beside her grandmother. Once he was aboard, he gave a light flip of the reins and off they went.

The Nelsons' home was just a short twenty-minute drive. Rolling down the road, they were accustomed to hearing the wagon creak and the clomping of Buddy's hooves on the hard dirt. Soon Lizzie was chattering about visiting her three friends.

"Do you think I can play with the puppies, Papa?" Lizzie asked as they approached the gate to the farm.

"I don't know, but I bet if you ask nicely, the answer just might be yes." He turned to see her face had lit up. It was plain to see she needed company. *Well, school will start in a few months for her. Whoa ... wait a minute. How will I take her to school and then pick her up?* He knew this would be a difficult question to answer. *If he asked Mom, he would have to listen to the constant complaining. Perhaps I could hold Lizzie out of school for a year. No. No. I cannot do that. If she had a mother, she could help Lizzie with school.* Now was the time to start on a plan. He must ask Owen for ideas on how to find a wife. This woman would have to learn to love his daughter and be accepting of farm life. It was a daunting notion, to say the least.

Driving up to the front of the Nelsons' house, Charles stopped. There was Owen already out on the front porch and waiting for them. Charles waved and smiled back to his old friend. Having set the brake on the wagon, he stepped down and walked around to help his Mom and Lizzie out.

"Hello there, Charles, Mrs. Baxter, and Miss Elizabeth. How are you all doing?" Owen inquired in a cheerful voice.

"Owen, it's good to see you. We've been looking forward to dinner with you and the family all week. This is mighty nice of you."

Helen walked up to Owen and gave him a light hug. "Elizabeth has been chattering like a jay bird."

Owen was a tall man with a medium build. His hair was the color of winter wheat, and his eyes were sky blue. It was easy to see why his wife, Daniela was so taken with him. He was a smart and good-looking man, and a little on the quiet side. However, he became very talkative when discussing horses, his business.

Within a few moments, Daniela rushed out of the house followed by three little ones. Daniela was a short Italian woman, with deep brown hair and light gray eyes. She had a happy and lively nature. "Good evening to everyone. We have been looking forward to this dinner. Our children have been buzzing around like bees, and for the moment, they are even clean." Daniela laughed. "Come on in. Supper is almost ready." She waved her hands backward and forward, ushering in her children first. Lizzie scooted up to join her friends.

"How are you feeling Daniela? Is the baby kicking yet?" Helen inquired as everyone walked indoors.

"Ah well, the baby is very active. She wants to come out and play with her brothers and her sister. At least, I hope it's a girl. Laura does not want to be the only girl." Daniela gave them all a quick wink, turned and led the way inside towards the kitchen. In front of him, Charles saw the little flock of children now clustered around Lizzie. He felt his heart warm as he watched the children.

Soon Daniela came out from the kitchen. Walking into the front room, she stopped and looked at her guests. "Excuse me. If you could please take a seat at the table in dining room, we can begin. I've just about got everything ready."

Once all the guests were seated, Daniela brought out a basket full of hot bread and set it in the middle of the table. Turning, she rushed back to the kitchen and returned with a large steaming bowl of vegetables and potatoes. Owen followed with a big casserole dish. A wonderful aroma filled the room and inspired appetites. Dinner conversation began with the appreciation of the tasty dishes. The main course was a chicken dish with mushrooms, onions, herbs, and tomatoes. Peach pie was on the sideboard for dessert.

Charles watched Daniela address the children as they had finished their pie. "Children, you may be excused from the supper table. Please go into the front room to play. If you promise to be good, your father will bring in the puppies for you to play with." Daniela turned to look at Owen and gave him an impish smile as her eyes twinkled with merriment.

"I'll bring in the puppies for them." Shrugging his shoulders,

Owen grinned and got up from his seat to walk towards the back-kitchen door.

"Daniela, I don't think I have ever had chicken prepared this way. It is delicious." Helen leaned forward. "You must tell me how you make it."

"It is very simple. This dish is what we call Pollo, meaning 'chicken' and Cacciatore meaning 'hunter' in Italy. It means hunter's stew. You see in the old days, the hunters would catch birds, rabbits or other game for their meals. The game meat would be mixed with tomatoes and other vegetables. So now, here we use the same recipe for chicken." She took a sip of water. "In my family, we sometimes use rabbit, instead of chicken. I can write it down for you before you leave."

"That would be nice of you. I'm afraid Charles is tired of the same old roasted chicken I make every week."

Charles decided it was best to continue to be quiet. So, he smiled and watched Daniela rush around the corner to the front room. Momentarily, she returned with paper and a pencil. She quickly jotted down the instructions she had just verbalized.

"Thank you, Daniela. This is so nice of you. I only hope I have the time to try this. It has been so hectic since Josephine passed on."

Feeling a sharp pain in his chest, Charles decided there was no need to make Lizzie any sadder by thinking of her mother and grandfather. He shook his head.

Before long, Owen had re-entered the room from depositing the puppies with the children.

"Daniela, who do we know that might be a fitting wife for this fine chap?"

Charles pulled at his shirt collar and cleared his throat. "Ah, hem."

Daniela responded, "Now, it has been over two years … you are entitled to be done with your grieving period, and your daughter needs a mother."

Charles cringed. This was not the conversation he wanted to have with everyone, just Owen. If he heard his mother tell him one more time, he should marry Francis Miller — he would go crazy. Then Charles considered the thought of courting a lady, and this idea had him breaking out in a cold sweat! Heck, if he had to admit it, marrying Josephine was a natural given. They grew up together, and she knew he was painfully shy. It was Josephine who took the initial steps of marriage. He wiped his now damp palms on the legs of his pants.

"What about Francis, dear?" Helen sweetly asked.

Shaking his head again, Charles gathered his composure to respond. "Mom, not Francis. Besides, I am not good at courting, even if there was anyone interesting in town." Charles noticed he was perspiring. *Great, a grown man sweating like a horse.* Charles moved a little in his chair.

Mrs. Nelson spoke up to fill the awkward silence. "The pickings around here are pretty slim, and all my sisters are already married. There is Ida Millhouse."

That name sent a shiver through Charles. "I'll pass on her." A small cough escaped Charles. *Ida has the disposition of mule and was almost as pretty.*

Owen turned to his wife, "Tell him about what your sister wrote in her last letter. You know … the bit about the mail-order brides that came from Cincinnati."

Daniela grinned. "Yes, that is a good idea. Charles, you know I have told you about my sisters Theresa and Isabella."

Charles nodded, pleased to move the conversation away from Francis and Ida.

"My sisters wrote that two men from their town sent for mail order brides. Both women arrived from the same agency located in Cincinnati."

Again, he nodded politely. However, now he wanted to hear more.

"As they tell it, the women are both very nice and accomplished. The men could not be happier. And they are pretty, too. At least, to hear the men tell it. It seems this agency requires references from both the men and the women. The agency owner matches the individuals, and through correspondence, they decide if they suit one another. They claim the agency has a spotless record of making good matches." Daniela smiled at Charles and turned to look at Owen.

Helen raised an eyebrow and gave Charles a pointed look. He ignored it….

"It sounds like quite a risk, marrying someone you have never met before," stated Helen.

"I think I need some time to consider this approach to getting married. Thank you for the suggestion, Daniela." *It did sound interesting.*

"Just in case, let me get you the advertisement for this agency. Isabella sent me one. I'll be right back." Daniela left the table and went in search of the clipping.

"Think on it, Charles." Owen said with a nod and continued, "Daniela's sisters are good judges of character. And I would put good stock on their recommendation."

"Thanks, I'll think about it," Charles replied, appreciative of Owen and Daniela's concern.

Glancing to his mother, he saw the perturbed expression. Familiar was the look. He continued, "Now mother, perhaps we should see if we can pry Lizzie away from those puppies and be on our way."

Daniela returned with the folded advertisement and placed it in Charles' hands. He took the neatly folded newsprint and put in his pocket. They said their goodbyes and thanked their hosts for the delicious supper. As he suspected, it took time to get Lizzie to leave the puppies.

Lizzie turned and said, "Thank you for the yummy dinner and PIE." With her right fingertip, she touched her mouth and said in a whisper, "I love your puppies. They give lots of kisses, and it is nice to pet their fur." She turned her head and waved to the other children and ran to the wagon to wait for her father to lift her up.

Owen smiled and said, "Well, young lady, I'm glad you love them because you get to take this puppy home with you as an early birthday present." He brought out the puppy he had been hiding behind his back and gave it to her.

Squealing as she took the puppy, she hugged him tight. "Oh, thank you! Thank you! I promise to take very good care of him," she responded and laughed as the puppy licked her face.

Smiling Charles stepped up to Lizzie and said, "We are very happy you like him. Mr. Nelson and I discussed this and decided you needed a playmate and some responsibility. He will need a name. And he will need to be fed and looked after." Turning to Owen, Charles gave him a handshake and said, "Thanks for the lovely dinner and of course, the puppy." Then he clasped Owen on the back.

Daniela went up to Charles and whispered into his ear. "Think about the mail order bride. You need some companionship as well."

Charles nodded. As they left, everyone made their final wave goodbye.

IT WAS MIDDAY, AND CHARLES HAD JUST FINISHED PLOWING THE north field. With a pull on the reins and the command of "whoa," his ever-faithful horse Buddy came to a halt. Plowing the field today had taken a little longer than normal. His thoughts had periodically drifted to the Nelsons' suggestion of getting a mail order bride. It was sounding like an idea worth considering. Goodness knows there were not very many potential brides here in Crystal Creek. In fact, they were practically non-existent.

Throughout the plowing, Charles had listed in his mind the advantages and then disadvantages of getting a mail order bride for himself. For each thought, he then added up the good and the possible bad outcomes. In the end, he reasoned he would be corresponding with his potential bride. And, in his letters, he could express what qualities would be useful in dealing with farm life in Montana. *After all, honesty is the best policy. It is so much easier for me to communicate in a letter. I could skip all the need to know stuff for courting a lady. Why this could be the best idea! And, hopefully, she wouldn't look like Ida.* That thought sent a shiver down his spine.

Charles walked up and stopped at Buddy's shoulder. He gave the horse a couple of hardy pats. "I'll bet you're hungry. Heaven knows I am. We worked hard getting this field ready for planting. And today it's done, so let's see if we both get some kind of a reward."

He unhitched Buddy, and they walked through the furrows of newly turned earth, back towards the barn. Buddy was always an excellent listener. "Don't worry I will give you a scoop of oats and maybe I'll trickle some molasses in your bucket too. Do YOU think I should get a mail order bride?" He let out a little laugh. In companionable silence, they walked back to the barn.

Finally rounding the back corner of the barn, Charles recognized they had visitors. *OH, NO. Not this again.* Tied to the front hitching rail at the house was a familiar horse and carriage. Letting out a deep sigh, Charles led Buddy into the barn. Once inside, Charles took off the harness and led Buddy into his stall. He poured a scoop of oats into a bucket and then grabbed the jug of molasses on the nearby shelf and dribbled a liberal amount over the oats. Buddy nickered. Charles chuckled and brought over his bucket. *Well, we know for sure this is your treat.* Placing the bucket into Buddy's feed bin, Charles stepped into the stall and gave his horse a good grooming. There were many things he prided himself on, and one was taking good care of his animals. He stood there for a moment and watched Buddy appreciatively gobble down his oats and molasses. Turning, he reluctantly left the barn. *I guess I can't put this off any longer.*

Striding past the horse and carriage, Charles stopped at the front door, gave his neck a quick rub and then pulled back his shoulders. Reaching for the doorknob, he remembered to paste a smile on his tired face. Entering the house, he saw three women chatting in the back of the kitchen. Glancing to the side of the sitting room, he found his daughter playing with her doll by the window. "What are you doing Lizzie?" At the sight of his daughter, his smile softened.

"I'm playing with Dolly and staying out of the way," Lizzie whispered as quietly.

Hearing this Charles lifted an eyebrow. He found himself irritated as he remembered one of his mother's favorite sayings, 'children should be seen and not heard.' Here was his daughter off by herself in a corner. *Couldn't they have included her for even just a short time?*

"Oh, I see. Well, you're a smart girl. Say, I'm hungry. How about you?" Lizzie answered her father with a nod.

"Well, Lizzie, let's go into the kitchen and see what is cooking." Sensing her discomfort, he stooped over and whispered into her ear. "Don't worry I'll protect you." Leaning back, he peered into her uneasy eyes. Seeing her expression, he gave her a wink and a big smile and hand-in-hand, they walked into the kitchen.

Suddenly, the chatter halted as the women turned to see him. "Good afternoon, ladies. How are Miss Francis and Mrs. Miller doing today?"

Charles' mother grinned sheepishly. The younger woman spoke first, "Good afternoon, Charles. We are doing very well, thank you." Each word was spoken with a generous amount of sugary sweetness.

The older woman just nodded her head along with each of her daughter's words, but at the end, she quickly added, "Just fine.

Thank you for asking Charles." Then she turned her head expectantly towards his mother.

"Good to hear. What brings you ladies out into this neck of the woods?" Charles asked. The stiff conversation made him feel uncomfortable, and he wondered if Lizzie could feel the moisture on his hand. Shifting his weight from one foot to the other, he tried hard to keep eye contact so as not to appear rude.

His mother stepped towards him and stopped. "Charles, I bumped into Mrs. Miller and Francis yesterday when I was delivering eggs to the Busy Bee Café. Francis has just returned from visiting her cousins in Bozeman, and I invited them to come over for dinner, remember?"

"Oh, I must have forgotten today was the day." *Now I know you didn't tell me....*

Francis sauntered forward to stand in front of Charles and coyly batted her eyelashes. "Charles, I baked two cherry pies for dessert today. That is your favorite kind of pie, is it not?" Another round of eyelash batting was presented to him.

Looking at the table, he saw five place settings. He turned to look at Francis. "Why, yes, it is. Thank you, Miss Francis." Charles then cocked his head and looked at his mother. "Mom, is there anything I can do to help with dinner?"

"No thank you, Charles. I am just about to put it on the table," answered his mother.

"Well, maybe Lizzie can help with that?" he offered and looked down to see Lizzie smile.

"Oh, Charles! Elizabeth is just a little girl. It is best to let us ladies help with the food," simpered Francis.

Charles felt his daughter's hand stiffen. He turned and gazed down at her. "Lizzie, how about if you helped me feed the chickens later?"

"Oh yes, Papa." Lizzie's hand relaxed, and a small smile came over her face.

Helen called out, "Dinner is ready. Please sit down." Glancing around the table, Charles noticed his mother had put out the good plates and glasses. He stepped around to pull out and hold the chairs for each of the ladies. Last, he walked to the head of the table and took his seat. He bowed his head and said grace.

Most of the mealtime was spent listening to the ladies discussing recipes. Occasionally, they asked if he liked a particular dish. Francis also tried to impress his mother with her knowledge of the latest fashions. *Has anyone noticed Lizzie and I are sitting here?*

Charles felt restless and bothered. Not once did anyone try to include Lizzie in the conversation. How was his daughter ever going to learn how to converse, if people never talked to her? Thinking to change the conversation, he seized upon a moment of silence. "Miss Francis, how was your visit with your cousins? Are your younger cousins still in school?"

Francis coyly raised her eyes to meet Charles and then took a deep breath. "The boys still are, but the girls are spending their time learning how to cook, sew and keep house. You know, girl things."

Charles proceeded to bait Francis. "What other subjects do you think are important in a young girl's education?" He could sense he caught her off-guard.

"Well, I think a little bit of schooling is fine. But studying numbers and history is wasted on a young girl." Francis professed.

Both older ladies nodded in agreement.

Once again, this idea that a girl shouldn't have a well-rounded education rears its ugly head. He tamped down his irritation. Charles didn't want to have this argument again and in front of company.

Lizzie will not grow up to be like her if I have anything to say about it. Leaning back in his chair, he forced a smile. "I think I heard someone mention there's cherry pie for dessert?"

～

AFTER PUTTING LIZZIE TO BED, CHARLES REFLECTED ON THE evening and the conversation after dinner. His mother was right about one thing. At some point, he would need to move on and consider marrying again. Helen had mentioned Francis more and more frequently in her talks with him. Tonight, she had been especially persistent, and each time he tried to change the subject. But there was no stopping her! She had a one-track mind.

Before retiring, he went to his dresser and retrieved Daniela's paper. It read–**'The Turner Bridal Agency invites eligible men to apply for brides of good character and disposition.'** He knew he could not muddle through the reading. His head was throbbing, most likely a result of trying not to argue with his mother earlier. *I'll think about this tomorrow.* He placed the advertisement back into his dresser and got ready for bed. *A mail order bride?* Owen and Daniela Nelson were the best of friends and very levelheaded. They wouldn't encourage him down that path if they didn't believe in it. But then, they didn't have to live with the consequences either. He hoped he would make the right decision. Blowing out the lantern, he climbed into the large bed. He felt alone.

The next morning as he was dressing, he could not shake the nagging concerns from last evening. Might a mail order bride be the right choice for him? He wasn't getting any younger. Surely Lizzie could benefit by having a mother to care for her? She had become a little withdrawn since her mother had died. He had to admit, Lizzie was probably as lonely as he was. Francis was out of the question and from his observations she was terrible around children. He would not subject Lizzie to such a fate.

He pulled open the dresser drawer and withdrew his shirt. Seeing the advertisement, he picked it up and started to read where he had left off last evening.

Applicants must be of good character and good standing in the community. Men must be of an appropriate age, have property and the means to support a family. Our brides will be honorable women, who have passed a rigorous check of good character. In addition, they will not be over 29 years of age and will possess good domestic skills. Interested parties may contact the owner of the agency, Mrs. Turner at the address below. Two written letters of references must accompany your request. The one letter of reference must be from your local minister, attesting to character and standing in the community.

Turner Bridal Agency
137 Myrtle Street,
Cincinnati, Ohio

After re-reading the advertisement, it seemed like a better chance of ending up with a suitable wife. At least, more so than placing an advertisement in a newspaper in the East and marrying whoever got off the train. He had heard a tale or two about how bad that ended up.

Exiting his bedroom, he found Lizzie sitting in the kitchen with her doll. The puppy was napping in its bed under the stove. Lizzie looked listless.

"What is the matter, sweetheart?" Charles asked, "Is Dolly OK?"

"She is sad. She doesn't have any friends to play with. She's all alone."

The words hit him like a sledgehammer. Lizzie was not talking about the doll. She was talking about herself. She was all alone with no sisters or brothers. Remembering the dinner at the Nelsons' house, Charles had noticed how all the children laughed and played with one another. No child there was truly alone because they were part of a large family.

It was now obvious what he needed to do. He wanted his daughter to be happy and to have brothers and sisters to play with while growing up in a safe and secure home. Lizzie needed to have happy childhood memories which she and her siblings could write about when they were older, just as Daniela Nelson and her sisters wrote to each other. *I will not allow myself to be that lonely old man in my dreams.*

He had to take a wife. His daughter needed it, and deep in his heart, he knew he needed it too.

Determined to take action, he prepared for the ride into town. He was going ask Reverend Winterthorpe to write a recommendation for him. His second recommendation would be from Mr. Alastair McCloud, one of the most upstanding cattlemen of Montana. Maybe he would even ask Mr. Holt, the Crystal Creek Hotel owner, to write a third recommendation for him. These individuals knew him well and perhaps having a third letter would stack the odds in his favor. Charles' course of action now seemed clear, and it felt as if a great weight was lifted from his shoulders. There was no reason to delay any longer; he was going straight-a-way to the church for the first recommendation.

CHARLES PULLED A CHAIR UP TO THE KITCHEN TABLE AND TRIED TO think of what to write in his letter to Mrs. Turner at the Bridal Agency. He reached up and moved the inkwell again, each time a little closer to his paper. *Well, I have to start my letter sometime...* so he dipped the pen in the inkwell and wrote.

June 23, 1882

Dear Mrs. Turner,

Greetings. My name is Charles Baxter. I am twenty-eight years of age, and I live in Crystal Creek, Montana. Just over two years ago, my wife died in Diphtheria epidemic. We were blessed with a daughter by the name of Elizabeth. Elizabeth is seven years old and has blonde hair and blue eyes. She is a good girl but sometimes shy. I am in hopes my future wife would be a good mother to my daughter and a companion to me, someone who enjoys reading and can appreciate the beauty of the land where I live.

The farm where I earn my living was inherited from my father. It is about a thirty-minute wagon drive from town. My farm is a good size being one hundred and sixty acres. I make a good honest living supplying food to many of the local businesses and the townsfolk. As for myself, I am over six feet tall. My hair is blond and my eyes are blue. I enjoy reading when my chores permit. My house is a four-bedroom, two-story home. We are a good Christian family and attend church regularly. However, attending church is sometimes difficult in the wintertime because of the weather. I believe I live in God's country. The town of Crystal Creek is in the Green Valley of Montana. The weather is more agreeable to farming as the winters are a little less harsh. We have beautiful rolling hills, large mountains and many rivers and creeks. While the summer is very pleasant, I would be remiss if I did not say the winters are long and very cold. I promise to be a good husband and to protect and honor my new wife. Thank you for your consideration.

Sincerely yours,

Charles Baxter

He glanced over the letter. Not his best penmanship as it had been a while since he wrote to his brother John, but he concluded it would have to do. Thinking he had written what was important, he wanted to mail it before he changed his mind. He put his letter into an envelope and included the letters from Reverend Winterthorpe, Mr. Alastair McCloud, and Mr. Holt. Pen to ink, he addressed the envelope to the Turner Bridal Agency. Deep in his heart, he felt this was right. He saddled his horse and left for town to mail his request to Mrs. Turner.

CHAPTER 3

CINCINNATI, OHIO — JULY 1882.

MARY WAS TIRED AFTER THE LONG TRAIN RIDE FROM
Philadelphia. Soon she would arrive at The Turner Bridal Agency.
The carriage driver at the train station assured her that he knew the
address. She glanced out the carriage window to look at the sites of
Cincinnati. The horse slowed his pace, and she glimpsed down to
check her appearance. Her eyes stopped at the hem of her traveling
dress as she noted it was trimmed with coal dust. *Oh, well, can't be
helped.*

Suddenly, the carriage surged forward and then back as the
carriage horse halted. She looked out the window and saw a large,
elegant two-story Victorian home painted white with blue trim.
With the help of the driver, she stepped out of the carriage as
gracefully as she could.

Mary endeavored to put her best foot forward despite her lack
of sleep. Straightening her back, she pasted a big smile on her face.
Turning, she saw the driver was already busy unloading her trunks
from the carriage.

Glancing around, she saw no sign proclaiming this location as that of the Turner Bridal Agency. Feeling apprehensive, she looked at the numbers on the door and saw it was marked as 137 Myrtle Street – that part was correct. She walked up to the front door and lifted the knocker. Before the knocker had made a sound to her surprise, a young lady wearing a blue dress with a white apron opened the door. "Good Afternoon, Turner Bridal Agency."

"Oh, good day. My name is Mary Schulman, and I believe I am expected."

"Mary, you're early!" Looking up the staircase, she saw Rachel rushing down. Her pretty apple green dress was billowing out all around her. There was Rachel's smile as broad and infectious as ever. She pressed forward and hugged Mary.

"I took the early train and got here as soon as I could," Mary replied as she dragged her overstuffed carpetbag past the threshold. She turned to the gentleman from the Carriage Service, paid and thanked him. Nodding his thanks, he hurried down to attend to his horse and carriage.

"This is so wonderful! I could hardly believe my good fortune when Mrs. Turner told me you were coming." Rachel motioned toward the hallway. "As soon as you have finished talking with Mrs. Turner, I will show you around. I can't wait to introduce you to the other ladies. We're going to have so many new friends here." Rachel was bubbling with joy.

"Oh, excuse me. This young lady is Bess Johnson. She works very hard trying to keep the house in good order, especially with all of us making such a mess of things. I'm not mentioning anyone in particular." And Rachel batted her eyelashes and laughed.

"Pleased to make your acquaintance, Miss. You can just call me, Bess." The maid smiled and took Mary's bag. "I'll arrange to have your trunks taken upstairs. Please allow me to show you to Mrs. Turner's office."

"Mary, this will be very exciting for us!"

Briefly, Mary closed her eyes and let out a huge breath of

relief. Walking towards the end of the hall, they stopped at a partly open Walnut paneled door. Rachel knocked, and they entered the office. A large wooden desk sat near the back wall. There was a pair of green velvet wing-backed chairs facing the desk and a few oil landscapes decorated the yellow walls. Behind the desk sat a handsome elderly woman with graying hair worn in a fashionable bun. The woman rose as they entered and walked around the desk to meet them.

"Mrs. Turner, I would like to present my good friend Miss Mary Schulman."

The handsome woman extended her hand in greeting. "It is so nice to meet you, Mary. Rachel has so many good things to say about you."

"My pleasure, ma'am. It is very nice to be here."

Rachael excused herself, and Mrs. Turner waved Mary to the closest chair facing the desk. "Sit, please." Mrs. Turner continued as she walked back to her chair. "I expect you had a long journey."

"Yes, it certainly was." Mary seated herself. The softness of the chair was a welcome change after the hard seats of the train.

There was a soft knock on the door, and Bess entered carrying a tray of tea and biscuits. After having poured two cups of tea, she quietly exited the room.

"Perhaps we should talk a bit about what you should be expecting. As you are aware, you are here to find a suitable husband — to become the wife of a man you have not met. And, probably end up living in an area of the country you most likely have never seen. This should sound either exciting or frightening to you, or perhaps a little of both." Mrs. Turner added with an easy smile.

Cautiously Mary answered. "Yes, ma'am. A little of both I believe." *However, staying in Philadelphia is definitely out of the question.*

Mrs. Turner continued, "You may be amazed to find men feel the same way. They are not as self-assured as they would have us believe."

Not having thought about it in this light before, Mary could believe it to be true.

"If you go through an agency such as mine, you have many advantages. First, we screen all the applicants. As you know, there is a severe shortage of women in the Frontier Territories, and there are many men wishing to find brides. Some of these men may be so desperate as to misrepresent themselves and their situations."

Mary's mind stumbled at that thought.

"No need to be concerned, dear. For this reason, I require a minimum of two references from all candidates and one of these must be from the local minister. When I finally receive all the information I require, only then do I evaluate the candidate. By offering only respectable ladies, the agency can afford to be very selective. I believe this procedure allows us the ability to avoid sending a lady into an undesirable situation."

That's a relief. But a first time is always a possibility?

Mrs. Turner paused. "However, this by itself does not always guarantee a good outcome. That is why we request the gentlemen abstain from marital relations until the lady has time to become acquainted with him and the surroundings."

Mary blushed and swallowed. She reminded herself WHY she was here and that she would think positive thoughts, hopefully about everything. She listened intently.

"In addition, my agency offers our ladies many lessons in the domestic arts. These would be tasks a prospective husband might expect his wife to know such as cooking, sewing, child rearing and so on." She paused to sip her tea and continued, "when I present you with a potential match, you will have the opportunity to go over his initial letter and the reference letters. If acceptable, you will write back and begin a courtship by mail. Your responsibility is to be as honest as possible about yourself. Your letter should include your capabilities, your qualities and what you expect of your prospective husband. He does not want to be trapped in a position where the two of you are not suited to each other, any more than you do. I should also mention he is not obligated to agree with the first lady I suggest. Nor are you obligated to the first man. I hope I am making myself clear?"

"Yes, ma'am." Now, Mary was feeling much better about her choice. She quickly responded. "This sounds quite acceptable."

"To reiterate," Mrs. Turner tilted her head and held her gaze. "You will be leaving your family, home, and friends behind. Your new home will be in a place quite different than a big city like Philadelphia. We will be considering men who will have property, for example, a farm or a ranch or perhaps even a business in town. However, life could be hard. The amenities may differ greatly from what you are accustomed to, such as, there may be no indoor plumbing."

Something more to consider, Mary shivered as she pictured herself trudging through the snow just to get to the outhouse.

MARY EXITED MRS. TURNER'S OFFICE, AND IN TYPICAL FASHION, Rachel grabbed Mary's arm, and they bounded up the stairs. Rushing down the hall, she led Mary into her new bedroom.

"I am so happy to have you here with me! We shall share this big new adventure together. First, we will unpack your bag and trunks. And then I'll show you the house!" They approached the third bed in the large room and stopped. Rachel then took and hefted Mary's carpetbag onto the bed with an exaggerated huff and puff, ending with laughter.

"Oh Rachel, it is so nice to be here with you!" Mary relaxed as she listened to Rachel chatter about the various happenings. She considered this home to be very elegant as she glanced around. The room had three small single beds, each with a two-drawer night-stand. Against the opposite wall were three narrow wardrobes sporting a different colored ribbon tied to each doorknob. Looking further, Mary noted that each nightstand had a corresponding colored ribbon tied to its drawer handle. *How VERY organized!* Bright colors of blue and yellow were used to decorate the room. And, of course, in the corner was a small ladies desk stocked with paper, pen, and inkwell. *I do admire the choice of the décor of this home, and I think I'll make notes on any details I might want to use for my new home.*

"Let's get you unpacked and settled," Rachel proclaimed.

Mary nodded, and the two of them began to unpack. "My second trunk will not take much time to unpack, only a few dresses. I will leave the books and other odds and ends in the trunk. Could you help me drag it to the foot of the bed like the others?"

"Of course," said Rachel.

Just then a few young ladies entered the room. They each gave a nod to Mary and settled themselves on the bed across from her. A pretty blonde lady spoke first with a distinct southern drawl. "We all personally wanted to say, 'welcome.' Rachel told us that you would arrive today. I am Charlotte, on my right is Jeannine and to my left is Adele. It is very nice to have you here." Charlotte looked to her companions, and they all nodded in agreement.

"Thank you for your nice welcome. It is good to be here, finally."

Hearing a sudden swish of satin, everyone lifted their eyes to the doorway. There stood another young lady. She did not attempt to enter. Her face was long and gaunt-looking which seemed to indicate a permanent scowl. She had ink black hair which was pulled into a very tight bun that sat slightly above her neck. It did nothing to soften her appearance. "I am Clara, and I believe we are to go down to the Parlor to attend a sewing lesson." And with that, she left. Mary watched her as she spun around and traipsed down the hall. *That's a very unhappy young woman.*

After a couple of moments of silence, everyone mumbled about going down stairs and took their leave. Rachel touched Mary's shoulder, "Do you need to freshen up first?"

"Yes, please. It has been such a long journey," Mary replied.

Smiling Rachel nodded, "I will go downstairs to the Parlor and save a spot for us. It gets very crowded, and it is best to get a well-lit seat for sewing."

Mary knew there would be questions later, maybe even as to what brought her to the Agency. And she had better start thinking about her answers.

FRESHENING UP FROM HER TRAVELS, MARY TOOK RACHEL'S advice. She splashed water on her face from the pretty blue wash-stand bowl. As the water trickled down, she picked up the yellow embroidered hand cloth and blotted her face dry. Now she was ready to attend the sewing lesson.

Mary entered the parlor and noticed the instructor was not yet present. This delay gave her a little time to study the surrounding décor. The first item to catch Mary's eye was the picture hanging above the fireplace mantel. Looking closer at the painting, Mary saw a younger version of Mrs. Turner sitting beside an older woman, most likely her mother. Standing behind the ladies were three men of various ages dressed in somber clothing. A printing press stood next to the men.

Soon she saw Rachel waving to her. Mary hastened over to sit beside her on the love seat. Leaning over, she whispered, "I noticed the portrait, and I was wondering if Mrs. Turner's family was in the printing business?"

"Yes, after her husband died in the Civil War, she returned to help with the family's newspaper. During this time, she noticed quite a few advertisements from men looking for wives to join them out West. Based on that information, she then formed the matchmaking agency. Her thinking was she could more accurately match respectable women to respectable men, and in the mean-time, the ladies living at the agency could learn domestic skills."

"Good gracious, I for one would appreciate being matched to a respectable man. Apparently, I am not very good at the matching part," muttered Mary.

"Now Mary, you promised me you would stop thinking about the past."

"You are correct, and I promise again."

Hearing someone entering the room, Mary turned thinking it would be the instructor. Instead, it was Clara. And here she was, later than everyone. Clara sauntered over to where Charlotte sat. She stopped and looked down at her, "I always sit in this chair as I require the additional light from the window." Charlotte flinched and then stiffened. She glanced around not knowing where to go.

Adele came to the rescue. "Charlotte, I would be pleased if you would sit by me on the settee. There is excellent light given off by the lamp behind. And, I have seen the lovely stitches you set. Perhaps that will inspire me!"

"Oh, thank you, Adele. You are very kind." Charlotte murmured as she stood and smoothed out her dress. Smiling, she walked over to Adele. In one graceful motion, she sat down. Mary watched Charlotte quickly scanned the room to see the smiles given to her by the other ladies. *Well done, Charlotte and Adele!* After a moment of uncomfortable silence, the ladies began to converse again.

"I know I will need more than good lighting to improve MY stitching or darning," Rachel stated to the ladies sitting close by.

Mary was enjoying the humor offered. "Presently if I were to darn any man's socks, they would unravel in the middle of a rain storm!" Everyone laughed.

A small round older woman rushed into the room. "I apologize for my tardiness ladies. It was unavoidable. I am Mrs. Davies, for those of you who are new to the Agency. Let's get right to your lesson. I would like everyone to please take a wool sock from this basket. Each sock already has a darning egg inside. I will demonstrate how to darn the hole, and then you may begin. I will be walking around the room to provide assistance." Mrs. Davies seated herself in the wing back chair and proceeded with her demonstration.

All the ladies began their task. Mary struggled to keep the wooden egg in front of the hole, so much so, that she began to giggle. Tightening her grip, she blew out a breath of air. *Finally, I got you! Now stay still.* By this time, laughter was heard throughout the room. Mary glimpsed around. The only person not laughing or smiling was Clara. Instead, she was staring down at her sock. Looking further, Mary saw that Clara's eyebrows were almost knitted together. *If she would only smile and spare a kind word for someone else, she could have more friends.*

Rachel caught Mary's eye and whispered, "I guess you were not kidding when you suggested that your husband's sock would unravel. Your stitches look awful. You need to ask Mrs. Davies for help."

"Oh, very well. What would I do without you? Let me see yours." Mary looked over at Rachel's sock, "Of course, the stitches are perfect!" Rachel gave Mary an impish smile.

Mary looked around and found Mrs. Davies. She called out, "it is Mary Schulman, and I would greatly appreciate your help when you have a moment, PLEASE."

"Why yes, Mary. I would be most happy to help." Walking over, she first stopped in front of Charlotte. "Charlotte, you have done an excellent job. It is evident you already know this task."

Charlotte glowed with the praise. "Thank you, Mrs. Davies. I did the darning for my family, being the eldest girl."

Mrs. Davies smiled and continued walking to Mary. She looked down. She stopped. "My dear, your stitches must be closer. You need to pull them together. Like so." Leaning over, she reached for the sock, pulled the yarn taut and returned it. Mary took it carefully, determined not to let the egg slip again.

"Do not worry. You will improve with time." She gave a brief nod to Mary.

Turning to face the entire group, Mrs. Davies gave a smile to all. "I have another basket of wool socks which I have given Mrs. Turner. I would greatly appreciate if you would darn these socks in your spare time. After which, they will be given back to the older members of my church community. Some folks are unable to darn their socks as a result of age afflictions, or they have no family members to help them." All the ladies eagerly pledged their support. Overwhelmed by their generosity, Mrs. Davies collected a hankie from inside her dress sleeve and dabbed at the corners of her eyes. She then continued her inspection of the ladies' progress. When she reached Clara, she stopped. Shaking her finger, Mrs. Davies stated, "one moment… you are holding your sewing too close to your face. I want you to hold it further away, so you do not end up poking your eye out. Is there some reason you feel you must hold it so close?"

Clara looked up in surprise. Her face turned beet red, and her mouth dropped open. "NO, Mrs. Davies, there is not. I will endeavor to hold it further away." Clara bristled as she spoke, her chin jutting out further in defiance.

Mrs. Davies nodded with a patronizing smile and concluded the lesson. She informed the ladies she would see them in three days hence.

LIFE AT THE AGENCY WAS ALWAYS BUSY AND TIME QUICKLY PASSED. Mary would often sit with a book in hand and watch what was happening around her. Sometimes she would see a person struggling with a task or maybe see the excitement of a young lady accepting a proposal. The latter always had Mary daydreaming of her future. *What will my husband be like? Perhaps he'll be an owner of a store in town, a cattle rancher or someone else entirely?*

Soon most of the ladies had become good friends, and they

shared their knowledge on many homemaking tasks and ideas. With the exception of Sundays, their days were filled with two or even three lessons. The most recent lesson was on making jam and taught by Mrs. Cameron, the cook. Not exactly a simple task. However, everyone enjoyed the fruits of their labors with the morning's toast. Today was their day to relax, and Mary had decided to do a little reading in the Agency library. Skimming the titles of the books, she was looking for something which would catch her interest.

After a while, Rachel sauntered into the library. "Mary, would you like to go into town for tea and scones?" Rachel coaxed. "Charlotte and Jeannine are coming as well."

Mary turned and contemplated the offer. She watched Rachel put her hands on her hips.

"Do come, Mary, you need an outing," she pleaded.

In a mocking gesture, Mary placed HER hands on her hips. "I thought I would stay inside and do a little reading. Maybe even copy down a few recipes. Mrs. Cameron said I should write down all those I thought would be of interest."

Rachel tilted her head slightly and then arched an eyebrow. "The weather is most pleasant today, and it's not always this nice. We could stop into Englebert's Bookstore and Periodicals Shop. It's just a little way down from the tea house," she offered.

Mary recognized this expression Rachel's face — the one that said, she would not take NO for an answer. She shrugged her shoulders and surrendered with "You win. I am convinced. Let me fetch my things."

"Oh, by-the-way, where is Adele? And, what about inviting Clara? I feel sorry for her sitting all by herself. What IS her story?" Mary quietly inquired.

Stepping closer, Rachel whispered, "Adele is visiting her local relatives now. And … the reason Clara is here, is her stepmother wants her quickly married off. Her thinking was to enable her own daughters to be free to marry the better prospects in their town. It's very sad. I have tried to include her, but she always refuses."

"We need to ask Clara to sit with us at dinner tonight," Mary stated.

"As usual, that is a commendable idea. Tonight then. You are a good person." Rachel waved her hands back and forth. "Go, Go. Jeannine and Charlotte are waiting for us. I knew I could convince you to say yes."

Hurrying up to her room, Mary grabbed her bag, parasol, and gloves and ran back down the stairs. She arrived in the foyer and saw that the ladies were chatting up a storm. They were all clearly in need of some exercise and a change of scenery. *This is a good idea.* "Come on ladies; I am ready! Let's go out for our tea and scones. After, we can walk over to the bookstore."

Jeannine's slender face lit up with impish delight. Bouncing up on her toes, "I am ready to go. No waiting for me."

Rachel instantly contributed, "I vote for getting tea and scones first. I'm hungry."

While tying the ribbons of her pretty flowered hat, Charlotte joined in, "this way, we will keep our books free of tea or jam stains."

Jeannine stopped twirling the point of her parasol on the floor and turned to Charlotte. "You are always the thinker."

The ladies laughed and then stepped out into the sunshine. After a brisk walk, they arrived at the Turtle Dove Cafe. The head waiter, evidently impressed with four such lovely young ladies, showed them to a table by the front window where they could watch the people walking up and down the street. Sitting down, they were presented with a menu. Admiring the variety of teas, muffins, donuts, and scones offered, they settled on a large pot of Oolong tea, scones with clotted cream and strawberry jam to be shared amongst the four of them.

The conversation started out with the latest fashions for ladies and moved to baking and cooking. Before long, it turned towards a common topic which was what traits each lady considered were desirable or undesirable in a husband. Mary watched Rachel take charge.

"Let's see, what do I find are good traits in a man? Well, I think the man should be quiet but answer when spoken to. He should be adventuresome but not stray too far from home. Someone, who will treat his wife as an equal. And do all the cooking himself." Rachel kept a straight face throughout her entire disclosure.

Knowing Rachel was waiting to see what the group's reaction would be, Mary glanced around. She saw Charlotte's eyes widen and her mouth drop open, probably at the idea of the man of the house doing all the cooking himself. Looking to Charlotte's left, Mary saw Jeannine had her hand covering her mouth. She was trying very hard not to laugh.

A moment of silence passed and Charlotte quickly figured out Rachel was putting her on. "Goodness Rachel, who would not like most of those traits? I, for one, would also like to be free of the cooking chores and have a husband who could cook. Who knows, he might even be a better cook than me, especially now. He should also be kind and strong. And, if he had nice teeth and a full head of hair it would be a blessing." The ladies were all grinning now.

By this time Jeannine had removed her hand from her mouth. "If I am going to dream, then I choose to add to your list — a generous man. One, who would want to open a bakery shop for me. He might also think of me as his princess. I could cook and care for him as if he were a king."

Last, it was Mary's turn to say something. She lightly tapped her forehead. "Wishes aside, and to be truthful, I would settle for an honest, faithful, hardworking man and one who bathes occasionally." The sudden burst of laughter drew immediate scowls from the three tables nearby.

After composing themselves, they finished their tea and decided it was time to walk over to the bookstore. They picked up their belongings and walked down the street, window-shopping along the way. Two blocks later, they arrived at a large carved wooden door with colorful leaded windows. Big black letters above the door proclaimed this store to be Englebert's Books and Periodicals.

Entering, they soon found their separate sections of interest. Splitting off from the rest of group, Mary decided to look at the magazines and news publications. Hoping to impress her future husband she thought to look for Frontier related periodicals. These would be useful later. A table near the payment counter held several stacks of magazines. She glanced through them. *Ah, ha. I see a few referencing the newest practices for ranching and farming.* The first magazine to catch her eye was the largest, and it was entitled **Farm and Fireside**. Turning the pages of the second publication entitled **The National Grange**, she became fascinated with an article entitled **Know Your Chicken**. *Apparently, chickens were not all the same.* Hearing footsteps behind her, Mary grabbed the last magazine near the front of the table. She recognized this magazine was the one her mother periodically purchased. It was **The Home Companion**. These publications were just what Mary needed to familiarize herself with what she thought was to become her new life. She wanted to be well informed on most aspects of life in the West. With her newfound wealth of information, she stepped up to the counter. Placing **The Home Companion** on top, she pushed the magazines towards the clerk. She promptly paid the clerk and folded her new purchases placing them into her bag.

Turning, Mary looked around the store to find her friends. Rachel was the first to approach her. "Sooo, what did you get?" And without even waiting for Mary to answer, Rachel showed off her purchase. "Look what I found, the **Buckeye Cookery and Practical Housekeeping**. And, it was published in 1877 — not too long ago. Therefore, it must have all the latest information on how to cure meats and – all KINDS of recipes as well medical ailments. Okay, now what do YOU have tucked away?" Rachel stepped closer and peered down at Mary's bulging net bag.

MARY HAD LEARNED THERE WERE TWO REASONS WHY ONE MIGHT be called to Mrs. Turner's office. The first was a potential match. However, she had only recently arrived at the agency, so perhaps that was not it. The second reason was being guilty of an infraction of the house rules. She could remember nothing she had done wrong. *What could this be? Has she found someone for me so soon?* Apprehensively, she knocked lightly on the office door.

"Come in, please."

Entering, Mary closed the door behind her. Mrs. Turner was at the sideboard pouring a cup of tea. Turning to Mary, "Would you like a cup of tea?"

Afraid her trembling hands were not steady enough to hold the teacup, she replied. "I have recently finished a cup." Swiftly she added, "Thank you for the offer, ma'am."

"Please have a seat, Mary." The older woman smiled and motioned her to the wing-backed chair. She then proceeded to get settled behind her desk. "I have something to discuss with you."

Nervous, Mary smoothed her skirt as she sat. "Yes, ma'am." She clasped her hands together in her lap to mask the trembling.

"Mary, I have a potential match for you to consider."

"So, soon?" She could hardly contain herself. "Please tell me more." She had been here a much shorter time than several of the other girls. It didn't seem right it should be her turn.

Mrs. Turner lifted the top few pieces of paper from the stack nearest her and read. "His name is Charles Baxter, and he lives in the town of Crystal Creek in Montana Territory." She took a sip of tea and continued. "He is a widower with a small daughter." Clearing her voice, she then read further, "he owns a farm a short distance from town, and he comes with excellent recommendations from Reverend Winterthorpe of the local church and, he has two other references as well. This is Mr. Baxter's letter and the other letters." The agency's owner extended the papers.

With her hands' shaking, Mary took the offered papers.

"Would you be open to a match with a widower and one who already has a child?" the agency's owner asked.

Eager to answer this question, she began. "I can already say this would NOT be a problem for me in any way. I am older than many of your Agency ladies, so having a daughter would give me a head start, so-to-speak."

"Dear, you should still consider those issues overnight, and you need to read the letters carefully." Mrs. Turner's voice became quite serious. "If you wish this match, the next step would be for the two of you to correspond before committing. However, if you have any doubts in the morning, it would be best to wait for another prospect." Mrs. Turner leaned forward in her chair. "As you are aware, this is not a decision to be answered straight away." The older woman's gaze was intense.

Mary sat up even straighter. "I understand. And, I will read the letters with a promise to consider them with the utmost care."

"Very good and thank you. I will leave you to your thoughts."

"One question, if I may?" Mary requested.

Mrs. Turner tilted her head to one side. "Yes, my dear?"

She glanced down at the papers in her hands and then looked at Mrs. Turner. "I have been here such a short time compared to some of the other ladies. Why did you select me for this man?"

"You have a maturity about you, Mary. A man with a child will need this quality. Also, I have found matching people of similar height is one good way to start. Men have strong bones and strong muscles, but can have weak egos." Mrs. Turner paused a moment. Mary nodded thinking this was one of Mrs. Turner's shared bits of wisdom. It sounded logical.

"A man most often wants to be bigger and stronger than his wife. However, this match is promising for other reasons. One being, you both enjoy reading – a common interest that will help to pass the time during those long winter months." She took another sip of her tea before continuing. "It is for all of these reasons, I first thought of you for Mr. Baxter. However, I do want this to be your choice."

"Yes ma'am, I understand and thank you." Mary knew her height had caused most men to shy away from her in the past. In this case, her height was an asset. Mary rose from the chair. Her heart was light with anticipation.

The elder lady smiled. "This is what I am here for, dear."

"When you go downstairs, would you be so kind as to please ask Abigail to come to my office." Mrs. Turner was now perusing through the second stack of papers on her desk. *Perhaps, there is good news for Abigail, too. I hope so for her sake.* Abigail had been at the agency the longest of all of her new friends. "Certainly, ma'am." And she left in search of Abby.

Mary couldn't wait to tell Rachel the good news. Believing she might have found her match, she hoped she would find nothing in the letters that would change her mind – at least not at this point.

THE LADIES WERE IN GOOD HUMOR LISTENING TO ADELE TELLING stories about her family. On a few occasions Adele had confided, she would not marry any man from Baltimore as they spent most of their time in the beer halls. She was an amazing story teller. Relaxing, Mary ate her supper. When it seemed polite, she excused herself. She knew she had some serious thinking to do.

Exiting the dining room, she went to the library and walked over to her favorite spot. There she snuggled up in the blue tapestry armchair and pulled out the letters to read again. She poured over each word and, in the end, became certain of her prospect for a good match. It seemed he was a good family man, well respected around town and an excellent farmer. She liked how he showed concern for his young daughter. She had enjoyed the occasions when she was asked to watch after her young cousins. Reading again the portion of the letter where he disclosed his love of reading, she was pleased they had this in common. She found her heart ached for Charles when she thought about him losing his wife and father. He was honest to admit the winters were very cold in the Montana Territory. And to Mary's way of thinking, a successful farmer must be a man of action with a good constitution. She did not want a man who had his head in the clouds, unable to see what was in front of him. Mary was determined she would not be so foolish as to give her heart to another wishy-washy man. Mary thought about her conversation with Mrs. Turner earlier and realized she liked the idea of being matched to a tall man.

The late hour had caught up to her, and she left her chair in favor of finding her bed. As she crawled between the sheets, she dreamed of life on a farm. She saw herself feeding the chickens and milking the cow, fixing supper and then reading to Elizabeth with Charles looking on.

Waking up the next morning, Mary knew she wanted to know more about Charles. Hopefully, he would be pleased to hear about her. Finishing with her toiletries and putting on her most perky and colorful dress, she picked up her skirts and ran down the stairs. Arriving near Mrs. Turner's office, she slowed to a subdued walk. Trying to gather her composure, she took a deep breath and then slowly exhaled. Stopping at the slightly open door, she smoothed out the billows of her dress and gave the door a gentle rap-tap-tap. "Mrs. Turner, it is Mary, are you available?"

"Good morning, Mary. Yes. Please enter."

Mary quickly entered and closed the door behind her. Turning, she saw Mrs. Turner gesture towards the green chair again. After sitting, she pulled the four letters out from her pocket and placed them on her lap. "Mrs. Turner, I am very happy to say I would like to begin a correspondence with Mr. Baxter. He sounds like a gentleman and someone I would like to know more about."

Mrs. Turner grinned. "Well, Miss Mary, this is exactly the response I had hoped you would give me. Please help yourself to the writing material on the corner of my desk and remember always to be yourself when corresponding. If you have any questions, please do not hesitate to call upon me."

Springing up from her chair, Mary clasped the letters to her chest. "Oh, thank you, thank you. I shall write my letter to Mr. Baxter right now."

Before leaving the office, Mary took some blank sheets of paper and envelopes. She brought them upstairs and thought about her correspondence with Mr. Charles Baxter. She sat at the bedroom desk and wrote,

July 2, 1882

Dear Mr. Baxter,

My name is Mary Schulman, and I was born and raised in Philadelphia, Pennsylvania. I am a bookkeeper's daughter and enjoy reading and helping my father with some of his extra bookkeeping tasks. In the past, I have taken care of my cousins' children and have greatly enjoyed doing so. It's always a pleasure to read to them. In addition, I also help them with their letters, reading, and their numbers. I understand your daughter is shy and I remember as a young girl, I was somewhat the same. I believe I can be a good wife and help you raise your daughter with love, understanding, and affection.

Although I was raised in the city, I would look forward to the living in the country with its beautiful mountains and plains. I know how to cook and care for a home, and I am willing to learn about the responsibilities of being a farmer's wife.

For myself, I am twenty-five years of age, tall for a woman, slender but not frail, and I have auburn colored hair and brown eyes. I have been told I am not unattractive.

I look forward to your next letter.

Sincerely yours,

Mary Schulman

Reading over her letter again, she was satisfied with the

content. Eager to get her letter on its way, Mary hurried out to the Post Office. She was hoping for a quick and favorable reply.

AFTER A COUPLE OF MONTHS OF CORRESPONDENCE, MARY HAD agreed to marry Charles. Last night she had written her parents telling them about Charles and her upcoming marriage.

She made a list of what she needed to do before she left the Agency. The first item was to get a few children's books for Charles' daughter. The second was to purchase warm winter clothing if she could find it. It was still warm in Cincinnati.

In the morning, she hurried down to the local bookstore near the agency. While there, she picked up a few books and the latest new publications on farming. Mrs. Turner had shared the thought they would be scarce in the Northwest.

Returning to the agency and walking into the parlor, Mary was greeted by Rachel and all her friends. She felt herself blush as she took out her new book purchases. The last book she drew up very slowly from her mesh bag. She knew it would catch Rachel's eye. It was the ***Buckeye Cookery and Practical Housekeeping*** – the same book Rachel had purchased earlier!

Upon seeing it, Rachel shrieked. "Great minds think alike! I have already begun to read mine and found it most helpful!" Then she dropped her voice to a playful whisper. "I need the most help."

Everyone laughed. Undoubtedly, they all remembered Rachel burning her batch of jam in class. Standing amongst her friends, Mary was thankful for the good wishes in starting her new life. Each of her friends insisted she write them and include all the details of travel, her new family, and home. Mary took a long look at them and realized she would be a little sad to leave. She stepped up to each of her friends, to include Clara, and gave them a kiss on the cheek. Not surprisingly, they all offered to help her pack. Thankful for the help, Mary laughed. 'Many hands make light work' was the moto day. And the trunks were finished in no time. Upon completion, they all left. Rachel stayed to help her change into her traveling clothes.

The door to the office was partly open. Mary gave a light knock.

"Please enter, Mary. Come sit down and we can discuss the final details of your journey." Mrs. Turner softly smiled. "I know you are nervous. However, I also know you are an intelligent young woman, and this is what the West needs." She extended a hand holding a thick envelope containing the travel itinerary. Mary took it. "You may now open the envelope, and we will discuss the contents."

Opening the envelope, Mary found a train ticket, ten dollars for the purchase of the stagecoach ticket and other travel costs, and a letter containing directions of travel to her future husband's home. Looking up, Mary felt her eyes become a little misty. "Thank you, Mrs. Turner, for everything. I am most appreciative of the classes offered here and for the opportunity of meeting such nice ladies. Most of all, I want to thank you again for all of your help."

Mary saw the agency owner's face beam with appreciation. Her facial features had softened and took on a more youthful appearance. Mrs. Turner gave a nod, stood up and walked around. She gave Mary a gentle embrace. "Mary, thank you for your kind words, and I wish you the very best!"

Blushing, Mary dipped her head and excused herself from the office. She thanked all the agency staff a big thank you and said a final goodbye to all her friends. And to Rachel, a kiss on each cheek was given and a promise to write soon.

CHAPTER 4

CRYSTAL CREEK, MONTANA – EARLY AUGUST 1882

CHARLES WOKE UP FEELING EXHILARATED. HIS CORRESPONDENCE with Mary Schulman at the Turner Bridal Agency had ended with their agreement to marry. He thought about introducing Mary to his family. He pictured her in his home. Then his vision slowly changed. First, it showed an old but well-built home in need of painting and some repairs. Next, it showed the barn missing a window shutter here and there, and finally, corral fences with a few missing rails. It was apparent he had spent much time mourning the passing of his wife and father. In hindsight, he had clung onto his grief for far too long. Feeling panicky, he wondered where to start. It seemed everywhere he looked there was something that needed to be fixed. He loved this old farm, and he wanted to make his home the place it once was so Mary would love it too.

It was time for some sprucing up. Charles remembered his father's favorite expression, 'ALWAYS PUT YOUR BEST FOOT FORWARD, SON!' He made a mental list of chores to do, and before long he realized it was quite lengthy.

The first chore on his list was to paint the house. Driving into town to get the needed supplies, Charles began to daydream. It was time for everyone to see the house in its original splendor. *What should I say if they ask about all this sudden fixing up? I do need to tell them about Mary, but I'll save it for tomorrow.*

Returning from town with cans of paint, he started in on the front of the house. Charles worked quickly, the brush moving in time with a song he was whistling. His thoughts drifted to Mary. *What will she think when she sees this place? Since Mary is an east coast lady, I am sure she will be used to an attractive home.* Distracted by the thoughts of his new bride, Charles didn't realize it was almost supper time until he heard the angry rumbles in his stomach. He stepped back and saw he had finished the bottom half of the farmhouse. *Not too shabby.*

He went to the barn and changed from his paint-spattered clothes. Having worked up an appetite, he was looking forward to supper. He hoped his mother wouldn't ask any awkward questions. Entering the house, he gave a hardy greeting, "Mom, supper smells delicious!" Stopping in front of his daughter, he bent down and gave her a kiss on the forehead. "Lizzie, did you help?"

Lizzie's slowly looked to her grandmother and then to her father, "I set the table and put out the honey for your biscuits."

"Ah well, it looks wonderful darling." He reached down and swept the hair away from her eyes.

Everyone sat down at the table to eat, and supper was finished in no time. Mom and Lizzie started to clear the table.

"Charles, I think it is nice you are repainting the house. Perhaps, we should ask Francis and her mother over for dinner again? Don't you want them to see how lovely the place looks now?" his mother suggested.

Quick to squash the wretched thought of entertaining Francis again, Charles lowered his eyes to Lizzie and dropped his voice, "Lizzie, please go and feed the chickens. They are looking a little thin."

Lizzie's eyes nearly popped out. "Again?" she asked.

"Yes… again."

She shrugged her shoulders and glanced to her grandmother and then again to her father. "Do I get a piece of pie later?" the little girl asked.

"Yes Lizzie, of course, you do. I will come get you in a few minutes when the pie is ready." *I will tell her later.*

Charles watched his little girl quietly walk to the front door. "Please leave the door open — so I can see you."

He then turned towards his mother. "Mom, please sit down. I have something important to tell you." Charles waited until she took a seat. "Well, as a matter of fact, I AM sprucing up the farm a little. However, I am NOT doing it for Francis. Do you remember when we had dinner at the Nelsons?"

"Oh, goodness, you aren't doing this because you want to invite the Nelsons over to dinner?" Her tone had an aggravated note.

Nip her remarks in the bud. "No, I am talking about the Nelsons' suggestion of a mail order bride. I thought about it and decided it was a good idea. So, I have already written to the Turner Bridal Agency, and I have agreed to marry a lovely young lady with whom I have been corresponding."

Abruptly, Helen got up from the table. She took her plate into the kitchen and slammed it on the counter. The crashing noise reverberated off the counter top and onto the walls and even off the ceiling. He heard the broken dish as it finally hit the sink and floor. Undoubtedly this was Mom's first attempt at voicing her displeasure.

His mother returned to the table and gave him a cold hard stare. "Charles, I did not think you would take that advice seriously. I cannot believe you did this without talking to me. How could you prefer someone we have never met over marrying a nice girl like Francis Miller?" Her voice grew louder with each word. Finally, she finished talking and just stared at him.

"Mom, I know you want the best for us, but this needs to be my decision. Please believe me when I say Francis is not what I want in a wife. On this, you will have to trust me." He paused for a moment. "You know better than most people — there is a lot of work on a farm. Do you honestly think a girl like Francis would lift a finger to help anybody but her silly spoiled self?" He watched his mother's eyes flash with anger.

"I do trust you, but Charles I cannot let you invite some unknown into our home. How could you do this to me?" his mother announced with a slow, deliberate enunciation to each word.

It doesn't seem like you trust me. Charles took a deep breath and reminded himself that he was a grown man. "Mom," Charles recognized his voice sounded like his father's. "I am the man of this house and the one who is getting married. She is coming here to be a part of this family and to help us whether you like it or not. And this is the last I want to hear of it."

Helen's face slackened and then grew red with rage. She stormed from the room. *Well, I guess it could have gone worse.* And Charles walked over to the table and cut two large pieces of pie, one for him and one for Lizzie.

CHARLES WALKED OUT TO THE BARN WITH THE PIE. AFTER THE confrontation with Mom, he thought giving the news about Lizzie's new mother would be better done in the barn. He saw Lizzie playing with the new chicks. "Lizzie, come here, and we'll sit down on the milking stools and eat our pie."

His little girl nodded and took the piece of pie he offered her. "All right, Papa."

After a few moments, Charles looked to his daughter. "Sweetheart, we need to have a little talk."

"Okay." She glanced at the straw in front of his feet and then to his face.

"It has been over two years since your Mother and Granddaddy have gone to heaven. I believe they are looking down and wishing us well. They knew how hard life was on a farm. It is often a lonely life. Your friends Tommy, Bobby, and Jane are never alone. As they grow up, they will have each other to talk to and will always help one another. It is for these reasons, and much more that I've decided to get a new mother for you." Charles paused when he saw the shocked look on Lizzie's face. Her mouth flew opened and her eyes watered … tears flowed.

She gasped. "A new mother?! But I love my old mother!" Lizzie paused to gulp in air and then coughed. She cleared her throat. "An — and, I miss her, very much! I don't want a new mother. No one will ever replace my mother. I'm not calling anyone else 'Mother'!" Her face was flushed, and the tears continued down her cheeks as she crossed her little arms in front of her chest.

Charles dropped his pie plate on the ground beside him. Reaching over, he gathered his daughter into his arms. He held her tightly as she continued to cry on his shoulder. It hurt him so to see her cry like that.

After several long moments, he whispered in her ear, "Lizzie, no one could ever replace your mother. She will remain in our hearts forever. You can take my word on that." He gave her another big hug, and the sobbing subsided.

Charles attempted to get the conversation back on track. "You know your grandmother needs help with her chores. School will start soon. And, I know how much you are looking forward to attending. I am sure you have noticed Miss Miller is around more than usual. It seems your grandmother has her eye on Miss Miller as a mother for you and a wife for me. She is not my idea of a suitable companion for either of us. But you must understand your grandmother is just trying to help."

Lizzie's eyes widen as she took a deep breath. Charles raised his hand. *That got her attention.*

He continued. "Instead, Auntie Daniela and Uncle Owen suggested I write a letter to the Turner Bridal Agency for help in finding someone for us. Her name is Miss Mary Schulman. Don't worry you do not have to call this new lady 'Mother.' Most importantly, you will always be my daughter. If you have any problems or questions about her, you are to talk to me right away. You know I love you very, very much. And we can always talk to each other, daytime or night."

Lizzie wiped her eyes with her dress sleeve and sniffed. Pulling back a little, she looked into her father's eyes. "Truly, I may talk to you anytime?"

Reassuringly, Charles smiled at his little girl. "Of course, anytime. Please give this new lady a chance. That is what you would like someone to do for you. She is traveling a long distance to be a part of OUR family. She is leaving HER family behind and will be lonesome at first. I know you will help her when she is sad. Surely, we all have room in our hearts for another. Now lastly, we can't call her 'lady,' or 'Miss Schulman,' or even 'Mrs. Baxter' all the time because that will not be polite. So since 'Mother' is rightfully taken, why don't you call her 'Mama.' Does this sound all right to you?"

Lizzie sniffed. "It sounds all right to me," she quietly replied.

Charles hugged his daughter once again, and they walked back into the house.

EXCITED, MARY ARRIVED AT THE TRAIN STATION WITH TIME TO spare. Today was the day, she would start her journey to meet her new family. She boarded the train and found a nice secluded place to sit down. It would be a long journey and to pass the time away, she decided upon reading. She opened her bag and pulled out the first book. It was ***Alice's Adventures in Wonderland***, one of her favorite childhood books. She had bought this book especially to read to Elizabeth. The next books were on farming. *No, not now.* She sighed and continued to look. She settled on the ***Buckeye Cookery and Practical Housekeeping***. It seemed fitting for her journey and would help to ease her nerves. The train ride was to take five to six days and had many stops.

As time crept by, Mary grew more restless with each day that passed. There were only so many times a person could reread 'How to Roast a Chicken' and make an apple pie.

It was mid-morning, and Mary woke up as she felt the train jolt. It was slowing down. After days of sitting and much-interrupted sleep, she was exhausted. This was the last stop of her train ride. Beaverton, Montana was finally here.

The nice conductor helped Mary off the train and pointed out the stationmaster for her. Men were unloading luggage and crates from the baggage car in the rear. Her trunks were just coming off.

The stationmaster was a portly fellow with a balding head. "Do you need some help, Miss?" he asked.

"Please sir, I need to take the stagecoach to Crystal Creek."

"Why, yes Miss. Welcome to Beaverton. You will catch the northbound stagecoach outside the Astor Hotel here in town. The hotel is to the right up on this street — in the middle of the second block. If you point out your luggage, I will have my porters take them over to the hotel for you." He motioned for two men to come over.

"Thank you very much, sir. My trunks are the two dark brown ones there, next to the lamppost. They have yellow ribbons tied to the handles, and the name on them is Mary Schulman."

"Very well, Miss."

The porters moved the trunks onto a short cart. As Mary walked towards the hotel, she turned to make sure they were following close behind. Entering the lobby, she walked up to the register counter. There sat a short older man. His vest buttons strained against his ample belly – the last two buttons missing. What little gray hair he had was combed over his bald patch. She tried to keep herself from staring … as she saw his mustache was curled out to his ears. It did not help matters that his neck stuck out like a turkey and with a beak-like nose, he reminded her of **Rumpelstiltskin** from **Grimm's Fairy Tales.** *So… this is the Western Frontier.*

"Excuse me, sir, could you please tell me when the northbound stage to Crystal Creek might be leaving?"

The man looked up from reading the newsprint. "Howdy Miss, I reckon the stagecoach should depart about one o'clock today. You can rest yourself in the lobby here while you're a'waitin. We keep the front doors open, so as to see when the stagecoach arrives. And, so you all can be cooler with the breeze. The restaurant will be open shortly if 'in you want for a bite to eat."

"Thank you, Mr…" Mary paused not knowing his name.

"Perkins, Miss. And it's a pleasure to help such fine little lady as yourself." And he gave her a pleasant smile.

"Thank you, Mr. Perkins. What can I do with my trunks?" Mary waved her hand to the two men standing on the boardwalk.

"Just have 'em set them right down here." Perkins waved to the men to bring her trunks inside. Mary smiled and paid the porters before they left. *I hope someday I'll be able to understand all they are saying.*

MARY DABBED AT HER MOIST BROW WITH HER HANKIE. THE BREEZE Mr. Perkins promised was non-existent. With loud gongs, the grandfather clock against the lobby wall announced it was three o'clock in the afternoon. The stage was very late, and she wondered if it would ever arrive. Quite a few people had traversed the hotel lobby to eat in the restaurant. And now, the smells from the kitchen made Mary hungry.

Across from her in the lobby sat a handsome cowboy with a gun strapped to his right hip. Her eyes widen as he shifted in his seat, exposing a row of bullets tucked in the loops of his gun belt. He glanced at her with his piercing black eyes, momentarily holding her gaze. *Could he be a gunslinger instead of a cowboy? One gun is probably typical for a cowboy in this town. I think a gunslinger would definitely carry two guns!* The cowboy had said only a few words since sitting down, and that was to inquire with the clerk about the northbound stage. The same stagecoach she was scheduled to board.

Mary shifted in her seat as the cowboy ran his fingers over the holster. *Maybe a gunman, after all?* He untied the leather string holding the holster to his thigh and stretched out his long legs. Mary quickly dipped her head so he wouldn't notice her watching him.

She had been reading the same section of her book over and over in order to avoid staring. The handsome cowboy was listening to what was being said out front. Mary considered the relaxed posture of the cowboy as it projected an easy manner. But she bet he would be ready for anything at a moment's notice.

All of a sudden, a loud clomping noise was heard. Mary turned her head to see what had caused the disturbance in front of the hotel. A young man mounted on a horse had slid to a halt. And with a high swing of his right leg, he dismounted. A couple of thuds were heard as his boots hit the hard dirt street. He entered – a cloud of dust followed as he walked over to the counter and stopped.

Mary was mesmerized. *He must be bringing news.* She eagerly listened for details.

"Billy, you not drivin' today?" The clerk scratched his head as he looked at the young man.

"We broke a wheel about ten miles south. You have any folks here waiting for the stage?" Timmy shifted from one leg to the other.

"The perdy one and the cowboy." Perkins pointed to the two of them, his Adam's apple bouncing up and down like a ball.

Turning to look at her and the handsome cowboy, Billy stroked his sparse beard. "We had a mite bit of trouble with the stage." He took off his hat and smacked it on his left trouser leg dispersing another cloud of dust. "Got a busted wheel and won't be able to go on till we get er' fixed. So, we won't be leaving here till mornin."

Mary placed her book firmly in her lap for the moment. "What bad luck!" Just then she realized she had not meant to voice her opinion out loud. *I hope this is not suggestive of events to come.*

Billy smiled and turned back to Perkins, "You got any idea where Smithers might be at? He warn't at the smithy or the livery, I done checked. I need him ta brung me out a new wheel. If'en he's got one." The young man stomped his boot, and even more dust settled to the floor.

"I'll help you find him, Billy." The cowboy swiftly rose from his seat and grabbed his hat. Then he strode over to the young man.

"Try the Wooden Nickel Saloon — spends about half his day there," the hotel clerk offered.

Billy limped out the door and turned right. The silent cowboy tipped his hat to Mary and followed.

This news is going to present a problem. Mary already knew there was no telegraph office in Crystal Creek. She had no way to tell Charles of this delay. Her mind began to picture Charles and Lizzie waiting for her until the sun had set. *Certainly, he will understand. Delays are inevitable if one was traveling by stagecoach, right?* Mary got up and went to the counter. She had to first deal with the problem of tonight's accommodations. "It seems I will need a room for this evening. Do you have one available?"

Perkins leaned over and examined the register. Turning it, he pushed it towards her.

"Have a large room in the front for two bucks or a smaller room in the back for a buck and a quarter."

Mary's father had always told her, 'it was easier to save a

dollar than it was to earn it,' and so her decision was easy. "The smaller room will be fine for me." Mary paused, this might be the last time she'd write the name she'd had all her life. Soon she'd be Mrs. Charles Baxter, and her husband would be the one writing their names in the hotel registers.

"Want a bath in your room for ten cents, Miss -" Perkins turned the book back to read her name. "Sc-Schulman. Want it now?"

"Yes, in about an hour," replied Mary. A bath sounded heavenly in this heat, but she decided food must come first.

As if Perkins had read her mind, "If'n you want somethin' to eat, not as fancy here — the Fussy Duck Café next door has mighty fine eats. Your trunks will be okay in the back room for the night. In the morning, I'll git them brung out to the stage."

"Thank you very much, Mr. Perkins. That is very kind of you." Mary took the room key from him and lifted her carpetbag. She was worried but what else could she do?

CHARLES STOOD ON THE BOARDWALK AT THE STAGE STOP IN FRONT of the Crystal Creek Hotel. The Nelsons, his mother, and daughter were waiting inside the lobby to meet Mary Schulman, his bride-to-be. Hopefully, Mary was everything she had stated in her letters. *Charles sent up a silent prayer.*

The Nelsons were to be witnesses at his wedding. However, it seemed the whole town was lingering outside waiting to see his mail order bride arrive.

Now the sun was setting on top of the hazy purple mountains behind the town. Watching the sun slowly slide away, Charles hoped the road would be visible for the drive home.

"Well, it should be along any time now." Owen turned to see the families had come out from the hotel lobby.

"Yep." Charles' stomach was in a knot with anticipation. *What had gone wrong with Mary's arrival? Maybe a broken axle, a lame horse or one of the passengers had become ill? Please let the problem be as small as that.*

Charles turned to see his mother walking towards him. He thought to distract her from any comments on the lateness of the stage … "how do you think I look, OK?" he asked.

His mother smiled. "You look very handsome. Don't you agree, Elizabeth?"

He glanced at his little girl.

"Oh yes, Papa. You look like a prince!" Lizzie's head bobbed up and down causing her blonde curls to bounce. She truly was the sweetest daughter a father could ever have!

"You look a far sight better than my Owen did when we got married." Daniela offered a playful smile.

This elicited a boisterous chuckle from Owen.

A lone rider came down Main Street. It was Shelby from the Twin Oaks Ranch. He pulled his mount to a stop in front of them. "Charles, the stage won't be coming today! I just came from Beaverton and heard them say they had a problem to the south. They lost a wheel. But the stage should be here tomorrow." He tipped the brim of his hat to the women folk and wheeled his dusty trail horse around and jogged off.

Well, at least Mary is okay, and she is waiting in Beaverton for the next stage. I hope. The knot in Charles' stomach started to unravel a bit with this new information. He rubbed the back of his neck and turned to his mother. "Why don't you take Lizzie down to get a treat at the Biscuit Box while I go notify the Reverend Winterthorpe."

"Elizabeth, start thinking of what you would like." Helen latched on to Lizzie's hand, and they started down the boardwalk.

Stopping a few feet away from her father, Lizzie turned. "I thought my new Mama was coming today." Her blue eyes grew misty.

"Sweetheart, she should be here tomorrow." The disappointment was written all over her face. Charles stepped forward, bent down and gave her a kiss on her cheek. *I cannot let her see how disappointed I am.*

He thanked the Nelsons for coming and understood when they expressed their desire to return home. One of Daniela's sisters was visiting and had offered to watch the children until after the ceremony. Before leaving, they reminded Charles to keep them abreast of any news and took their leave.

Charles turned to walk towards the parsonage. It was a small single-story house located to the right and behind the church. Through the years Charles thought of the Reverend and his wife as a second set of parents. He knocked lightly on the partly open front door. Shortly, Beatrice Winterthorpe appeared. "Good afternoon Charles. Come on in. And where is your young lady?" She tilted her head to the side and tried to glance behind him.

"Afternoon. Ahem ... Mrs. Winterthorpe there's been a slight problem. Her stage didn't arrive today."

The older woman froze. "Oh, my dear, I hope she's all right."

"As do I. I'm sorry for the inconvenience. I need to talk to the Reverend."

"You will find the Reverend in the Church. He is waiting for you," she replied.

He caught a glimpse of Mrs. Winterthorpe slowly shaking her head as he walked off.

Entering the church, he saw the Reverend turn to gaze upon him.

"Are you and your bride ready, Charles?" The Reverend looked around.

Unlike his wife, Thomas Winterthorpe possessed a strong booming voice. It always seemed surprising, given his slight frame. Many a Sunday, it was this voice that kept Charles and others awake during the services.

"I am sorry Reverend; the stage did not come in today. They lost a wheel south of Beaverton. So, it looks as if there will not be a wedding today. I am expecting her to be on the stage tomorrow." He watched the Reverend's posture stiffen.

The Reverend sighed, "Well, Charles, this will present a problem."

Charles felt a slight shiver down to his toes. *What else could go wrong?*

"I did not tell you earlier, but my mother's taken ill in Cheyenne. From what I am given to understand, it is serious. So, I'm committed to traveling there tomorrow. I cannot marry you until I return. I am leaving in the morning before the stage arrives from Beaverton."

Charles couldn't believe what he was hearing. He shifted from one foot to the other, "and, ahh — what shall I do in the meantime?"

"In the meantime, son, do you have a spare bedroom at the farm?"

"Well ... yes. In fact, we do have one. It was my brother's room."

"Then she can either stay at the hotel in town or, if she is comfortable with it, at your house. I'm sure your mother would act as a chaperone. And, since you two won't be married yet, I suggest you court her until I get back." Charles knew the Reverend was a kind and romantic sort of man. *Courting? I am not good at this sort of thing. Just how AM I to court her?*

Uncomfortable, he pulled at his collar. "And how soon might you be returning?" he muttered.

"I will send word to you after I get to Cheyenne. I expect it to be around three weeks or so. Still like I said, I will send word." Thomas Winterthorpe looked at Charles as he had when Charles was young. "Do you want to know what I think?" The Reverend's brows arched.

Sheepishly, Charles tried to maintain eye contact. "Well, yes, please Reverend."

"I think this is a blessing in disguise. It might make this transition easier for her. You know, it can be very hard for a woman to travel all the way across the country to marry a man she has never met."

Charles nodded. "I understand, and I thank you." Leaving the church, he noticed his shirt felt damp. Slowly he headed back up the street to the Biscuit Box. *Mary will think we are to marry after she disembarks from the stage. What will she think of this new predicament? And how am I going to break this fact to her? And I haven't even told her about Mom living with us yet.* He looked to the sky ... *Lord, please help me!*

Fortunately for Charles, the gathering out in front of the saloon had dispersed. Soon word would spread his bride was delayed and undoubtedly some folks would speculate she had gotten cold feet. He did not relish the thought of being the subject of some embarrassing gossip.

On the drive home, he explained the pertinent part of his conversation with the Reverend to his mother. When he finished, she whispered. "I think this is for the best, son. I am not too fond of this idea of marrying someone you have never met before. Now if she comes, the two of you can get to know each other first, like it ought to be." She lowered her voice even further, "And, then you can see how you feel."

For the rest of the drive, his mother was unusually quiet. From the corner of his eye, he thought he saw a bit of a smile on her face. One thing was for certain; he did not want to know WHY she was smiling.

CHAPTER 5

TODAY WAS A NEW DAY. AFTER A RESTLESS NIGHT, MARY DRESSED again in her traveling clothes. She was hungry but decided on a light breakfast. So, it was back to the Fussy Duck Café. The stagecoach ride wouldn't fair too well on a full stomach.

Returning to the hotel from breakfast, she found her trunks were out front as Mr. Perkins had promised. Mary collected her carpetbag from her room and descended the stairs. She approached the front desk and greeted the clerk. "Good morning and thank you for the stay. I hope to make it all the way to Crystal Creek without another stopover."

"It was mighty fine having you stay in our hotel," he said, adding a farewell nod.

She smiled and walked out to the hotel boardwalk. Waiting outside, she noticed the handsome young cowboy from yesterday. He gave a nod and tipped his hat in her direction. Also, nearby was an old man with unkempt hair, a mangy red beard, and clothes that had not seen a washtub in some time.

All at once, a large cloud of dust announced the arrival of the stage. It rounded the corner near the train depot and pulled up in front of the hotel. *This is earlier than expected. A good omen?*

The old man stepped towards her. She stared at the gun tucked into his pants. Quickly she looked up into his eyes. "You gettin' on this stage, Missy?" he asked and then spit out a stream of tobacco juice into the street.

This allowed Mary a view of his rotten brown teeth — that is, of the few he still had left. His breath washed over her and, if possible, it smelled even worse than his rotten teeth looked. Overwhelmed, Mary took a step back. "Yes sir, I am." *Just my luck....*

"You sit right next to me, Missy. And I'll keep ya safe from them bandits." He spit more tobacco juice, missing Mary's skirt by inches.

She moved further back to get away from the man. She thought of as 'Mr. Smelly.' "Bandits?" Mary questioned in a high squeaky voice.

"Yup, Missy. You can't never be too sure in these here parts. Better you be safe, then sorry."

What happened to that good omen? And why do things always seem to happen to me? Two young men hopped out from within the coach and skedaddled over toward the saloon. Meanwhile, the stage driver and the guard climbed down from the top seat.

"Which of you folks is going north with us this morning?" the driver asked.

Mary could only nod her head in acknowledgment. She wanted 'Mr. Smelly' to board first so she could take a seat as far away from him as possible. Lingering some distance away, she proceeded to rummage through her carpetbag.

The cowboy walked up and stopped in front of the stage. He put down the small bag he was carrying. Next, he pulled a ticket from his shirt pocket and presented it to the driver. Turning in Mary's direction, he walked over to where a large riding saddle sat next to the luggage. The tall cowboy bent down and grabbed the saddle and hefted it over his shoulder. He then walked over to the guard. Mary's eyes grew wide with admiration. *Hmm, he is awfully strong.* The guard took the heavy saddle with a little less ease and loaded it on top of the stage. Then the cowboy climbed inside the coach.

Low and behold, 'Mr. Smelly' showed his ticket next, handed his one small bag to the guard and gave one last tobacco spit – followed by a leering glance at Mary as he climbed into the stage. Mary then came forward. "And please, my trunks are here in the front."

"Hank, can ya get those trunks over there for the little lady. They'll be going with us. If'n they fit," said the stagecoach driver.

Mary waited until her trunks were loaded onto the top of the stagecoach. Unable to avoid it any longer, she climbed into the dirty, dusty stage. Looking around, she was relieved to see there was a space available next to the cowboy. Oddly, the seat had her facing backward, but it was preferable to sitting on the other side.

"May I?" she asked.

"Why certainly, ma'am. My name is Harlan McCloud," the cowboy replied in a deep husky voice. He scooted over to make room. "I believe we were both forced to overnight here in order to catch the stage this morning."

Mary sat next to Mr. McCloud. "Yes, you're correct. I am Miss Schulman. Pleased – to make your acquaintance." *I recognize that name from Charles' reference letters.*

"And my name's Francis Sessions, Missy. But just call me Frank." And he proceeded to cough causing everyone to turn away.

As to dissuade further conversation, Mary responded with a nod and turned to look out the window. Just then she heard someone yelling from the hotel lobby. She turned to see a tall, lanky man rushing forward. *So, this is the man who had the last two trunks.* With much effort, the stagehand was finally able to get both trunks loaded onto the top of the stage. *This stagecoach is so top heavy, it will probably turn over on the first curve out of town.* Mary soon found herself considering which window she should dive through if the need arose.

Opening the door and climbing in, the tall man took the seat next to Frank and opposite Mary. *Oh well, that's what he gets for being late. At least there is more weight inside, but those poor horses.*

Mary breathed a small sigh of relief as the stagecoach began traveling to the little town of Crystal Creek. The rolling and bumping of the stage had Mary appreciating the fact she opted for the light breakfast. She looked at the other passengers to see if they were accustomed to the movement.

The tall, thin man turned to the cowboy. "Good morning. I am Nicolas DeForest."

"Mornin, I'm Harlan McCloud," the cowboy replied with a nod of his head.

After a moment, Mr. DeForest continued, "How far are you two going?" He waved his right hand to Mary and McCloud.

Harlan answered, "Oh, we're not together, but for myself, I'm going on to Crystal Creek."

Thinking to clear any misconceptions, Mary bravely began, "pleased to make your acquaintance Mr. DeForest. My name is Miss Schulman, and I am also going to Crystal Creek."

"It is a pleasure to meet you, Miss Schulman." Mr. DeForest forged ahead, "I will be taking over Braunsteins Mercantile there."

Everyone nodded and politely smiled – except Frank. He was busy spitting out tobacco juice through the stage window. *What will happen when the wind is blowing?* Mary tried hard to keep herself from shuttering. The stagecoach started on a straight path and all four of the passengers settled into a period of quiet.

Glancing out the other window, Mary observed the countryside outside Beaverton. It was rolling grasslands with the occasional shrub. As they traveled farther north, they crossed several streams and encountered more trees. The sky outside was getting gray and threatened rain, BUT it was still dusty. *It is as hot as an oven in here! Perhaps it will rain — does it rain mud here? Where's the breeze?* Just then ol' Frank let loose another stream of tobacco juice. *Be careful what you wish for....*

"So, you're the fella that's buying out Braunsteins?" The cowboy leaned forward and continued. "They told me they were headed out to California and had found a buyer. I reckon you're a lucky man. They ran a fine store."

"And I intend to keep it that way. I am hoping to expand as well." Mr. DeForest turned his gaze to Mary. "Are you from Crystal Creek Miss Schulman?"

"No," said Mary.

"Coming to visit, I presume?" McCloud questioned.

Not wanting to explain her exact situation, "I'm on my way to meet a friend, Charles Baxter, in Crystal Creek."

Suddenly waking up, Frank interjected, slurring his words. "Charlie Basser — that lousy lying drunkard of a horse thief. Where you say he be? Why I'm goin' kill that pole-cat."

"Now, listen here." McCloud interrupted angrily, "You might want to take back what you just said about the lady's friend."

Frank just looked out the window and spit another stream of tobacco juice. He then muttered, "horse thief."

Horse thief! Oh Lord, what have I got myself into now? Am I going to marry a HORSE THIEF? But the Reverend's letter had been quite glowing. Mary felt nauseous as McCloud pulled the gun out of his holster and laid it across his lap. He leaned forward and in a menacing voice said, "I don't think you got my meaning Frank."

Frank quickly sat upright and meekly replied, "Must have the wrong Charlie, I reckon."

"I reckon so," McCloud said, holstering his gun. Turning to Mary, "You have my word, ma'am. The Charles Baxter I know is definitely not of those things Frank said. He is a very good friend of mine and a gentleman."

With that, the churning in Mary's stomach slowed. *I would like to ask questions of this handsome cowboy, however, I know it is not polite to do so.*

Just then the stage slowed, and the driver called out, "Miller's

Crossing coming up. Get out, stretch your legs, and have a quick bite to eat while we change the horses. We'll be headed for Crystal Creek in twenty minutes."

When they re-boarded the stage, Frank was nowhere to be seen. "You seem to have scared him off," DeForest said to McCloud with a grin.

McCloud leaned back and stretched his legs. "I hope so. I had to sit down wind of that old coot, and he smelled worse than a hog pen in the heat of July." The men laughed, and Mary smiled. *They sure do have very apt expressions out West.*

THE MORNING CHORES WERE FINISHED, BREAKFAST WAS EATEN, AND Lizzie was in her room. However, Charles still felt a little uneasy. And then like clockwork, his mother started in. "Just what are you going to do if she doesn't come on today's stage? And what makes you think she's late instead of just changing her mind?" Her hands were on her hips as she stared at him. "You know those Eastern women aren't as dependable as the women out West."

Charles responded, "Mom, as we were told yesterday, the stage had a problem, and she is probably just late." He moved closer to her. "I will go into town today, by myself, to meet her." *Heaven above, please help me to be a more patient man.*

"What do you mean? Are you so all-fired sure she's coming in, today?" Her eyes narrowed, "I think we should both come with you." And with a huff, she crossed her arms. Her tone made it clear she was not happy to be left at the farm.

He stared at his mother. *Do you think you should interview Mary before I'm allowed to talk to her? Who is marrying her anyway? Besides, I gave my word when I went through the agency.* Charles finished his coffee and took the cup over to the sink, giving his mother more time to compose herself. He turned to face her. "Mother, I would like our meeting to start off with a quiet dinner at the Cattlemen's Restaurant in the hotel… just the two of us."

"Well, when do we get to meet her then?" Her voice sounded agitated.

"If she doesn't arrive today, I'll be back this afternoon. If she arrives, we will have supper and spend the night there. And of course, I WILL get two rooms. Then I'll bring her home tomorrow morning, first thing after breakfast."

"Off with you then. I hope this works out for the best." Her lips flatten in a straight line, and a frown appeared on her face. She probably realized this line of questioning was going no farther. Spinning around, she made a beeline up to her room.

Charles heard his mother's voice echoing down the staircase. "I told you what I think of this." *Always the last word. Well, at least she had not mentioned Francis.*

◠

THE STAGE CAME TO A SLOW AND DUSTY STOP IN FRONT OF THE Crystal Creek Hotel. Charles was waiting outside, eager to see his new bride. He prayed she would be on this coach.

When the stage door opened, he saw only a handsome couple and his old childhood friend, Harlan McCloud. The couple exited first, and they were still engaged in an animated conversation as Harlan stepped out of the coach. *Perhaps Mary was delayed two days, instead of one?* Dismayed, Charles turned and started to walk slowly towards the hotel entrance. He would have to, once again, change his hotel reservation and come back tomorrow. How he wished Crystal Creek had a telegraph office. *Oh, great. I can hear Mom now.*

"Charles, hold up there," Harlan called out. Charles turned back and took a couple of steps forward. He stopped. The lady who had been talking earlier with the other gentleman was now standing by Harlan.

Wearing a sly smile, Harlan said, "I do believe this lady is here to see you, Charles."

"Miss Schulman?" Charles asked, ashamed he had made the incorrect assumption about the couple. He felt the fool. Embarrassed and anxious, he exclaimed, "I was hoping you would arrive today!" Swiftly he removed his hat and stepped up to her. "I'm Charles Baxter. And welcome!" He presented her with the bouquet of flowers he had been holding behind his back. *My goodness, she is so beautiful!* Charles assessed his good fortune. The young woman that stood before him was tall, slender, had thick mahogany hair and honey brown eyes.

"It's a pleasure to meet you, Mr. Baxter. I must apologize for the lateness of my arrival. I am so happy you are here, especially as I could not send word earlier. And please, you must call me Mary."

"Oh, I'm just so glad you're here. It's finally a pleasure to meet you, Mary. And please call me Charles." He was now beside himself with excitement. This woman was here for him. *What a lucky man, I am!*

"Ahem, I should get along now. It was sure nice meeting you, Miss Schulman. And Charles … you better take good care of her." He tipped his hat to Mary and then winked at Charles.

"Thank you very much and goodbye, Mr. McCloud," Mary said.

Appreciative of Harlan catching him before he walked further away, Charles stepped closer. "Thank you, Harlan, and I'll see you later."

The cowboy took his leave and walked down the street humming.

The stage drivers were taking down luggage from on top of the coach and placing them on the boardwalk.

He took a moment to organize his thoughts. Turning to Mary, Charles asked, "Which of these are yours?"

She waved to the two large brown trunks on the near side of

the pile. "Those two brown trunks and this blue carpetbag are all I have." She was still smiling as she looked to her trunks. *There is no hint she is disappointed.*

Charles flagged the two young boys sitting on a bench in front of the hotel. "Timmy, could you and your brother bring in those two brown trunks and place them into this lady's hotel room? Say, for a nickel each?" Charles questioned.

"Yes sir, Mr. Baxter!"

He gave the boys a wink and offered his arm to Mary. "Miss Schulman, I thought we would take dinner here in the hotel this evening. I have arranged for two rooms. We can spend a relaxed evening in town before going out to the farm tomorrow morning. Since I wasn't sure when the stagecoach would arrive, I thought it best if Lizzie and her grandmother stayed at home tonight."

"I understand. Dinner and a relaxing evening sound lovely. I am most anxious to meet Lizzie. I brought some presents for her. I hope she will like them," she shyly suggested.

Charles smiled broadly.

～

TAKING CHARLES' ARM, MARY HOPED THE BUTTERFLIES IN HER stomach would calm down. *My goodness, what a handsome man!* She could easily listen to his deep melodious voice all day long.

They walked along and every now and then, she looked up to notice him smiling at her. *He is so very tall.* She smiled shyly in return. Nervous, she considered the fact that they would probably be married in the morning with all the family in attendance – wouldn't they? *Be patient, my girl and you will find out.*

Entering the hotel, Charles called out, "Mr. Holt, if you please, I have two rooms reserved."

"Certainly, Charles," the older man cheerily responded. Mr. Holt moved the register book around and leaned towards Charles. "How's the family?" he asked.

"Very well, and thank you for asking." Charles put down Mary's carpetbag and signed the register for both of them. Looking up, Mr. Holt exclaimed. "Oh, this must be your new lady! I see she has finally arrived."

Charles brought her forward. "Mary, this is Mr. Holt, owner of this fine establishment and one of my references."

Blushing, she took a step forward. "Pleased to meet you, Mr. Holt and I do remember your nice letter."

She watched the older man raise his head with pride. After an awkward moment, Mary turned to Charles and saw his cheeks were faintly pink. "As it was a long and dusty ride, you will want time to freshen up before we meet later. May I show you to your room first?" Charles asked.

"Thank you." She turned back to Mr. Holt. "A bath would be appreciated," she said in a whisper. *I probably should get rid of the stagecoach dust before meeting Charles' family and the preacher.*

"After you have freshened up, I will meet you in the lobby at four o'clock. Or do you need more time?"

"Oh, four o'clock would be lovely and again, thank you."

Charles turned and waved to the two young boys with Mary's trunks. They nodded and followed. Extending his arm to her, she smiled and linked arms. He escorted her up to her room on the second floor, unlocked the door and stepped inside. He gave the key to Mary. The two young boys carrying her trunks entered the room. Charles gestured to them to put the trunks in front of the window. Ruffling their hair, Charles dropped a nickel into each boy's hand. Next, he placed Mary's carpetbag near the bed.

Mary watched him walk around the room as he checked the window and behind the change screen. *What a gentleman. And apparently, no outlaws were hiding.*

Satisfied, he walked to her. "Everything looks fine. I am across the hall if you need anything. I will meet you downstairs at 4 o'clock."

She gazed up at Charles. "Until then."

CHAPTER 6

MARY SLIPPED ON HER FAVORITE YELLOW DRESS. LOOKING IN THE mirror on top of the dresser, she noticed the lace on the collar and sleeves were a bit wrinkled. However, it was just going to have to do. After making a few adjustments to the front pleats of her dress, she looked at herself again. All in all, she couldn't be more pleased, the dress had been packed well enough to avoid the majority of wrinkles. She wanted to be at her best for Charles. *What a strong figure of a man, and he has a full head of hair to boot.* When she thought about his thick wavy hair, she smiled. *I wonder what Rachel would say?*

Today she would endeavor to arrive downstairs on time. *No more delays. Four o'clock, downstairs.* Feeling refreshed, excited and happy, she began to daydream. *Will he take me to the Preacher and then to supper? Or is the wedding ceremony to be tomorrow, when his daughter and mother can attend? Mother, Father, and Jenny – I think you'll be pleased.*

She checked the pins in her hat and tucked a stray lock of hair behind her ear. Next, she glanced at her watch pin, and it read a few minutes before four o'clock. Turning to leave, she took one last look in the mirror. Well, here I am. Trying to calm her nerves, she took a deep breath. She walked out of the room, shut the door, turned and locked it. Her heart was still beating fast as she walked downstairs. Reaching the lobby, Mary looked around and saw Charles smiling as he walked towards her. *Goodness me, I think I should pinch myself.* Perhaps, my fortune has changed. She sent up a quick prayer.

She saw his eyes light up with appreciation. He stopped in front of her. "Mary, you look positively beautiful! I am a lucky man. Are you ready for a stroll?" He offered her his arm.

"Yes, I am kind sir." Mary felt herself blush as she took his arm. "Please lead on.

They started walking out into the town. Strolling along the boardwalk, he explained where all the different stores were located. Mary took mental notes knowing she will most likely have to call upon a good many of these businesses. Towards the end of the street, they walked up to a pretty little white church. Seeing the church, Mary felt her heart pounding. *Finally, we will meet with the Preacher.*

"Ahum, hem, Mary, this brings me to a point which I need to discuss with you." He then glanced from side to side and finally met her gaze. "The Reverend had to leave town this morning to visit his very sick mother. We were expecting you yesterday, and the marriage ceremony was to have been held last evening. I am so sorry this happened." He averted his eyes from hers to stare down at his boots for what seemed like an eternity.

Mary felt her heart stop. Not getting married! For the second time? Her mind was racing, and her head was beginning to hurt. She felt a wave of nausea. *Why me?*

"Mary?" Charles asked tentatively. "Are you feeling unwell? What can I do for you?"

Marry me as you promised! Mary tried to think of something else to say other than what was rolling around in her head ... at last, she spoke, "I understand. Of course, the Reverend had to leave and attend his mother." Her voice had dropped to a low murmur. She was absolutely crushed. Life had left Mary in a mud hole in the middle of a down pour of rain, she found herself light-headed and stuck.

∽

CHARLES DID NOT KNOW WHAT TO DO OR SAY NEXT. AS USUAL, the wording he had used to tell her the wedding ceremony had been delayed was clumsy at best. It had caught her off guard. He decided to hurry her to the Cattlemen's Restaurant, thinking her pale color was due to hunger. *Well, at least she will have a full stomach to consider things before deciding to leave or stay. How am I going to smooth this out? Perhaps I should have approached someone for advice? I should have asked Owen! Too late....*

He held the door for Mary. They stepped inside. Charles spotted a young man walking in from the kitchen area. "Herman, may we please have a table by the window?"

"Yes, of course, Mr. Baxter. Right, this way." He led them to a table in front of the largest window, facing west.

At least this way she can watch the beautiful Montana sunset before she leaves me. What a bumbler I am! He attempted to smile and held her chair for her.

Herman, the manager of the restaurant, presented them with menus. "I will give you a few minutes before I return to take your orders. May I bring water?"

"Yes, please," Mary replied with a tiny smile.

"That sounds great. Thanks, Herman." On the basis that food cured all ailments, Charles looked at his menu.

The tick-tock, tick-tock of the wall clock near them, filled the room. *Well, it seems she's waiting for me to begin the conversation. Maybe I can clear up a few of my blunders. Here goes.* "Mary, Reverend Winterthorpe will return in three weeks or so. He told me he would marry us then. Until that time, he suggested my mother could act as our chaperone on the farm. Does this meet with your approval?"

Just then Charles saw Herman standing beside them. *This is poor timing. You, too, must wait for an answer.* Embarrassment and the need for privacy overtook Charles. He addressed Herman none too subtly, "Oh, Herman, I think we will need a few more minutes. Thank you." Turning to look at Mary, he noticed her eyes were as round as saucers.

Mary could not believe what she was hearing! Why did he not continue with this thought while they were standing in front of the church? *So, the ceremony just delayed? He might have stated this information first.*

Taking a sip of her water, she found her voice. "Why yes, that will be most acceptable. Is your mother available and nearby?" A slight sensation of relief was occurring. *Perhaps, he does not realize how he comes across?* She remembered her mother saying, 'men often assume you know what they are saying, but do not completely say so themselves.' She could also hear her mother's laughing voice say, *'proceed with caution, my dear.'*

"Yes, since my mother lives with us, she has already agreed to act as our chaperone." Charles grinned, looking oblivious to what he had just disclosed.

His mother lives with him? This was a forgotten piece of information not covered in his letters. Mary blinked. "Oh, I see. That is very nice."

She had heard enough stories to know this was not always good news. New daughters-in-law were often given many tests. Unfortunately, the common outcome was usually, 'this apple pie is not as good as the one Mom makes.'

Charles continued to talk, "you will meet both Elizabeth and my mother, Helen, tomorrow morning."

She turned to see Herman was back.

Charles then addressed the young man, "Herman, what's the specialty tonight?"

"The specialty is beefsteak with potatoes in jackets, green beans, and carrots." Herman smiled.

Pausing, Charles looked to Mary. "Mary, have you considered what you would like for supper?"

Mary glanced through the menu again. "I believe I would like the special. Slightly pink on the inside for the beefsteak would be most appreciated. Thank you, sir."

Herman turned his head to Charles, "And for you?"

"Oh, I'll have the special as well but make mine rare, please."

While listening to Charles describe his family and farm during supper, Mary continued to ponder. There was always one reoccurring thought which popped into her mind. *I hope there are no dark clouds on the horizon for me.*

CHAPTER 7

IT WAS SIX-THIRTY IN THE MORNING, AND CHARLES WOULD HAVE
to wait for breakfast. He had told Mary they would have breakfast
at seven-thirty reasoning she was probably exhausted from her
long trip. After dressing, he went to the Livery Stables where Hans
was already hard at work. Charles made use of the time by
brushing out his horse. No sense in paying for what he could do
himself.

Returning to the hotel, he found Mary waiting in the lobby as
agreed. They walked over to the Busy Bee Café. He felt the eyes of
the early morning risers upon them. Trying to enjoy a pleasant
breakfast of eggs, ham, and biscuits, Charles broke the silence. "I
know Lizzie, and my mother are most eager to meet you."

"Oh, I am so very excited to meet them as well. I brought
several children's books with me, and I believe Elizabeth will
enjoy the stories. It will also be very nice to meet your mother.
Perhaps, she will share recipes."

Unintentionally, his eyes glanced over to the hat and coat rack
by the door and then back to Mary. The thought of his mother
relinquishing any kind control of the kitchen to Mary was almost
laughable. Feeling the start of perspiration on his forehead, he

opted to change the subject. "I will fetch the wagon while Mr. Holt is arranging to have your trunks brought downstairs," he mumbled.

"I will be ready."

Smiling, he nodded. He walked over to the rack and picked up his coat. And with the tip of his hat to Mary, he promptly left.

Some minutes later, Charles pulled the wagon up, stopping in front of the hotel. He saw Mary standing on the boardwalk. His heart lifted to the clouds upon seeing her — there stood the newest member of his family. She was smiling while holding her carpetbag and her trunks sat next to her. *She sure is a prompt and organized little lady.* "Are you ready to go to the farm?" Mary nodded, and her eyes glowed with excitement.

After everything was loaded in the back of the wagon, he lifted her by the waist and onto the seat. His hands tingled from her warmth. Climbing aboard and sitting down, he gave a flick of the reins. That was all it took to get Buddy homeward bound.

Charles saw her grab the seat as the buckboard lurched into motion. "It is not far from town." The front seat lurched back and forth on its springs with almost every stride of the trotting horse. *For certain, she's a city girl....*

Today he was the proudest man in town. He was finally taking his bride-to-be home. "You look very pretty this morning. I think the fresh Montana air agrees with you."

"You say the nicest things, Mr. Baxter." She put one hand lightly to her heart and smiled. "I cannot wait to see Elizabeth, your mother, and our new home. Well, not new for you, but new to me." She quickly grabbed the edge of the seat with both hands as the wagon bounced over a rut in the road.

"And, I cannot wait to show it to you." He slowed Buddy's gait and tried to make the ride smoother. *She had said OUR home.* Charles continued to look straight ahead. He knew he had little experience making small talk with women and he felt tongue-tied already.

THIS MORNING, CHARLES HAD SAID SHE WAS PRETTY. THESE compliments were so very nice to hear, especially after Robert. She shuddered at the thought of him. And just like a cobweb, she was determined to brush that memory away forever.

At long last, they were headed to their home. *Home, that sounded wonderful.*

The seat of the buckboard continued to lurch back and forth as the wagon made its way along the hard-packed dirt road. *At least it was better than the rough ride of the stagecoach.* So, the better part of valor had Mary holding on with both hands. Falling off would not be the right way to impress Charles.

As the drive went along, she slowly loosened her grip. It was becoming easier to understand the motions of the horse, the wagon, and the seat. Now she had time to notice the countryside through which they were traveling. Large trees were dotting the edges of the creek on her left. The leaves of the trees shimmered in the wind as the sunlight touched them. Pewter-gray clouds hovered over the distant purple mountains that surrounded them. And, the bright blue sky was like nothing she had ever seen before.

Charles had not said too much since leaving town. Glancing at him, she saw he didn't look upset, but he was silent. *I wonder what he's thinking? Is he pleased with me?* She flexed her fingers slowly realizing they were stiff. As they passed a patch of cottonwood trees, a handsome log and lime mortar ranch house came into view. It had a large red barn and several smaller buildings. "Is this your home?" Mary gestured to the house in front.

"No, that is the Nelsons' place, our nearest neighbors."

"Oh. How close are they to your farm?"

"They live a little less than a half hour drive away. You will get to meet the Nelsons tomorrow night. They have invited us over for dinner." He smiled at her for a couple of moments and then turned back to look at the road.

"Is this the family that encouraged you to write to the Agency?"

"Why, yes, they are," he replied and continued, "Mr. Nelson, or Owen, is a real horse expert. He raises the best draft horses around here. Daniela, his wife, is quite a good cook, and she will talk your ear off. I think you will like them. They have three little ones, whom Lizzie likes to play with."

"I can't wait to meet them. They sound like very nice people."

Before long another fork in the road appeared. Charles took the left road, and the wagon slowed as it went up the incline. Upon cresting the hill, another house and barn came into view. As they approached, Mary could see this property differed from the horse ranch they had just passed. She could tell this place was a farm.

The house was a freshly painted white two-story farmhouse. Cultivated fields of different grain crops and vegetables surrounded the house. The barn was very large, and there were several fenced-in areas around it. Mary thought back to her earlier reading and remembered the fenced-in areas were referred to as corrals.

Fascinated, she continued to look further at the animals. There were cows, goats, and a few horses in the corrals and pens. Waddling around in the smaller enclosures were ducks and geese. They were all pecking at the presumably tasty morsels on the ground. *This is the largest number of farm animals that I have ever seen in one place. Those magazine articles are going to be of help.* Nearing the house, she could see there had been some additional painting started, but it was not quite finished. She could not keep herself from smiling as she saw the partially painted blue trim of the window frames and the eaves of the roof. *He has been busy.* In her heart, she felt secretly pleased with his attempt to dress up his home.

ONCE AGAIN, CHARLES MENTALLY THANKED THE NELSONS FOR suggesting he write to the Agency. Mary had a way about her that made him feel special – if only he could do the same.

As he drove towards the house, the front door opened and Lizzie rushed out and stopped in the courtyard.

Mary's face lit up. He continued to watch her and soon found her face was positively glowing. This was the reaction he had desperately wanted. Charles set the brake and jumped to the ground. He lifted Mary down from the buckboard. It felt wonderful to have a woman to hold once again.

His eyes followed her as she walked over to Lizzie and bent down to see his little girl at eye level. *Francis would never have done that.*

"Well, hello. You must be Elizabeth! I'm so happy to meet you. Your father has told me so much about you," Mary sweetly said.

The little girl replied with a meek, "Hello."

Charles saw Lizzie slowly look Mary over. She then gave her a small, shy smile.

The front door opened and his mother descended the steps. "You must be Mary. My name is Helen, and I'm pleased to meet you." She said, placing her hand on Charles's shoulder.

MARY FELT SOMEONE STEP UP BESIDE HER. LOOKING DOWN, SHE saw it was Lizzie. The little girl went up on her tippy toes to whisper, "My name is Elizabeth, but you may call me Lizzie like my Papa."

Blinking back the mist forming in her eyes, Mary felt her heart swelled with joy. "My apologies to you for my late arrival. Do you think I can make it up to you tonight by reading a few stories?"

The little girl's eyes grew wide with excitement. "Yes, please. I love hearing stories."

"Until tonight, then." Mary could see Lizzie took after her father with her blonde hair and blue eyes.

Just where is Charles? Mary turned back to see Charles had headed back to the wagon to unload her carpetbag and trunks.

"I'll bring these into your room. And ladies, please go inside and get acquainted." Charles' smile was fair to bursting.

Everything must be going well since he is smiling. Happy and pleased, Mary continued to hold Lizzie's hand while they entered the house. Helen showed them into the parlor. Glancing around, Mary saw a stonework fireplace, a blue velvet settee accompanied by two small mahogany tables on each side, two wing-backed chairs and a rocking chair near the fireplace. The walls were painted a light yellow. A braided carpet was on the floor. It was apparent the room was well used as it had a comfortable look. Mary smiled at Lizzie and let go of her new daughter's hand to take off her hat. She glanced at the top of the fireplace mantel to see a pretty carved wooden clock. A rifle was mounted on the wall above. Mary blinked. *Well, maybe I shouldn't be surprised — this is the wild Northwest.*

"Would you like some tea and biscuits?" asked Helen.

"Thank you. That would be wonderful." However, Mary's mind was still on the rifle.

"Come see my room." Lizzie took her hand and guided her up the hallway stairs and back to her bedroom. It was a small room with one single bed against the back wall. There was also a small desk in the corner and a wooden toy box with hand-painted animals on the top and sides. Reaching her bed, she turned and held up a small patchwork doll. "This is Dolly."

"It is nice to meet you, Dolly. My name is Mary."

"We play together all the time."

"I had a dolly I played with too, when I was your age. Her name was Sally."

"Tea is ready," Helen called from the bottom of the stairs.

"Would you and Dolly like to come have some tea?"

"Dolly would like to come, but she doesn't like tea."

"Then she can come and, perhaps have a glass of milk?"

"Oh, yes, please. I think Dolly is feeling thirsty." Lizzie replied smiling.

Mary took Lizzie's hand again, and they started down the stairs.

Charles was hefting a trunk up the stairs. They moved back and up to the top of the hallway in order for him to pass.

"I see you've met Dolly."

"Yes. We are on the way to tea."

"I'll join you in a few minutes," said Charles, shifting the trunk from one shoulder to the other to make room for them to pass.

Hmm. Strong AND handsome!

CHARLES FINISHED UNLOADING MARY'S LAST TRUNK FROM THE wagon and brought it upstairs. She would use his room while he slept in his brother's old room. This arrangement would be satisfactory for chaperoning purposes as his mother's bedroom was between the two.

Returning downstairs, Charles found the two women and his daughter having a good time in the kitchen. *All seemed to be going according to plan.* He stood for a couple of moments to admire his new bride-to-be. Then he caught his mother's inquiring look. *Is she curious about how I feel towards Mary already? With women, a man could never tell what they were thinking.* "Mary, how about I show you around the place?"

"I would love to see the farm. Your mother has been telling me some stories about when you were a little boy."

"Don't believe a thing she says. I only stole three of those pies."

Smiling, Mary raised her left eyebrow. "A pie thief?"

"Just kidding. Of course not, well … maybe not. Harlan was in on it, too."

Mom bristled. "You were a rascal, you were."

"Like I said, time for us to take a walk around the place." He wanted to spend more time alone with Mary.

Helen put the biscuits back into the jar. "All right, you can move along. But remember, I am your chaperone, and I will be keeping an eye on you."

Did she need to say it like that? Charles felt his face flush. "Lizzie, why don't you help with the dishes? And when you're done, you can come out to the barn and show your puppy and bunnies to your new Mama."

"Yes, Papa." With that, Lizzie quickly started picking up the cups and saucers from the table.

"Thank you for the tea and biscuits, Helen. They were delicious. Lizzie, I shall see you shortly."

Charles held the front door open. A brief hint of lavender drifted by as Mary passed through the doorway onto the porch. It was most agreeable to have another woman back in the house.

WHILE WALKING OUTSIDE WITH CHARLES, MARY CHUCKLED TO herself. *Well, better a pie thief than a horse thief.* Approaching the barnyard, she could see the weathered boards on the north side of the large two-story barn. She had read the winters were very harsh in the Montana Territory. Thankful she arrived in August, she knew there was time to adjust to the weather changes.

"Well, Miss Mary, it is wonderful to have you here." Charles opened the large heavy barn door for her. "Watch your step inside. It is always darker when you first enter."

As described, the barn was dim. However, Mary's eyes soon adjusted. She could make out stalls for animals on the left and right sides. Each stall had a back door which opened to an outside paddock. Above the center of the barn was a hayloft which could be accessed by the ladder beneath.

"What a big barn and how organized it is. This is very exciting for me. I would love to see all the animals."

"Yes, indeed. In the summertime, the larger animals usually spend their days and nights outside. However, they are kept inside during the winter when the weather is harsh. As I wrote, it gets very cold here. The hay bundles are stored in the hayloft above."

Mary looked up. All at once, two pairs of eyes peeked down. Mary took a step back. "Meow, meow, mew." She saw it was two green-eyed orange tabby cats. Mary burst out laughing. "And who do we have here?"

Charles chuckled. "Oh, those two are the barn cats, Becky and Polly, and they are a little shy when greeting people. Their job is to keep the mice away from the grain. And over here are the milking stalls for Daisy and Tilly. The larger stalls are for the horses. Buddy's is the largest."

He even has names for the cats, milk cows and horses. She hadn't considered it would be normal to name the cows as well. "Do all the animals have names?"

"No, just the barn animals we plan on keeping. As you can imagine, it makes it difficult when some of the animals become our food, or we sell their meat in town." He paused for a moment to see if she would react to what he had said.

Mary nodded her head. "I quite agree."

"Lizzie can tell you all their names."

"Through this door is the chicken coop. The chickens bring in good money as we supply eggs to Braunsteins Mercantile and a few other places in town. Actually, most of the animals bring in money in some way or another."

He walked around to the outside door of the chicken pen and noticed the chickens were still in the coop. Apparently, Mom had forgotten to let the chickens out. *She was most likely cleaning the house.* Opening the door of the coop, a steady stream of chickens came tumbling out, clucking and flapping their wings. They were running in every direction, only stopping every so often to peck at the ground. "When you first come in the morning, you need to be very careful not to step on them. They are always in such a hurry to get outside. Well, maybe not the ones sitting on their eggs."

They entered the coop. It smelled faintly of chicken manure. The floor had a light coating of straw, and on both sides, ramps were leading up to three levels of nesting boxes. Two of the hens were still on their nests having chosen not to go outside with the others.

Grabbing a large black speckled chicken on the upper level, he set it outside the coop. "There are usually eggs in all of the nests. Except in the winter when the hens lay less.

"These chickens are Plymouth Rocks. They are good layers."

Charles grinned. "That's right."

She enjoyed listening to Charles as he explained how things worked on the farm. "I have done a little reading on farmyard animals and more reading on chickens. Can I help with the chickens?"

"I hope so. This chore needs to be done every day to keep the chickens happy and laying well."

"So, after letting them out, what do I do next?"

Mary followed him as he walked back into the barn. "Next, we go over here to get the feed from the barn bin." The hens followed him, it seemed to be their routine. "This is the feed room, and the door needs to be kept closed, except when you are going in or out. We do not want the animals getting into the grain feed as they will get sick if they eat too much. ESPECIALLY the horses! They can become very ill when they eat too much grain."

He pointed to a barrel on the floor. "This is the chicken feed." He scooped out a small amount and showed her the cracked corn and other seeds. "The measuring scoop is here on the shelf. You will need to put two scoops into this pan." He handed her the scoop and gestured with his hands. "Go ahead."

This should not be difficult she thought. She scooped the seeds as he held the pan.

"Now bring the pan outside, and we will scatter the food in their pen." Charles grabbed a large basket off the wall before closing the feed room door. With Charles leading the way, Mary and the chickens all walked back to the pen in a straight line, like children following the Pied Piper.

She started to put the pan on the ground.

"Hold up. You need to spread it around." He grabbed a handful of grain and flung it across to the ground.

Mary blushed. "Oh, I understand now."

"The reason we spread it is, so they all get some. If you make a big pile, the stronger ones will shoo the smaller ones away and eat all the food. They're not very good at sharing." He was very understanding of her inexperience around the farm. *Good to have a patient man.*

Flinging several more handfuls around, Mary watched the chickens scattered in all directions. *This is fun.* She hoped her other lessons would be as easy.

Charles went back to the coop. He paused and said. "Now here comes the tricky part, learning to retrieve the egg from under a bird still on the nest."

Mary moved toward the bird. It clucked and flapped its wings. When she quickly reached out to try for the egg, the bird pecked her hand. Recoiling from the attack, "Why do you keep this mean one?" Mary looked up to Charles with her left eyebrow raised. She then glanced down to her hand and noticed the bird had not broken the skin. A laugh escaped her, as she recognized she had only been surprised.

Still laughing, Charles said. "Here, let me show you a trick. Well, we keep her because she is the second-best egg-layer in the flock." He took a wooden shingle hanging on a hook above the nest. He then held the shingle in his left hand, levering up the squawking bird, while sliding his right hand under the shingle to reach the egg. He turned to Mary, "Now you try it. Don't let her scare you."

Taking the shingle, she made the same movements Charles had. The bird protested, but the shingle did its job and kept the chicken's beak away from her hand as she retrieved the last egg from the nest.

"Now, in a moment or two, she will discover her egg is gone. Then she will go out with the others to eat."

Accomplishing this task without getting hurt or maiming the chicken had Mary feeling pleased. *Perhaps this farm work will be easier than I first thought.*

An overpowering unpleasant odor wafted through the air, and it got worse the closer they walked to a set of sturdy pens. She stopped. "What is that smell?"

"It's the hogs. Pork and bacon are fine for eating, but you do not want to spend much time around these pens. The hogs can also be pushy and aggressive as they are always hungry."

Looking into the first pen, she saw one large sow and many piglets. "I guess, this is the nursery?"

"You could put it that way. Those little guys have to be kept separate from the daddy." He motioned to another pen about ten yards away. "Or at least, until the piglets get big enough to fend for themselves. Just so you know, these animals may look peaceful to a city girl, but they are big, mean and will eat anything. Therefore, I do not want you to go into their pen. Do you understand? I hope I didn't scare the daylights out of you. But hogs are not to be trifled with."

She had read about the aggressive behavior of the hogs in her farm magazines. "I understand." *There it is — City Girl. Well, I can see I'm going to have to prove myself.* Stepping backed away from the pigpen, she turned and tried to smile. The stench was overwhelming. It was obvious why these pens were located farther away from everything else.

Charles led the way around the back of the barn to another set of sturdy enclosures. She saw that these pens contained a couple of goats and five sheep of various ages. The other pen was full of geese and ducks enjoying the big mud puddle in the center. "Just be aware, the goats like to get out and eat everything in sight, especially the vegetable gardens around the house. On the other hand, you give the ducks and geese a big mud puddle, and they will be quite happy." He chuckled.

CHAPTER 8

WHILE WAITING FOR DINNER WITH HER NEW FAMILY, MARY AND Lizzie were enjoying a game of spinning tops. It had been ages since Mary played tops with her sister and she delighted in hearing Lizzie giggle. Mary had dreamed of having a family such as this.

The smell from the kitchen was mouthwatering. Perhaps there would be some upsides to having his mother in the house. Mary was looking forward to learning how to cook some of her future mother-in-law's specialties. Most importantly, living in the frontier with an experienced woman was a comforting thought.

Having eaten little in the days before her arrival, Mary was reminded she was hungry. She hoped the rumbling noises of her stomach were not so loud as to be heard by others. Mary glanced around the room until her eyes met Charles. They smiled at one another.

Interrupting the moment, Helen stepped out from the kitchen. "Dinner is ready."

Mary picked Lizzie up from the floor. "Oh goodness, it's time for us to wash up."

"Yes, Mama." Lizzie ran over to the kitchen wash basin.

There is that word again – 'Mama' how wonderful that word

sounds. Mary followed Lizzie into the kitchen to wash up. Drying her hands on a towel, Mary looked to Helen and then Charles, "Where would you like me to sit?"

"Right here next to me, if you would." And Charles pointed to the chair on his right.

"Mrs. Baxter, this all smells delicious." Mary looked at the feast laid out before her. Helen had certainly prepared a special dinner for the evening. It was an appetizing combination of ham with peach sauce, mashed potatoes, and a side dish of green beans mixed with a few fried onions and bacon.

"Oh dear, you must call me Helen. A special meal – for a special occasion." Mary watched Charles' mother sit down across from him. They all joined hands and bowed their heads while Helen said grace. Mary could see Lizzie mouthing the words silently along with her grandmother.

Helen looked to Mary. "Schulman, a nice German name I assume?"

Mary lifted her head. "Yes, my grandparents came to New York from Germany and later moved to Baltimore. My parents now live in Philadelphia. I have a younger sister, Jenny and we visited our grandparents on holidays."

"I see. The Germans are organized and disciplined people, unlike some others. Hardworking too, like the Swedes." Helen continued to hold Mary's gaze, expecting a confirmation no doubt. Mary smiled and nodded her head. She was becoming uncomfortable with Helen's line of questioning. It seemed Helen wanted to know how she felt about the different ethnic groups. Mary became determined not to give a judgmental statement on any group of people. Her father's old adage was true for her – 'Never judge a book by its cover.'

"Now Mom, perhaps we should hear about Mary's trip out here."

"Charles. I just want to learn about her family."

It became apparent his attempt fell on deaf ears. "Yes, Helen, I would say my family is very organized." Mary felt a little awkward at using Helen's first name. Charles' mother did not emit a feeling of warmth and friendliness. "Organization and diligence are most important in my father's line of work. He is a bookkeeper." Mary hoped this was enough of a response.

"No doubt." Helen paused. "Is school work important in your family?"

Now Mary was wondering at the depth of all these questions. What had brought on all the scrutiny? "Very, and all of us did well in school. We were taught to read at an early age. In addition, we all learned a high level of arithmetic as a result of my father's efforts. Also, my sister and I learned to speak and write German. He said learning a second language sharpened the mind." Mary smiled and took another bite of food, hoping this might defuse the current line of questions.

Helen returned to her food. Her questions seemed to have been answered for the moment. Perhaps Helen was concerned that Lizzie might not grow up in a disciplined environment with the proper respect for schoolwork and learning. Charles also expressed this concern in his letters. Mary was most happy to assume this responsibility.

"I brought books for Lizzie so we could practice reading and writing."

"What books?" Little Lizzie practically squealed with excitement. "Can we read one tonight?"

"Yes, of course. However, we must first help your Grandmother clean up after dinner. Later, we can read from a book called ***Aesop's Fables***. It was one of my favorite books when I was your age."

"Can we, Papa?" Lizzie eagerly looked to her father.

"Of course, we can." Charles gazed at Mary appreciatively.

Mary glanced to Helen. She felt determined and would show her future mother-in-law that she could teach her granddaughter quite a lot. It would start with tonight's reading. Hoping this approach met with his approval, Mary looked to Charles. He was nodding.

Charles turned to his mother. "What is for dessert, Mom?"

"I made a chocolate cake." Helen looked to Mary. "I hope you like chocolate."

"It is one of my favorites. Thank you, Helen."

"Mine too," Lizzie timidly contributed. Mary saw Lizzie look shyly at her. *I think she is a bit bashful — I can help her get over that.*

CHARLES THOUGHT THE DINNER HAD GONE VERY WELL. MARY seemed to enjoy his mother's cooking and rightly so. This evening's meal was a special treat and a big improvement over his normal fare.

Ever since the first introduction, Lizzie called Mary by her new name Mama. He had been a little concerned Mary may have been taken back a little. But quite the contrary, he had seen her eyes grow misty after Lizzie addressed her as Mama. It warmed his heart to see the budding relationship between Lizzie and his wife-to-be. Mary looked happy, and he was more than pleased with their first day at the farm.

He accompanied Mary upstairs to fetch the book she had suggested for story time. Arriving at the outside of his old bedroom doorway, he leaned up against the doorframe and watched. Mary brought out her books from the trunk. *Now I know why that one was heavier. What a lot of books.* As Mary continued to search through her trunk, he saw a few magazines and publications. What got his attention was the titles, **Farm and Fireside**, and **The National Farmer**. Stunned, he felt his heart beat faster. *Did she buy farming magazines to study in preparation for life with me?* He felt his breath catch for a moment. Not knowing what to say, he said the first thing that popped into his head. "I wondered what you had in that particular trunk." He watched Mary blush. She stopped and stood still. Charles blurted out, "I was just kidding." She tilted her head and then laughed. Walking over to him, he saw a children's book clutched in her hand.

"I was told books are scarce out West, so I brought a good amount with me."

"They are hard to come by. This town is not large enough to have a library like your fancy cities do." Charles said.

"Children enjoy being read to, and I thought Lizzie would like me to read to her. This book is called *Aesop's Fables,* written by Reverend Thomas James. He's the one who illustrated *Alice's Adventures in Wonderland* by Lewis Carroll." She took a few small steps closer to him and opened the book to show some of the drawings.

Charles looked on with curiosity. "Oh, the illustrations are beautiful. I am sure Lizzie would love seeing them." Glancing through some of the pages with her, he looked up to see Mary's face soften as she studied the drawings. *What a thoughtful idea to bring these books for my daughter.* A deep sense of admiration and appreciation came to him.

Helen called up the stairs, "We're ready for story time."

"We are coming, Mom." Watching Mary shyly step around him, Charles made a note to become more mindful of his manners. He realized he wanted to impress her. *Why was this beautiful, educated young lady willing to become a mail order bride? And how did I get so lucky?*

Charles followed Mary downstairs and into the parlor. He sat in his usual chair and Mary sat on the settee. Helen entered the parlor with her knitting and headed for the rocking chair.

Mary asked, "Lizzie, why not come here and sit by me? This way you can see the beautiful pictures."

"Yes, Mama." His little girl walked over to sit beside Mary.

He watched as Lizzie scooted up a little closer to Mary. Then she arranged her skirts as Mary had done. Watching his daughter bask in the attention of her new Mama, he felt extremely pleased. He heard his mother's needles clicking and saw she looked comfortable in her rocker. Charles relaxed. This scene was how he pictured his happy family.

With Mary reading, he had made a mental note he needed to purchase a couple more lanterns for added light. Listening closely, Charles heard Mary read the first story from *Aesop's Fables* entitled *The Fox and the Grapes*. She spoke in an elegant manner. While reading through the story, Mary changed her voice to reflect scene and mood changes described. Soon, everyone was listening. The knitting needles had stopped clicking.

Mary leaned back in her seat and began to mimic the fox's final retort. "Well! What does it matter! The grapes are sour!"

Charles laughed along with them. Even Helen smiled and gave a nod of her head with the truth of the story.

Charles liked how Mary took time after each story to discuss the bigger words, meanings and moral of the story. At the conclusion, he noticed Mary would ask Lizzie what she thought about the story and if there were any questions. He could see this approach made Lizzie feel important. His little girl was talking and opening up. It had been bothering him to see Lizzie become more withdrawn after her mother had died. He had to admit they had all become withdrawn since then.

The second story was read and discussed as well. The third story of *The Wolf and the Crane* was a story everyone enjoyed. In the end, the wolf had told the crane she was lucky to have removed her head from his throat. After hearing this, everyone was laughing. Again, the story discussion was joined by all. Every one added his and her interpretation of the story's moral.

Charles looked at his daughter's questioning expression and offered his explanation. "Lizzie, I believe the story is saying — people who look for thanks from bad people should not be surprised to receive nothing more than sneers." Again, everyone nodded their agreement. *Perhaps we will be able to have a deeper marriage than just an arranged one?*

～

CHARLES HAD SUGGESTED THEY SIT OUT ON THE PORCH THIS evening and watch for shooting stars. He claimed the night sky in Montana was always beautiful at this time of year. However, Helen had stated it was too windy and cold. *Was Helen going to be a stickler as a chaperone or was it something else? Am I to be skating on thin ice?* The only comforting thought was Charles did not look pleased with his mother's retort either.

As the evening was still young, Mary decided to write to her Mother and Father. However, she did not relish the thought of telling her parents the wedding was delayed. With Rachel's pen in hand, she began:

> **Dearest Mother and Father,**
>
> **I have arrived safely in Crystal Creek, Montana Territory. The town is small but quite nice. Mr. Baxter's farm is not far away, and the countryside is beautiful. The trip out was very arduous but most worthwhile. You would both certainly approve of Charles. He is caring and most considerate. As you know from the letter I mailed in Cincinnati, he is a widower. In addition, he is much more of a gentleman than many of the men in Philadelphia. He has a wonderful daughter named Elizabeth. She is seven years old. Elizabeth is shy, sweet and polite. I believe she is taking to me. I could not have asked for a better start to my new life. Charles's mother also lives with us at the farm. She is quite a good cook and a pleasant lady. I expect we will get along well.**

Mary paused in her writing. *At least I hope we will get along. What to write?*

Sharing any thoughts of Helen might cause concern when it could very well iron itself out. She did not wish to go into the details about the problems of her journey. There was no need to worry them. However, she would have to tell them about the delay of the wedding. *What is it with wedding ceremonies and me?*

She continued writing her letter,

We have scheduled our wedding for three weeks hence. This delay is the result of my arriving a day late because of a broken stagecoach wheel. Unfortunately, the Reverend had to travel to Cheyenne to attend to his very sick mother. Charles' mother is acting as our chaperone until the ceremony.

The countryside here is so beautiful it allows me to appreciate the beauty of God's green earth. I feel blessed by my good fortune. I miss you all and will write more soon. Give my love to Jenny.

Your loving daughter, Mary

Pleased with her letter, she addressed the envelope and got ready for bed. She was told mornings came very early on a farm.

CHAPTER 9

AFTER A RESTLESS NIGHT, CHARLES DECIDED HE MIGHT AS WELL get up. His thoughts were of the beautiful woman in the house, and it was darn hard falling asleep. All his observations told him that Mary was thoughtful, intelligent and lovely. *I could go on, but what more could I ask for? The question is — will I be good enough for her?*

Rubbing the back of his neck, Charles decided it was best to concentrate on the chores of the day and to check on Daisy. This was to be the first time for Daisy to calve. The signs were there, and the birth would be any day now. Quickly, Charles dressed and grabbed his coat, pausing at the bottom of the stairs. Hearing noises, he stepped around to glance into the kitchen. There was Mary with a dusting of flour in her hair and on her forehead, making the daily bread. *Up early as well.* He stopped to watch her knead the dough. What a pretty sight she made. *I like seeing her like this.*

Mary turned to see Charles and smiled. "Good morning, Charles."

Startled, he recognized she must have heard him approaching. *I hope she did not see me staring.* He made a mental note to fix the bottom step of the stairs. "Good morning to you. Did you sleep well?"

She paused shaping the bread dough. "Very well and thank you for asking. Did you?"

So polite and proper. "Yes, and I am on my way to check on Daisy. She is about to have her first calf. I should be back shortly for breakfast." He gave her a wink and turned to walk over to the hat rack by the front door. Putting on his hat, he stepped out and closed the door behind him. It was five in the morning, nippy and still a bit dark.

He was pleasantly surprised his city girl was already up and at it. *Yep, things are definitely looking up.* Charles strode out to the barn. Hopefully, Daisy's calf was already here. Reaching the barn door, he gently opened it. Entering, he lit the lantern on the nearby post. After a few moments, he gazed down towards the end of the barn. Low and behold, in the far stall was a wet and shiny little calf standing right beside Daisy. It stood on long and wobbly legs, swaying back and forth … trying desperately to keep its balance as Daisy licked its back and face. Charles quietly walked over to mother and baby, all the while giving them soothing words of praise. Upon closer examination, it was apparent that Daisy had done a good job cleaning her calf. Stepping up to the edge of the stall, he noticed it was a heifer. *Well, this is something! I should fetch Mary to come and see this little miracle of life.* Charles flew out of the barn and back to the house. He opened the front door.

"Mary, Mary come with me," he softly called. "I have a surprise to show you, and I know you will love it!"

"Oh, I love surprises!"

She popped the newly shaped loaves of bread into the oven and hurried to him. Charles wrapped his old coat around her shoulders, and they hurried to the barn.

Stopping at the door, Charles turned to her and brought a finger to his lips. They crept into the barn and continued walking until they stood in front of Daisy's large stall. Before them stood one of the most precious sights a person could see — a newborn calf being washed by its mother.

He glanced at Mary. She stood transfixed. She looked at Daisy and her calf – her eyes became soft and dewy.

"So, what should we name her?"

"Oh, Charles. She is so beautiful! I don't think I should be the one to name her, though. Let Lizzie name her."

How very thoughtful. What a far cry from what Francis would say....

"I'LL BRING LIZZIE OUT TO THE BARN TO SEE THE NEW CALF," Mary called as she rushed to the house. Opening the front door, she smelled the baking bread. Thinking to take a quick peek, she opened the oven door and peered in. *Good, it needs more time.* Closing the oven door, she ran upstairs to wake Lizzie. Entering the room, she walked over and gently touched her. "Lizzie — dear, wake up. There is a newborn calf in the barn, and your father thinks you should be the one to name her." Lizzie wiggled around in the bed and then opened her eyes in a flash.

"What? Did you say Papa wants me to name the new calf?"

Excited, she leapt out of her bed in a flash. She ran over to her chair and quickly donned her clothes. All at once, Lizzie raced out of her room and thundered down the staircase with her hair was flying all directions. Mary took off after her.

Both of them raced towards the barn to see the new baby calf. Mary caught up with Lizzie at the barn door and opened it wider for them to enter. Once inside, Charles again put his finger to his lips. "Shhh, Lizzie, slow down. You do not want to frighten the baby."

Mary took Lizzie's hand, and they crept to where Daisy was stalled. Looking down at Lizzie, Mary saw she was fairly bursting at the seams with the excitement of it all. Watching her, Mary thought it was a small wonder the little girl could contain her enthusiasm. *What a good girl.*

With a light squeeze to Lizzie's hand, Mary began to question. "Lizzie, what do you think of this surprise?"

"I think she is pretty. What do you think I should name her?" Excited, Lizzie then rattled through about six names as possible suggestions. But in the end, she shook her head in rejection.

Charles scratched his head, "I know. Lizzie, what are the names of some flowers?"

"Oh. I know! I know! How about Lily? I think it is a wonderful name for her! We'll call her, Lily!" Lizzie exclaimed and then softly giggled.

Hearing footsteps behind them, they all turned.

"Well, good morning. I got up and saw the house was deserted, so I thought I would check here. She sure is a sweet thing. It looks like Daisy is very proud of her too. I like the name you choose for her, Elizabeth." Helen said as she joined them.

At that moment, Mary remembered she had bread baking. She hoped it wasn't burnt!

Dashing back to the kitchen, she called over her shoulder, "I'll be back later for another visit." Mary was discovering things were always happening on a farm.

TODAY WAS DINNER AT THE NELSONS' HOME. EVERYONE WAS seated in the wagon and Mary watched Charles as he lightly snapped Buddy's reins. Slowly, the buckboard started down the road. Mary could feel Charles bump up against her with every bounce of the wagon. Lizzie was busy chatting about her playmates while sitting beside her grandmother on the bench seat in the back.

While driving along, Charles pointed to a long wooden fence on the left and said, "The Nelsons' place starts at that fence line."

Mary nodded, as she continued looking at the wide-open countryside. In short order, they arrived in front of the large log ranch house that Mary had seen on her trip out from town. Bounding out of the barn to greet the wagon were three small children and several brown and white puppies. And, by some miracle, the puppies were able to dodge Buddy's hooves. Mary could see the resemblance to Lizzie's puppy, Skippy.

As Charles set the wagon brake, a man emerged from the house.

"Charles, right on time I see."

Mary made a mental note to remember that about Charles. *Be Punctual.*

"We would not dare be late to one of your wife's marvelous feasts." Charles jumped down from the front bench seat and walked around to the other side. There he grasped Mary around the waist and lifted her gently to the ground. Mary enjoyed the sensation of having his hands on her waist, even if briefly. Stepping back, he took Lizzie out from the makeshift seat in the back of the wagon and stood her on the ground. He turned his attention to his mother, helping her out of the wagon as well.

He put a hand under Mary's arm, and they stepped forward. "Owen, I would like you to meet Miss Mary Schulman from Philadelphia."

"Pleased to meet you, Miss Schulman." Owen Nelson took off his hat in a sweeping gesture as he bowed his head.

Laughing, Mary gave a quick curtsey. "I am very pleased to meet you. Please call me Mary. And who are these little darlings?" She waved to the children. Soon Lizzie was fidgeting by her side.

Mr. Nelson pointed to the two boys in order of height. "The oldest boy is Tommy, and the other is Bobby. And...."

Lizzie pointed to the little girl. "And that's my best friend, Jane." Mary smiled and gestured for her join her friends.

A pretty short woman with dark brown hair came through the door. "Good afternoon, everyone. And you must be Mary. I am

Daniela Nelson, and it is so nice to meet you after all this time." The young and very pregnant woman hugged her and stepped back, her brown eyes twinkling. "Charles has told us much about you. Come in, please. We have so much to talk about. I want to hear all about your trip and the big city of Philadelphia." She ushered Mary and Helen through the front door. "We were so excited to hear you were coming." She continued talking nonstop as they walked back into the house. "Ladies please join me in the kitchen while I finish up the dinner."

The aroma wafting from the kitchen was mouthwatering. There were several pots bubbling on the stove and soon Daniela was cutting a loaf of bread with small green specks in it. Mary was intrigued, "What kind of bread is this?"

"Oh, this is rosemary bread from my Tia Angelina's recipe. But I do add a bit more rosemary and a little more honey." She cut off a small morsel and tore it in half. "Here, try a taste." Daniela handed Mary and Helen a warm piece of bread.

Carefully placing the morsel into her mouth, Mary chewed and then smiled. "This is wonderful. Who would have ever thought to add rosemary to bread?"

"The best cooks in the world come from Italy, and my family is Italian." Daniela happily continued with a discourse on Italian cooking.

Mary felt herself relax while listening to Daniela. She thought back to what Charles had said about her earlier and realized he was correct. This lady could talk a mile a minute. *Tonight is going to be fun.*

ONCE THE WOMEN WERE INSIDE THE HOUSE, OWEN TURNED TO Charles. "Well, she is a pretty one. How did YOU get so lucky? Is everything going well?"

Charles knew Owen was joking but also talking in earnest.

Since sending for Mary was Daniela's idea, Charles knew they would both be curious. "I am lucky to be sure. And, it is going extremely well with the one exception of the Reverend having to leave. However, she took the news fairly well. She is all I had hoped for. Last night she even read stories to Lizzie. Lizzie's already calling her Mama, and I believe Mary likes hearing it. I even think Mom is a little pleased."

"I am very happy to hear that, and I know Daniela will be too!" Owen clapped Charles on the back.

Thinking to redirect the conversation, "Owen, how are the new foals doing?"

"They are doing great. Why don't we take a look at them?" Owen led the way to the barn.

While walking, Charles shared he was thinking about getting another work horse. And Owen was just the man to help. His specialty was the large Percheron draft horse. Charles remembered Owen would always laugh and say, 'you could set a table on their back.' It was known these horses were terrific pullers, great for plowing, logging and other heavy tasks. Owen also suggested these gentle giants could also be ridden to town when the need arose. *That is, once you hauled yourself up on top of one of those monsters. I am a tall man, but I think if I tried, I'd be the laughingstock of the town. Two giants — what a sight that would make. It's tempting, though.*

Watching Owen talk and work with his horses was always a special treat. Owen opened the sliding barn door, "We have two new colts and a filly since you were last here."

They walked into the large barn. Inside, the light was dim, but one could see both sides of the center aisle were lined with sturdy wooden stalls. Owen led Charles over to the first stall on the left. "Here is Midnight and her new filly. We haven't named her yet." Midnight was a solid black mare and clearly deserving of her name. The filly was a wobbly legged little thing standing next to her massive mother.

The children came running into the barn. Charles saw the boys were leading the way, and Lizzie was bringing up the rear with their sister. They stopped at one of the other stalls.

"This baby I'm going to call Hercules." The eldest boy Tommy announced as he showed Lizzie one of the young colts on the other side of the barn.

"You are all to be very careful and look only from this side of the stall doors." Owen cautioned the children.

"We will," Tommy answered. The rest of the group nodded their heads.

"Say, Owen, I'd like to see about getting one of your trained horses for my plow work. Buddy is getting a little long-in-the-tooth. I am thinking of letting him do the lighter chores — maybe making him the wagon horse. Lizzie will be going to school soon. So, we'll need another horse."

"Sure thing, anytime you're ready Charles. Just let me know."

MARY WAS ENJOYING HERSELF WHILE VISITING WITH DANIELA AND Helen in the kitchen. It was nice to meet a friendly woman. While they were talking, she could not help but smell the wonderful spicy scent coming from the pots on the stove.

"Well, are you ladies hungry? I think I am about ready to serve."

Helen offered, "should I call everyone? No need for you to do any extra running around in your condition."

Daniela sighed. "Oh, that would be lovely and thank you, Helen."

"When is your baby due?" Mary inquired.

Her new friend's face lit up, "In about two months or so."

"How wonderful! If you ever need anything, please let me know. I am only a short drive away. Perhaps I could watch the children or bring over a dinner?" *I may know nothing about birthing, but surely, I can help with something.*

"Thank you, Mary. That certainly is nice of you. I will remember." She lightly touched her stomach. "Let's see, are we ready?"

Daniela went back to stirring one of the pots on the stove. Mary noticed the kitchen table was set for the children. Their bread had already been placed in a basket. *What a good idea. The children can have a good time as well.* The dining room table, she saw, was set for the adults.

Helen returned a short time later with the four youngsters. The sound of the front door opening again announced the men were back.

"What else can I help you with?" Mary inquired.

"Perhaps you could bring the bread and water out to the dining table. I have everything else ready."

Pausing, Mary watched Daniela serve the children. This scene brought wishful thoughts. *Maybe someday Lizzie will have brothers and sisters.*

Quickly turning, she walked to the oven. She retrieved the bread and picked up the water pitcher from the washboard and placed them on the long dining table. She could hear Daniela tell the children to behave and to mind their manners.

Daniela brought out one pot, followed by a bowl. She set them on top of a hot plate on the dining room table. Sitting down, she took a plate and with a pair of forks began to capture the elusive thin noodles from the first pot.

Mary looked intrigued. On top of the noodles, Daniela ladled a large spoonful of red sauce with meat chunks and passed the first plate to Helen. She then repeated these steps until each person had been served.

Owen said grace.

"This is a dish we call macaroni with red sauce in the old country. The sauce is an old family recipe with tomato, meat, and lots of spices."

"This is delicious, Daniela." Mary took another bite. "I would greatly appreciate if you would show me how to make this dish."

"The noodles have to be formed and dried. I can give you some until you learn to make your own. I make all my pasta in the summer. You can't dry them properly in the winter. But the secret is in the sauce. In the summer, I can use fresh tomatoes, but in the winter, I use my canned tomatoes as a base."

Owen added, "My wife can't just cook standard simple country fare, we are often treated to her Italian dishes."

"Are you complaining about my cooking now?" Daniela asked as she lifted her eyebrows.

Her husband raised his hands. "Absolutely not, it's the best in the Territory. You know that because I'm always telling you so."

His reply elicited a laugh from Daniela. "Just checking, because we can go back to eating salt pork and hard tack — if that's what you want."

Mary was enjoying the taste of this meal immensely. "Daniela, would you be willing to teach me how to can tomatoes? I noticed there are quite a few in our back garden."

"Why yes. You must come over, and we will have a canning day."

Charles looked up from his empty plate. "Daniela, I am always ready for seconds of your cooking. May I, please have a bit more?"

As Charles and Owen ate their second helping, Daniela asked Mary about her family and life in Philadelphia.

Owen turned to Helen. "When I was in town yesterday I noticed the Braunsteins were not at the mercantile any longer. In addition, the name was changed to The General Store. I know you take eggs to the store a couple of times a week. Do you know what happened to them?" Helen straightened up. "I do." She took her napkin and blotted her mouth. "They asked me not to mention it, but since they are gone, I suppose it is all right. They went to San Francisco to start another store with a brother of his. They sold the store to a fellow that one of Mr. Braunsteins' brothers knew. His name is Nichols DeForest. You know how private the Braunsteins were. They told only Sheriff Abbot and me, or SO they said."

Mary joined in the conversation. "I met Mr. DeForest on the stage ride to Crystal Creek. He seems to be a nice man. He is from Denver where his family has a clothing business."

Owen sighed and added, "I'm sorry to see the Braunsteins leave. They are good people and always extended credit during times of need."

~

EARLY THE NEXT MORNING, MARY SAT DOWN AT THE KITCHEN table. She had decided to start a letter to Rachel while the bread was baking. Her letter was overdue, and the most obvious time to start it was now while the house was quiet. She needed to finish the letter today as Rachel was not the most patient of people when it came receiving news.

Dear Rachel,

I write this from my new home on the Baxter Farm in Montana Territory. This land is so open and beautiful compared to the crowded city of Philadelphia. The rivers run clear, the sky is a vibrant blue, and the mountains are BIG — like nothing you have seen before. It is very much as you had described it.

As of yet, I have not married Charles. The reason being, I arrived in Crystal Creek a day late, and that led to complications beyond everyone's control. The Reverend left town to visit his mother, as she became seriously ill. He is not due back for two to three weeks, so we will be wed when he returns.

My Charles is wonderful, and unlike our fears at the agency, he has ALL his hair and his teeth. He is quite handsome and every bit the gentleman. In point-of-fact, he is the exact opposite of our fears. Please share this information with our friends. I feel very fortunate. You encouraged me to take this journey, and so far, I could not be happier.

His daughter Elizabeth, or Lizzie as I call her, is such a darling and she already calls me Mama. We have already started to read Aesop's Fables. I am extremely pleased to be here with this wonderful family. Lest you think ill of me for being in his house before the marriage, his mother is living here with us as our chaperone. Her cooking is splendid, and I think she approves of me, but I do sense she has reservations about Charles sending for a mail-order bride.

I hope things are well with you and all our friends at the agency. Perhaps soon I will hear about a match for you. Be fore-warned, the train trip will be long and tiring. The journey is even dirtier than Mrs. Turner told us. Wear an old dress for traveling, one you are prepared to throw out. I tried to clean mine, but in the end, I may have to resort to burning it.

I will write to you again very soon.

Your friend forever,

Mary Schulman

Pleased with her letter, she folded it and placed it in an envelope. Mary then sealed it knowing Rachel would soon have news of her journey and arrival. It was now time to do the morning farm chores.

CHAPTER 10

THE NEXT MORNING HELEN WAS UP EARLY AND FIXING BREAKFAST. Charles was already feeling irritated with his mom for squashing his idea of sitting out on the porch last night again. *How am I supposed to court Mary?* Trying to move past his annoyance, he looked into the kitchen and saw his mother telling Mary to do this and that. *Is she trying to establish the kitchen as her domain?* Charles wondered if Mary might like to do more of the cooking. However, cooking was an area he hoped would be resolved between the two women. 'Too many cooks spoil the broth' as his grandmother had frequently said. For now, this was a good time for him to head out to the barn and do some work.

Returning for breakfast, he sat down at the table. Charles detected there had been a little problem with the cooking. It seemed the one thing his mother had allowed Mary to do was to cook the bacon. The ends of the strips were burnt, but he was going eat it without comment. It was obvious his mother had told Mary to use the left back burner knowing it was the hottest! *Hm...I can only guess what's going on here.*

After finishing his breakfast, he pushed the chair away from the table. He glanced over to Lizzie and saw she was staring off into space. He waved his hand in front of her eyes, and when he had her attention, he gave her a wink. "Lizzie, please do your chores and most importantly watch after your puppy. Do not let Skippy chase after the chickens again."

Lizzie's eyes grew solemn. "Yes, Papa. I will do my chores and keep Skippy out of trouble."

"I know you will, sweetheart."

"Mom, I will take Mary out to the barn. There are a lot of things she needs to know. Besides, I am sure she already knows how to wash dishes."

Helen frowned.

Noticing the frown, Mary became uncomfortable. However, she untied her apron. "Lizzie, I have put two books out on the front room table. When you are done with your chores, you may look through them and pick a couple of stories for me to read to you tonight," she offered. Mary added a warm smile for Lizzie.

Charles saw Lizzie stop chewing her bacon and come to attention. "Oh, thank you, Mama." Mary gently swept a few strands of hair out of Lizzie's eyes. He thought his heart would melt right there.

Stepping outside, Charles turned to Mary, "That was very nice of you. There are times when Lizzie gets a little left out with so many chores to do."

Walking closer to the barn, they encountered a large white goose. The huge goose stepped towards Mary. It spread its wings and gave an ear-piercing honk. They halted. Charles leaned over and whispered, "don't be afraid." He put his arm around Mary and greeted the goose, "Good morning, Millie. How are things?" He glanced down at Mary and saw she was both startled and puzzled. He laughed, guessing there was a question in there somewhere. "Millie is our barnyard watchdog. You just heard her loud voice, and this tells us there is something unusual happening. When I hear her, I always check to see what's going on." Losing interest, Millie meandered off to the other side of the yard.

Mary's eyes widened, "Ah, ha. I am learning all kinds of things."

Charles nodded. "You know, I was thinking. How do you feel about horses? They are an absolute necessity out in the country for traveling and accomplishing chores."

She looked him straight in the eyes, "I have to admit I know very little about horses. And, I don't know how to drive or ride. However, I do like them."

He saw her face light up as she continued to talk about the horses. "That's good to hear. I would like to teach you how to drive Buddy. Who knows, maybe later you might want to learn how to ride. Currently, we have been using the buckboard wagon when we go back and forth to town. However, I also have a carriage to use for church and visiting. It is currently at the blacksmith's being fixed but should be ready soon."

"I would love to learn to drive! I could make deliveries and take Lizzie to school and pick her up. Once I am a good driver, that is."

Just what he wanted to hear.

MARY WAS EXCITED ABOUT LEARNING HOW TO DRIVE BUDDY. Being able to do this task well would enable her to make deliveries and pick up supplies, as well as drive Lizzie to and from school. It was hard to contain her excitement, so much so, that the next morning she rose early and prepared for what she hoped would be her first driving lesson. She entered the kitchen and saw Helen was already there slicing the bacon.

Helen turned to Mary. "Could you please fetch the eggs from the chicken coop." She passed her the large basket.

"Certainly." Turning to the front door, Mary observed Lizzie quietly sitting at the table." Lizzie, would you like to come with me?"

"Please, I can be a big help," little Lizzie replied.

And they walked outside to the chicken coop. Mary took care while slowly opening the coop door. And, as if on cue, a continuous flow of chickens poured out. After feeding the hungry birds, Mary declared, "Now, let's see about getting the eggs."

"Goodie!" Lizzie announced.

Mary saw all the chickens had left their nests. *Ah, so far, so good.* After placing the basket on the ground behind them, Lizzie gathered the eggs from the bottom nesting boxes and Mary retrieved them from the top. They placed their eggs in the basket. Not a one was missed. Stepping out, Mary closed the coop door.

"Would you like to carry the basket into the house?"

"I can do that. I don't get to help very often."

Mary gave the basket to Lizzie, "Hold on — with both hands."

They started back to the house. Exiting through chicken pen gate, Mary saw a board on the threshold was protruding into the gateway. Before she could sound a warning, she heard an 'ouff' and 'thump.' Lizzie went head over teakettle. Out flew the basket like it had wings of its own. Eggs went in every direction, and many landed with a splat. Lizzie immediately began to cry.

She rushed to little Lizzie's side and lifted her up. "Shh, darling, are you all right?" The little girl nodded her head as the tears streamed down her cheeks. She rubbed her left knee. Mary continued to console her. "Besides your knee, do you hurt anywhere else?" Lizzie shook her head and started to cry again. "Oh honey, it will be all right. There'll be more eggs tomorrow. Don't worry Lizzie. I wish I had seen that board sticking out earlier. I am so very sorry." Mary gathered little Lizzie into her arms and hugged her while whispering soothing words.

After a few moments, Mary stepped back to brush off Lizzie's pinafore. Taking a hankie from her sleeve, she began to wipe Lizzie's tears away. "Accidents do happen, sweetheart. Not to worry." She only hoped everyone would feel the same.

CHARLES CHECKED DAISY'S PADDOCK AND FOUND THE FENCE boards were secure. No sense in allowing the new calf an exit to go exploring. Feeding the larger livestock was his next chore. The horses nickered as he pitched their hay into the mangers. He then allowed them back into their stalls to eat. Last, he would ask Mary and Lizzie to feed the chickens before breakfast. This was a fun chore to start their day.

Rounding the corner of the barn, he looked toward the house and came to a dead stop. *What happened?* Mary was brushing off Lizzie's dress. Lizzie was crying. Now Mary was wiping her tears away with a hankie. Streams of dripping yellow blobs covered the two of them. The surrounding ground was dotted with white shells. The egg basket was turned over and lying in the dirt. He heard Mary trying to reassure Lizzie. Mary was lamenting the fact she had not seen the board sticking out into the doorway soon enough to prevent the fall.

"Son of a gun!" Charles called out and began to rush over. He had not gotten around to fixing that board yet, and this accident was his fault.

As he arrived at the scene, Mary quickly straightened up. "This was my fault."

"No, it was not. Are you hurt?"

Mary looked Lizzie over again and glanced to Charles. "No, we are fine."

"Are you sure?"

"Yes, Papa."

"Good to hear. However, it was I who forgot to fix that board."

"Whew!" Charles uttered in relief. *They were all right. Mom was going to be highly annoyed about the eggs, but at least no one was hurt.* He made a mental note to himself that from here on out, he should write his fix-it list on a piece of paper.

CHAPTER 11

THE RIDE INTO TOWN TODAY WAS A QUIET ONE. CHARLES HELPED everyone out of the wagon. Mary glanced over to Lizzie. Helen was fixing her curls and plumping the bow of her pinafore. Charles took the crates of eggs and fresh vegetables out of the bed of the wagon and Mary followed him to the mercantile. The bells above the door jangled as they entered.

Mr. DeForest was at the back counter comparing stock items with the books in front of him. The shopkeeper looked up as Charles walked to the counter and set the crate of eggs down.

Mr. DeForest smiled at Mary. "Good day Miss Schulman. And this must be Mr. Charles Baxter."

She returned his smile. "Good morning Mr. DeForest."

Charles quickly extended his hand, "Charles Baxter, good morning to you. And, welcome to our town."

The store owner took his hand and gave it a firm shake. "Nicholas DeForest, at your service."

"Nice to meet you." Charles straightened to his full height.

Mr. DeForest leaned slightly away. "Yes, sir. And I am happy to be here."

Charles raised an eyebrow. "I see you changed the name of the store."

"Yes, sir. I thought it would be easier with the change in ownership." Mr. DeForest gave a partial smile.

Nodding, Charles pushed the crate of eggs closer the new store owner. "First off, I want to apologize for the late delivery of our eggs — a slight accident befell us yesterday. However, I can assure you we will be able to continue to deliver eggs to your store twice a week. This is the same schedule the Braunsteins requested. Is this acceptable to you?"

"Certainly, Mr. Baxter. Most appreciated."

Mary gave Charles a list of items she needed for her canning lesson. He placed the list, along with his mother's, on the counter top.

"I would like the items on these two lists, please."

Mary glanced at Charles, "please gentlemen, I will allow you to continue your business."

"Certainly, Miss Schulman. Please feel free to look around the store. I am still making changes at present – for the better, I hope." Mr. DeForest gave Mary a dazzling smile and a lingering appreciative gaze.

Charles stepped closer and touched her shoulder. "Let me know if you see something you would like."

My, he certainly is a tall man, Mary could not help but smile. "That's very kind of you, Charles. And Mr. DeForest, I am sure you will have your store looking splendid in no time."

With a nod of her head, she turned and walked down the aisle in search of Helen and Lizzie. It felt nice to have two polite gentlemen being attentive. And, she was pleased to see Charles was a man of business. *No head in the clouds with this man.* Stopping, she saw some nutmeg. Remembering her mother's most wonderful nutmeg jumbles, she thought to try her luck at making these biscuits for her new family. Ever practical, Mary had brought her mother's recipe. She hoped they would be as delicious.

THE TWO MEN WATCHED AS MARY WALKED DOWN THE AISLE. Charles turned and saw Mr. DeForest was continuing to watch a little longer than he liked. *Does he have to look that long?* With a shake of his head, Mr. DeForest came out of his trance. Leaning closer to Charles, "I rode the stage into town with Miss Schulman. She is a most engaging young woman — intelligent and beautiful." He paused and continued, now whispering in an even lower voice. "After meeting her, I am thinking of getting a mail order bride myself. It might be just the thing."

"She is a wonderful woman, to be sure." Charles was now feeling a little uneasy about the last part of their conversation.

Mr. DeForest picked up the lists. "I don't see any items here that will present a problem. Give me a few minutes. I am still getting my bearings as to where everything is." The store owner walked towards the back-storage room.

Charles raised his voice loud enough to be heard. "No problem. We are not in a hurry. I will be back with the buckboard to pick up the goods up later if that's all right."

"Absolutely. Mr. Baxter, anything you want."

The bell above the door jingled again and in stepped Francis with her mother. They were walking in his direction. *Oh, no. Just what I didn't need to add to my day. But what can I do?* He stood transfixed. Before his eyes, he could see his mother, Lizzie, and Mary were slowly walking up to him from the center aisle, from the far side of the store. A quick glance to his side told him that Francis and her mother were nearly upon him.

His eyes darted back to the center to the see Lizzie skipping ahead of his mother and Mary bringing up the rear. They were all coming towards him. He looked for a quick way out, but he was corned – like a rabbit caught in a trap. Looking back to his side, as usual, Francis was a step-in front of her mother. She sallied forth, gave a slight lift to her posture, and gushed. "Good afternoon, Mr. Baxter."

Pasting a smile on his face, Charles prepared to greet the ladies. "Good afternoon, Miss Francis and Mrs. Miller."

Quickly stepping towards the front door, Charles called out, "Oh, please excuse me, ladies, I'm late for my appointment." *Surely, I'm needed somewhere else?*

Just then he felt a tug on his pant leg. Charles stopped short and looked down. There was Lizzie.

"Papa, may I please, have a couple of peppermints," Lizzie asked.

Francis giggled. "Oh Elizabeth, little girls should not have candy. It's not good for your waistline."

A seven-year-old girl has to worry about her waistline? Charles could not believe what he heard. He looked down to Lizzie's fallen face.

"I believe a few peppermints would be in good order, especially since you have been doing such a good job keeping Skippy out of trouble." And he motioned for DeForest to get the candy.

"Charles, she might ruin her appetite for dinner." His mother looked to Francis who was nodding her head in agreement.

Nope. Not going to let them do that! Charles straightened to his full height and looked at DeForest, who seemed to be amused by it all.

"If you please, I would like a quarter of a pound of peppermints," Charles stated with determination. Feeling set upon, he looked behind the group for support from Mary. *Had she stepped farther away?* Their eyes met and smiling, she gave a nod of her head in approval.

"Yes, sir!" DeForest scooped out a generous portion of candy into a small paper bag and set it on the scale. Charles glanced at the new store owner and saw he was grinning.

"THANK YOU." And Charles took the bag, bent down and offered a piece to Lizzie.

Lizzie's eyes brightened. "Thank you, Papa." She stared inside of the bag for a couple of moments and then withdrew a large white and red striped piece.

Turning, he extended the bag of peppermints to the three ladies near him. All shook their heads in unison. Stepping past them, Charles offered some candy to Mary. She tilted her head and came forward.

"Yes, please and thank you." She slipped her long slender hand into the bag and withdrew a peppermint and popped it into her mouth. Charles did the same.

Francis' jaw dropped to the floor. With a curt nod, she and her mother turned and left.

Charles took Mary's arm. "I will escort you to the ribbon shop and then take my leave to see Hans." He and his ladies headed across the street to Berta May's, Ribbons and Buttons.

Looking back, Charles saw DeForest chuckling. *He certainly must have sized up that situation.*

~

WALKING TO THE RIBBONS AND BUTTONS SHOP, MARY THOUGHT of the recent conversation at the mercantile. *What a lot of nonsense! To think a little girl can't have a candy now and then.* Mary watched as Lizzie skipped down the boardwalk with Helen in tow. She and Charles followed.

Abruptly, Charles tugged on Mary's arm. They both stopped. A man in an old worn wool suit bumped into them. He reeked of cheap alcohol.

"Ahh ha, excuse me. "He squinted. "Oh, iteez you, Char-les. I needs to find my ree-port. Orz'it back in zee office?" He immediately turned and walked off.

Watching the him stumble around, she stepped in closer to Charles. The man continued weaving down the boardwalk. He stopped, fumbled with the doorknob and lurched into a small office. The door slammed with a loud bang.

Charles bent down to whisper in Mary's ear. His breath was warm and smelled of peppermint. "That man is Mr. Telford, the local surveyor. We used to see him in much better shape, especially after he married. Come to think of it, I haven't seen the Mrs. lately. This town has a few interesting characters as you will soon discover."

Stopping at the fabric shop, Charles opened the door. Mary saw the satin ribbons swaying in the breeze. Stepping inside, she looked at the many colorful bolts of fabric, boxes of threads and yarns, and yards of lace wrapped around pink paper.

Turning to find Helen and Lizzie looking through the buttons cards and boxes, she walked over to join them. *School will start soon, and Lizzie could use a couple of new dresses.* She saw some fabric out of the corner of her eye. It was an adorable blue calico print. She imagined it would make quite a pretty school dress for Lizzie. *This one will bring out the color of her eyes.*

Picking up the bolt, she promptly walked over to the older woman at the front table. Whispering, Mary said, "This is to be a surprise. May I have enough material to make a young girl's dress?" The older woman's face crinkled as she smiled. Anxiously, Mary watched her cut the fabric. The woman folded it, placed some matching blue thread on top and wrapped it all in brown paper. She tied it with string. Mary paid and quickly put the package into her mesh bag. Glancing around to see if Helen and Lizzie were watching, she was relieved to see they were still busy with the buttons.

She heard the shop door open and turned to recognize the same two ladies who had been at The General Store. They were standing an aisle over with their backs towards her. She could not help over-hearing.

"Francis, you should set your sights on another man. You know

Helen said Charles' mail order bride has arrived. And, you just saw her at mercantile."

The younger woman waved a hand back and forth, "Yes, however, Helen also said, they were not yet married either."

Mary's ears were ringing. *Oh, No! Not the gossiping again.*

MARY WAS QUIET ON THE RIDE HOME FROM THE BUSY BEE CAFÉ. It was very apparent she was on thin ice with Helen and Francis. She could sense Charles straining to keep the conversation going. After hearing what Francis said about keeping her sights on Charles, she did not feel like engaging in the conversation. Conniving women and gossip were exactly the type of situation she was hoping to avoid.

Although, from her observations, it seemed that Charles did not seem to enjoy being around Francis. But could she trust him? The expression, 'Fool me once – shame on you, fool me twice – shame on me' came to her mind. However, she knew Charles was an entirely different man from Robert. Judging by the honesty expressed in his letters and the way she had observed him with his family and friends, she felt a little relieved.

She blinked. The slight rise of Charles's voice brought her out of her thoughts.

"Hans said he would have the carriage fixed up shortly. Though, I am not sure when that will be. It's probably anyone's guess. You can push a friend only so far." Charles gave a little chuckle. "But when it's fixed, we can look forward to driving out in more comfort. I was thinking, maybe after church, we could go on a picnic? How does that sound to everyone?"

"Oh! Goodie! Can I bring Skippy? I promise to watch after him." Lizzie bounced up and down on the makeshift seat.

"Why not, but you will have to keep him on the leash and close to you. There will be no taking him to the creek without Papa. Are we understood?" Charles looked over his shoulder to stare at his daughter.

"Yes Papa," she replied and began to hum happily.

"Well, that means a lot of cooking and extra preparations," grumbled Helen.

"I understand Mom. However, with the weather being favorable, it will be a good time for us to relax. Mary has never seen our picnic spot."

Perhaps, I can find a way into her good graces.

"Helen, please tell me what I can do to help with the preparations," offered Mary.

MARY HAD A TERRIBLE TIME FALLING ASLEEP. THE CONVERSATION she overheard at the ribbon shop had brought back the awful memories of being left at the altar. On top of everything, she had accidentally overheard another disturbing conversation before last night's supper. When she had gone in search of Charles, she had stopped outside the barn door. She could not help but overhear the loud conversation Helen had with him. What was Helen going on about Francis being a better cook than Mary? *How would she know? She had only ever let me cook on the hottest burner on the stove. Of course, I burned the bacon.* Nonetheless, having another woman after her betrothed was not what she expected, much less wanted. *Who was Francis to Charles?* Mary did not think Charles was the sort of man to send for a mail-order bride if he was in love with someone else. *Why would a man go to the bother to correspond with a mail order bride, if that was the case?*

While lying in bed, Mary mulled over her situation. Being a bookkeeper's daughter, she liked knowing how things would add up. Once she knew of any issues, she wanted to be able to reconcile any odd pieces of information. She knew life, in general, was not this simple. However, there were always things which could never be arranged or understood. Mary knew she was a good and caring person. The question was, would Helen give her a fair opportunity to prove herself? Furthermore, she also knew she liked a challenge. However, if the numbers were stacked against her, she might have to revise her future plans.

Finally, in the wee hours of the morning, Mary decided she was tired of being placed aside. Charles had sent for her. She had accepted Charles and traveled to the West to become part of a new family. Meanwhile, Helen would have to accept she was here to stay.

CHAPTER 12

THE NEXT DAY MARY AWOKE FEELING BETTER. SHE WAS determined to do something right by Helen. With the egg debacle still hanging over her head, she thought to surprise everyone. She would show Helen that she was more than worth her salt. And, she would start with washing the bed linens. Washing the linens was a cumbersome task, and hopefully, Helen would appreciate her efforts. The timing could not be more perfect. It was a nice sunny day with a gentle breeze. She knew everyone was busy with other tasks. Lizzie was inside practicing her letter writing with a Dixon pencil and some paper Mary had brought out. Helen was busy churning the butter at a rapid pace. And, Charles was working on smoking the meat from a pig he had recently butchered.

And, so it began. Mary heated water in two large pots on the stove. From the back shed, she lugged out the washtub with its wooden ribbed washboard inside. She placed the tub near the outside water pump. Grabbing a large wicker basket from the shed, she entered the house. After stripping the beds of their sheets, she put them all in the basket. Next, she hefted the basket to her hip and brought it outside. Arriving at the tub, she shifted the basket front and center and bent down to place it next to the tub. It was time to retrieve the soap. She marched back to the shed and retrieved the only bar of soap on the shelf. While inside she picked up the wash dolly. She returned to the tub and placed the dolly inside. Carefully the soap was unwrapped from the wax paper, she then smelled the bar. *No fragrance.* Mary thought of the lavender bath soap she had brought from home. *Home, ahh ... NO, wait – the word 'home' should no longer apply to Philadelphia, or at least I hope so.*

Thoughts of her new home drifted in her head. Mary knew she loved little Lizzie as her own. Further, once she let her guard down, she felt she would fall in love with Charles. The farm and its animals were also a growing attachment. While living on a farm, she could see there was always some appreciation given or received. Sometimes it was from the animals being feed or seeing a new life having entered the world. Living in the countryside seemed a rewarding life for a person, assuming one was willing to work hard. Mary thought of the women in Philadelphia and their tea gatherings. She doubted many of those ladies ever did any physical labor.

Returning her thoughts to the task at hand, she placed the soap and paper on the ground beside the tub. Mary then fetched several buckets of water from the pump and poured them into the tub. With it filled half way, and she then went inside the house and brought out the two pots of hot water. She poured the hot water into the cold and watched it mix. Picking up the dolly, she inserted it into the tub and stirred. It was warm outside for early September. She wiped her brow with a hankie from her apron pocket. Gathering a few of the sheets, she plopped them into the tub. Naturally, the sheets kept rising to the top of the water. So again, she pushed them down and continued this for several more turns. Snagging the sheet at the bottom, she knew it was wet enough to soap. Pulling up a portion of the sheet over the washboard, she grabbed the soap and in no time at all, she had washed all the sheets.

After hanging the sheet up on the clothesline, she looked up to see Charles and Helen were both watching her. Helen was smiling. *Finally, it seems as if I may have pleased her.*

CHARLES WAS DELIGHTED WITH MARY FOR TAKING THE INITIATIVE to wash the bed linens. He noticed Mom looked pleased as well when she saw the full clothesline. *Perchance was Mom taking to Mary?* This was a welcome thought, especially after that conversation in the barn yesterday. Of course, she had to bring up Francis again by saying she was a better cook than Mary. All he needed to remember was the burnt bacon. To that statement, he could only huff in reply. He knew she had given Mary the hot stovetop burner. How could Mom make a comparison when she had not yet given Mary an opportunity to cook anything? But she had baked bread, and it was good. However, the kitchen was an area they had to work out between the two of them. He did not want to enter that domain. He might accidentally imply to Mary that she needed to do more cooking. That would be another blunder for his side, especially if she didn't like cooking. But most importantly, his mother shouldn't be discussing such things when Mary could walk into the barn and overhear what they were saying. *What was Mom thinking?!*

Charles decided it was time for the whole family to take a break from the house and farm chores for the rest of the afternoon. He did not want Mary to think farm life was just one chore after another with no break at all. And that could happen if his mother got the notion to have Mary do more hard chores today. *Who knows what Mom might suggest next, cleaning out the root cellar?* It was definitely time to take everyone into town.

"Lizzie, guess what? We are going to town. Care for a donut or some biscuits?"

His little girl popped up her head from tracing letters on the kitchen table. "Oh, yes Papa. Look what Mama has me practicing. It's the letters of the alphabet."

"What a fine job you have done, too! Perhaps you can do more when we return home?" Lizzie nodded and got up. Looking down, he noticed a large piece of paper and on it was the alphabet written in Mary's hand. He was touched. Mary had already engaged Lizzie in school work. She had started working on what they had discussed in their letters to each other. This scene reminded him that additional writing supplies should be purchased while they were in town. He went in search of Mary and Mom. Work was going to stop, and they were all going into town.

LOOKING FORWARD TO THE TRIP INTO TOWN, MARY CHECKED ON Lizzie and saw that Helen was already combing her golden locks into a semblance of ringlets. So, she went out into the barn and watched Charles hitch up the Buddy.

Charles presented her with a soft smile. "I noticed Lizzie was working on her letters. Thank you. I also noticed the graphite pencil and paper you gave her. That was very nice of you."

"It's my pleasure. She is a very bright young girl. And as you know, her letters will become easier after practice." Mary stepped a little closer. "I believe she will enjoy school."

After adjusting the harness, he looked back to Mary. "I hope so. How are you doing on your letter writing supplies? We can get some additional paper at the mercantile. You need to keep in touch with your family. They might like to come out to visit you sometime.

Tomorrow is Sunday, and I plan to introduce you to more people at church." Mary felt touched at Charles' thoughtfulness. *Some new friends will be most welcome.* "I would appreciate that. Thank you, Charles."

He nodded, and Mary continued to watch him harness Buddy.

She walked closer and patted the horse on the neck. "Such a good boy, you are," she softly said while stroking his neck. Buddy turned his head towards her and gave her a nudge. Mary laughed.

Charles' eyes flashed with delight. "He likes you. That is a big compliment as he is normally a quiet sort."

"I like him very much as well. He is strong and gentle." *Perchance he is a bit like you?*

The ride into town was filled with chatter. Charles stopped the wagon in front of the mercantile. Everyone filed into the store. Mary glanced around the shop and saw Mr. DeForest had given Lizzie a couple of peppermints. Helen was looking at the canned fruits. And, Charles was bringing up some writing supplies to the front counter as he had promised. Mary turned from admiring her future husband and started to walk down the nearby aisles.

Soon she was distracted by an argument outside the front of the store. It was followed by some scuffling and clanking noises. Next came some muffled voices, whining and finally a soft cry. Alarmed she rushed to see what had caused the disturbance. Mary walked to the store front entry and saw three boys. They looked about eight to ten years of age. The smallest boy had apparently been shoved to the boardwalk floor, and the tallest boy was reaching down to take the coins from the smaller boy's outstretched hand. The boy on the floor was in a precarious position.

Despite the bullying the older boys had given him, he held his head up and stared defiantly at them. Tears clung to his little checks. His clothes were too small for him. The fabric was worn thin from repeated use and washings. A threadbare grayish shirt clung to his thin body, and a shirt button was lying on the floor beside him. She saw one of the knee patches on his soft brown pants had loose stitching and was now close to falling off. *The poor boy! And he has no shoes, too. Just look at those cuts and dirt.*

Angered, Mary walked forward and stood in a position where she was behind and towering over the two older boys. "Ahemm

...." Heads spun around. They looked shocked — their eyes were wide, and their mouths were gaping open. *Sometimes being a tall woman has its benefits.* The bigger boys' faces turned a brilliant shade of crimson. And they quickly fled away and into the street. Offering her hand out to the small boy, "Here, please let me help you up."

He allowed Mary to pull him up from the floor. "Thank-you, Miss. I am Johnny, and I'd best be going now." With a nod, he skedaddled off as fast as his legs could take him.

After returning home, Mary followed Charles into the barn for the afternoon feeding chores. Mary stopped feeding the chickens and glanced at him. "Charles, can you please tell me anything about a boy who is around eight years old? He answers to the name of Johnny. The reason I ask is two boys a couple of years older were bullying him and almost ran off with his money. The little boy looked ... well, in need." Mary watched Charles' face grow deeply concerned as she continued to explain what had happened earlier. She saw Charles frown and shake his head.

"Mary, I am pleased you told me of this event, and I am even happier you stepped in. Johnny's family is having a hard time. His father is off on a cattle drive, and his mother is recovering from a long bout of influenza. I will see about discreetly dropping off some food supplies."

"Charles, thank you. And I would be happy to help you in any way I can."

ALTHOUGH IT WAS STILL EARLY IN THE DAY, MARY ALREADY FELT a little tired. All night long thoughts spun around in her head. She tossed and turned and kept thinking of the upsetting conversation she overheard in the fabric shop. To top it off, when she did start to fall asleep, Helen's footsteps were heard in the hall announcing the start of the day. Mary worried that with such an aggressive young woman after Charles, it would not hurt to say extra prayers in church today.

While driving into church, Mary heard Helen say, "Now Elizabeth, I want you to pay special attention to the sermon today. I helped Reverend Winterthorpe pick out this Sunday's topic."

Helen's forehead had developed a deep furrow. "Mr. Parsons will give this sermon today. I know he won't be able to deliver it as well as the Reverend would, but he will give it his best. I do hope the Reverend's Mother is on the mend and he will return very soon."

Everyone nodded his and her head in agreement, especially Mary. It was then she noticed the light sprinkling of rain from last night had dampened the ground. It was enough to settle at least some of the dust. She took in a deep breath and smelled the crisp, clean air. *Certainly, much better than the big cities!*

Soon the small white church came into view. It was nestled in a large grove of huge pine trees, at the end of Main Street. She could see the church's white steeple standing tall. As the wagon moved closer, she saw a crowd had already formed out front. There were two long hitching rails located alongside the parsonage. Charles drove up and tied Buddy amongst the other horses and carriages.

Helen scurried off. "I will meet you inside. I am going to see if Mr. Parsons' needs any help."

Entering the church, Charles removed his hat and guided Lizzie and Mary to their seats in the third pew, left front. Mary could feel all eyes were following her, especially those of Mr. DeForest. At the conclusion of the service, she thought Mr. Parsons had done a fine job with the sermon.

A large gathering had formed out in front of the church and Mary was looking forward to being introduced to the family friends. She felt Charles slipped his arm through her elbow as he began to guide his newly enlarged family over to join the group. Mary held hands with Lizzie as they all strolled around the large congregation. While walking, Mary glanced back to the church steps and found Helen was still busy talking with Mr. Parsons. *No doubt she was sharing her opinion of the sermon with him.*

It felt nice to be walking on a handsome gentleman's arm with her new daughter at her side. After a short while, Mary noticed the Nelsons waving. She stopped and looked up at Charles. He glanced over and took Mary's meaning,

"Lizzie, you may go over and play with your friends. Mind you, be careful of your Sunday clothes." With a firm nod of her head, Lizzie was off like a cat after a mouse. Smiling, Mary and Charles watched her greet her friends.

They continued walking until they were standing next to Harlan McCloud and his family.

"Ahem." All eyes turned to Charles and Mary. "I would like you all to meet my betrothed, Mary Schulman. She has recently arrived from Cincinnati, originally from Philadelphia."

A tall and handsome gray-haired man removed his wide brimmed black Stetson. His eyes held their eyes. "Good day and it is a pleasure to meet you, Miss Schulman. I am Alastair McCloud, and this is my wife, Emma." Mary recognized Mr. McCloud as the author of one of Charles' letters of recommendation. He was an impressive looking man. Mary could see where Harlan got his good looks.

"It is a pleasure to meet you, Mr. and Mrs. McCloud," Mary answered.

Mrs. McCloud stepped forward with a gracious smile. "I am very pleased to meet you, Miss Schulman, especially after all the nice things Harlan has said about you."

"Thank you for the compliment. Your son was quite the gallant gentleman during the stagecoach ride and upon my arrival."

Harlan chuckled. "Gallant, now that is something I've never been accused of before. Is that a good thing or a bad thing?"

"Now Harlan, stop horsing around and let Charles finish with the introductions." Emma McCloud chided her son, only to smile a moment later.

Charles rolled his eyes. "All right then, next to Harlan is John, Ethan and last, the pretty looking sibling, Miss Fiona."

Harlan shifted his shoulders and began again. "You know, I feel responsible for bringing you two together. I hope the Baxter family is treating you well. If they are not, they will have to answer to me." He grinned.

What else could she do but nod her head in a playful acknowledgment of the honeyed words? *He's a mischief-maker, and I bet he has all the ladies charmed.*

The conversation quickly turned to the topic of ranching. Mary followed the discussion on the merits of introducing a new polled breed of cattle into the area. Until now she had thought all cattle had horns.

Soon Mary noticed Daniela waving. She shuffled over and, linking her arm to Mary's, proceeded to introduce her to a group of ladies.

Mary glimpsed over towards the church and saw Charles walking in her direction. Within moments, he stopped. She saw that blonde woman had cornered him again.

"Good morning Mr. Baxter. Is it not a lovely day?"

That voice! So again, that woman had found her way to Charles.

ON THE DRIVE BACK TO THE HOUSE, CHARLES' MIND CENTERED ON the look of admiration DeForest had given Mary during the sermon. Then there was the resulting blush which appeared on Mary's face. This attention DeForest was giving Mary did not sit well with him. *But what can I do?*

As was her custom, his mother discussed the sermon with Lizzie. It was a good thing his mother hadn't asked him for his opinions. He had not paid that close attention. It seemed all the single men of the community, and even some of the married ones had all sneaked glances of appreciation at his bride-to-be. *When is Reverend Winterthorpe returning?* Charles tried to relax and think about the upcoming picnic.

He could feel the warmth of Mary sitting next to him on the wagon seat. Taking into account the time she had been with the family, he knew he hadn't much of an opportunity to court her as the Reverend suggested. And, as sure as rain falls from the sky, his mother's attitude wasn't helping matters. Perhaps while the family enjoyed their picnic, he could attempt a little courting.

CHAPTER 13

THE TWO LADIES SET ABOUT PACKING THE FOOD FOR THE PICNIC. They managed to fill two large picnic baskets.

Mary listened to Charles whistle as he walked back and forth between the house and the buckboard. He was carrying the picnic baskets and blankets. Returning for the third time, Charles announced, "Well ladies, I think we are ready. Lizzie is already in the barn putting on Skippy's leash."

He stood anxiously and watched the two ladies walk out the front door. Finally, Charles exited giving the doorknob a good pull to close it. Next, Charles assisted the ladies into the wagon and then gave a loud whistle. "Miss Elizabeth. If you and Skippy are ready, please join us," he shouted.

Abruptly everyone turned towards the noise coming from the barn. Exiting was a very excited puppy pulling Lizzie along at the end of his leash. As the two neared the wagon, Charles bent down and scooped up Skippy and handed the squirming puppy to Mary. He then lifted Lizzie into the back seat and returned the puppy to her.

Mary cautioned, "Hold onto him with the rope and maybe

snuggle him up into your arms for at least part of the trip. I can see you are both excited. I know I am."

"Yes, Mama. I will introduce Skippy to our special picnic spot."

Mary's heart warmed upon hearing Lizzie's reply, a gentle flick of the reins and they were off. Mary stretched her legs – her foot bumped into something. Looking down, she saw a shotgun lying on the floor. "Ah … Charles, why are you bringing a shotgun with us? Are you going to do a little hunting?"

He began to explain. "When driving into the country, we always bring a shotgun or rifle, depending on what we are doing. Today, it is for protection … in case a coyote comes around and wants our tasty chicken. We will scare him off with the shotgun. It is better to be safe than sorry. The shells are in my pocket. Rest assured, it is not loaded."

She thought it best to change the subject. "How far does your land extend?" inquired Mary, hoping her voice sounded nonchalant.

"That's a good question, especially since the trees lining the creek hide where our property stops. I also have land on the other side of Crystal Creek. That land is leased by the McClouds' for their cattle. Their family pays a yearly fee and gives us some beef as well."

Remembering an article, Mary read in *The National Grange,* "Do you rotate the land after seasonal grazing?"

Charles turned to look at her. "Well, I see you have been doing some reading. Good for you, Mary! Mom, did you hear?" Charles then pointedly looked his mother.

Helen smiled politely. "Yes, I did."

"The Cattlemen's Association and The Grange are implementing suggested plans for land rotation. It seems quite beneficial to me."

Along the roadside, Mary noticed the same flowers Charles

brought to her on the day she arrived. *Oh, he drove out and picked them.* She felt touched.

From the back of the wagon, "My Stephen use to bring me flowers from here."

Continuing to look beyond the dark green top line of the trees, she saw the mountains were various shades of gray and purple.

Nearing the pine trees, Charles turned towards her. "We are almost there."

"Oh, this is so exciting," exclaimed Mary.

"Goodie, goodie gumdrops! Do you hear that, Skippy?" Lizzie practically shouted.

Charles drove through a stand of trees and into a small clearing. Mary was in awe. It was simply beautiful! *If ever, there was a fairyland, it would be like this! No small wonder Lizzie was so very excited.*

Looking through the flickering glow, she saw a thousand shades of green, brown and silver surrounding them. There were clusters of exotic white flowers on single stalks. Indigo blue flowers winked in and out of the ribbon of light within the secluded hideaway.

Bending over, he took the shotgun off the floor and loaded it. Mary shifted in her seat to give him room.

"Please stay in the wagon while I check to ensure the area is safe from critters." He winked and then handed the reins to Mary.

She kept a watchful eye for bears and other creatures. All of a sudden, a rustling noise was heard from the trees ahead. Momentarily, she stopped breathing — a grinning Charles soon walked through the branches. "Our area is secure, and the creek is running steady. I'll come help you all down after I tie Buddy to the hitching post and put his feed bag on."

The first priority for the ladies was to spread the blankets. Charles reached into the back of the wagon and retrieved the baskets.

He glanced at Mary and then at Lizzie and his mother. "Now,

everyone follow me. Lizzie, dear, please keep Skippy on a short lead." And, he whistled a little tune as they all followed.

What Mary saw in front of her was a vision! She could see some sawed off tree stumps meant to serve as seats. Looking towards the back of the clearing, Mary saw a small log horse, complete with mounting block. Immediately Lizzie ran over and climbed onto the block and then over onto her stead. Try as Skippy might, he could not manage to join her.

The picnic spot had a magical feeling, and she would not have been surprised if she saw a fairy stealing a glimpse of them.

"This is truly the most beautiful spot I have ever seen! If I were an artist, I would paint it. Just to remember it as it is today."

Helen looked to Mary. Then she softly gazed at her surroundings. "Yes, my husband Stephen, God rest his soul, found this place many years ago. He, Charles and our youngest son Matthew, cleared away the small trees and brushes. It has always been beautiful."

"If I may ask, where is Matthew?"

"He is in the Oregon Territory living with his wife's family. I have never seen those grandchildren." Helen answered in a wistful tone of voice.

"Oh, I see. Well, I hope someday they will come for a visit."

Helen looked up at her and nodded. The ladies started to unpack the baskets. They finished setting all the goodies out.

"Time to eat." Helen then sat down to serve.

"Great! I'm hungry. Time to come on over, Lizzie," Charles said.

Helen served the plates. They were filled with fried chicken, biscuits with homemade butter, hard-boiled eggs, and potato salad. Last but not least, they enjoyed a slice of apple pie and a piece of cheese.

"When I was younger, my family and I went on picnics as well. And we brought along sour pickles made from my grandmother's recipe. Has anyone ever had a sour pickle?" Mary inquired.

Charles perked up. "Yes. It was some years back, at a wedding dinner of a neighbor's son. It seems a relative of the bride brought pickles for the guests to eat at the dinner. They were very tasty."

"Now, I remember. It was the Weber Family. Yes. And the pickles were delicious." Helen added.

"What does a pickle look like?" asked Lizzie.

"Oh, it's a type of treat made from a cucumber, which is a vegetable. It is as round as my thumb and about as long as my hand. It is usually a little curved and has tiny bumps it. They are put through a curing process in a stone crock or wooden keg filled with a salt and vinegar brine. I shall draw a picture of one for you later as they are not easy to describe. It is a type of German food. Many people enjoy them." Mary answered smiling down at Lizzie.

"I was thinking of making pickles from my grandmother's recipe. And if you think they are tasty, perhaps we might put them in a barrel and see if the General Store will sell them, and put the proceeds in our account. The mercantile stores in Philadelphia sell the pickles directly from a large barrel. We would just have to get some cucumber seeds and plant them next spring. What do you think of the idea?"

"What a great idea!" Charles answered.

"Will cucumbers grow here?" Helen asked with some interest.

"I believe, they will. They grow in Germany, and it is cold there as well." Mary answered thoughtfully.

"It is settled then. We will see about ordering the seeds, and shortly, we will be eating Mary's pickles." Charles gave Mary a quick wink.

Charles extended his hand to Mary, "Let's all go to the stream near the Cottonwood tree and we can introduce Skippy to running water. It's not deep there. Lizzie, bring the pup. He will have loads of fun splashing around – and will probably get us wet as well!"

Mary took Charles' hand and allowed him to pull her up from the blanket. Once she was standing, he did the same for his mother. Lizzie was already up and waiting.

"Lizzie, you hold on to Grandma's hand." He leaned over and picked up his shotgun.

All at once, Mary turned and ran over to the blanket area and grabbed a book. Since everyone enjoyed *Aesop's Fables,* she had decided to bring it along. She ran back to Charles. He gave a quick squeeze to her hand and led the way through a narrow path between the pine trees stopping after some distance. Before them was a small running stream.

"Okay everyone, let's enjoy ourselves. However, my only rule for today is – to stay in this area where I can see you. No wandering off, please." Charles smiled at everyone and settled a reassuring gaze on Mary. Hearing the puppy whine, he turned to his little girl. "Now Lizzie, let me introduce Skippy to the water and then you can hold the lead after he becomes a little tired."

"Oh, okay Papa." Lizzie begrudgingly gave the leash to her father.

"Lizzie, I have an idea. Why don't we take off our shoes and dip our toes into the water?" Mary looked at Charles, who then gave her a big nod. "Helen, would you care to join Lizzie and me?" Mary could see from Helen's expression that she was considering the offer.

"Thank you but maybe next time." She sat down and adjusted her hat to keep the sun off her face.

Mary nodded and turned back to the bank of the stream. They had their shoes and stockings off in no time and were dipping their toes in the bright clear water. At first, the water felt very cold, and that brought on a round of laughter. Mary reached over and took Lizzie's hand. They walked down stream to where the water up to their ankles. Another string of laughter began. Lizzie shrieked as she tried to sidestep over each mossy rock in the creek bed. Watching her, Mary thought it looked like a dance step. Soon she brought Lizzie to her side and gave her a big hug.

"Are we done with letting the water tickle us? And, if so, how about I read you a couple of stories?" asked Mary.

"Yes, please Mama. Can I hold Skippy so he can listen too?"

"Certainly, sweetheart." Mary turned to see Charles walking towards them with a tired and soaked Skippy.

He handed the leash to his little girl. "Here you go, Lizzie. I think he's tuckered out now. He should be ready for a story too." Charles reached out and took Mary's hand and motioned for Lizzie to follow as he led them back to the bank of the stream. Mary put her stockings and boots back on and finished helping Lizzie.

Everyone sat down, and Lizzie snuggled up to Mary for story time. Mary picked two stories to read. The first was ***The Angler and the Little Fish***, which seemed appropriate. The second was entitled ***The Fox and the Crow***. Everyone agreed that story was the best as the fox had cleverly outwitted the Crow with flattery.

As they all discussed the moral of the last fable, Mary felt a few drops of light rain.

Suddenly, they heard a loud commotion. What could it be? *They were all at the stream.* Turning, Mary looked towards the picnic area, and as she did, she heard Charles whisper, "Shh, shh. Wait a few moments and then follow me at a safe distance. Mom, please hold Lizzie's hand. And Mary ... please hold Skippy." Charles swiftly grabbed the shotgun and carefully stepped forward trying not to make any noise. Mary was now feeling very nervous. Unable to see Charles, she became worried. *Surely, he would shout if he needed help?*

She slowly walked after Charles. Helen and Lizzie following closely behind her. The light shower had turned to a downpour making it difficult to walk quietly, much less to see any distance ahead. Skippy started to whimper. Mary stopped and peeked around a nearby tree only to stare at the picnic spot. Her breath caught as she looked at the scene in front of her. The two picnic baskets were turned over. Dishes were askew, and the jug of milk had been knocked over. Small pieces of biscuits, plums, and other goodies covered the blanket. A large striped skunk was standing in the middle, nibbling on the fried chicken. Near their mother were three baby skunks happily eating the apple pie and hard-boiled eggs!

AND, hiding behind a tree a few feet to Mary's left was Charles. He was staring at the scene. The shotgun was pointed directly at the ground in front of him. Hearing them approach, Charles turned his head and held his right hand up. He then brought a finger up to his lips and held it there. Mary nodded her head in agreement.

Helen poked her head out to see what everyone was watching. A loud clanking of dishes brought her stepping out from behind Mary to shout and waved her arms at the little invaders. Mary joined in the shouting, thinking it made sense to scare them away. They looked so cute and amusing but, they were EATING their picnic!

"Be Quiet!" Charles said in a very deep whisper.

Mary, Helen, and Lizzie stopped and turned their heads to him. Waving his arms in a grand gesture, he put a finger to his lips and tapped it several times. His face looked fearful. *Why?*

Everyone turned their attention back to the intruders. As if on cue, the whole skunk family turned their backs to their audience. And, with a shake of their tails, a powerful odor wafted through the entire picnic area.

Laughing, Charles shook his head. "I tried to warn you. We cannot be too angry with them. The food was there to be eaten. At least we had some of the food earlier. It looks like scrambled eggs for supper. I sure hope Buddy does not take off with the wagon trying to escape the smell."

∾

Buddy was not pleased with the odor emanating from his passengers as they climbed aboard the wagon. However, the old horse refrained from bolting – and instead picked up a very brisk trot as he headed towards home. Everyone was looked forward to a good scrubbing upon arrival.

Later that evening they all gathered for a late supper of scrambled eggs and toast. Upon finishing, Mary once again sat down with Lizzie on the settee in the parlor for story time. Helen was already in her rocking chair knitting away. Skippy was fast asleep in front of the fire. Stepping around the puppy, Charles took his normal seat next to the fireplace. The flickering of light from the fire made the room even cozier. Stretching out his long legs, Charles was looking forward to Mary reading a story. He looked around. *I certainly made a good choice. This scene is every man's dream.*

He watched as Mary opened the book and an excited Lizzie looked through the pages to pick her first story of the evening. Lizzie's head popped up, and she looked up into Mary's face. "Awe, a bunny! Can we please read about the bunny?"

"Certainly, we can. This one is called ***The Hare and the Tortoise***. And it is one of my favorites."

Charles smiled. He remembered the fable, and it was a favorite of his as well. He listened to Mary read. To his mind, this story brought out an important and interesting life lesson to be understood. Being a farmer, he could appreciate how slow and steady was often the best approach. After all, some things just took time. One could not rush Mother Nature, the weather, or even a person falling in love. On that last note, he knew he would try harder to find opportunities to court Mary. At every turn, it seemed his mother was interrupting his attempts.

Continuing to listen to the story, he smiled as he heard Mary read about the over-confidence of the hare. He always believed he would win the race. Of course, in the end, the tortoise prevailed.

Closing the book, Mary turned, "Lizzie, can you guess the lesson of this fable?"

"Does it mean you shouldn't take naps?"

"Well, taking a nap certainly did not help the hare. However, the moral is slow and steady wins the race. And if we desire something we must be steady and diligent at working towards it."

Charles thought about how these actions applied to his situation. He wanted Mary to fall in love with him. Hm, slow and steady as the story said. He smiled to himself. This woman was one to be treasured.

CHAPTER 14

MARY WOKE UP EARLY. SHE HAD BEEN UP LATE LAST NIGHT cutting out and basting the blue calico material for Lizzie's new school dress. Every little girl needed at least one new dress for the start of school.

It was time to start the breakfast. When she finished making the bread dough, it was placed on the back portion of the warm stovetop. Ever organized, Mary sliced several pieces of bacon for cooking. While waiting for the loaves to finish rising, she decided to pick the vegetables she would need to take to Daniela's. Collecting a couple of baskets near the back door, she walked out to the vegetable garden. The sun was barely over the horizon, and the air was damp and crisp. Taking a deep breath, she savored the solitude. She leaned down and placed the baskets on the ground. Then she picked tomatoes, green beans, onions, and herbs — as much as two baskets could hold. Most all of these vegetables were going to Daniela's today for canning.

Finished, Mary came inside the house and placed the baskets on the kitchen counter. Ever mindful, she remembered to check on the bread dough. *Good, they are ready! Thank you, Mrs. Turner.* She popped the two loaf pans into the oven. Pausing to catch her breath, she thought of her dear friend, Rachel and her kitchen mishaps. *I will have to write another letter to her soon.*

Hearing footsteps, Mary's mind snapped back to the present. The door opened, and Helen walked in with a full basket of eggs. "Good Morning, Mary."

Ah, she still does not trust me with the eggs. Can't say, as I blame her. Mary wiped her hands on her apron. "Good morning to you, too, Helen. I'm trying to finish a few chores before going over to Daniela's for my canning lesson. There are two of loaves of bread baking in the oven."

"I see. And, you sliced the bacon as well. Thank you. Do you need anything else for your lesson?" Helen set the egg basket on the kitchen counter.

"Just some peaches. Is there anything you would like me to do?"

Helen looked up to Mary and gave a slight shake of her head. "No thank you, dear. You just finish collecting what you need for your canning. I never really did like to can. However, I do admit fruit and vegetables from the jars are quite tasty and a welcome change from the dried fare we have in the wintertime." Turning back to the counter top, Helen proceeded to busy herself with the breakfast preparation.

That was polite but brief. Well, slow and steady. Exiting the kitchen, Mary walked outside to the orchard. On the ground near the peach tree, she retrieved two pails and began to pick the peaches within her reach. When the first pail was nearly full, she considered whether she should use the ladder to pick more. She decided against it.

As if by some miracle, Charles appeared by her side. He was carrying a couple of additional pails. "Sweetheart, how about I fetch a few more for you? This way you can leave some with the Nelsons."

"I am sure they would enjoy them, and it would be a nice thank you." *He called me sweetheart. She felt her heart skip a beat.*

Charles stepped up the ladder and began picking the ripe fruit. Chuckling, he turned down to look at her, "You must have been thinking hard. Did you even hear me walk up to you?"

Mary started to laugh. "No. I was thinking about my first canning lesson."

Smiling, he looked down and suggested, "Since I am going into town after I drop you off, could you make up a basket of food for Johnny's family? I left a basket for you by the kitchen door."

"Thank you, and I would be most happy to do that. It will be filled with bread, butter, bacon, eggs, and even peaches." Her heart warmed at the thought of helping Johnny and his family.

WITH BREAKFAST FINISHED, CHARLES KNEW THEY NEEDED TO GET a move on if they were going to arrive at the Nelsons on time. He stepped out to the barn to ready the wagon. Mary followed him with the first two pails of peaches.

He turned to watch a soft curl fall out next to the side of her face, framing it beautifully. However, his shyness took over and he thought helping her load up the wagon was best. Who knew when his mother might step out? "Here Mary, let me load the rest of the fruits and vegetables into the wagon for you. Do you have everything you need? Don't forget the jars. I'll be going on into town after I drop you off. I have to purchase gunnysacks for storing the dried corn."

"Yes, I believe I have everything."

"And, I will see about getting you some work boots. What size should I buy?" As soon as the words escaped his mouth, he knew he had made another possible blunder. *Great, now she is going to think I want her to work harder.*

"Well, I could use sturdy work boots, thank you. I wear a size five."

He realized she had not misinterpreted his offer of new boots.

Watching her rush back into the house, he remembered he had not even kissed her as yet. Lately, he had been thinking about that a lot. He slowly shook his head. *I will not get much done today if these thoughts keep popping into my mind.*

Walking into the barn, Charles imagined Buddy would be looking for some of the dried apple pieces Mary had been giving him. Reaching into his pant pocket, he found a couple of bits. He realized he had picked up one of Mary's habits. This was a good habit, and he didn't want to disappoint the old horse. It was interesting how the influence of a good woman was changing things.

Charles pulled the buckboard around to the front of the house, and he loaded the rest of the canning supplies. He looked around at the farm. Things were changing for the better. It had been a long while since he felt content.

Hearing the front door open and then close, he saw Mary step out onto the front porch and tie the ribbons of her bonnet. He watched her with admiration as she approached. The fact that she was excited to learn how to can all their fruits and vegetables as well as spend time with his friends, pleased him to no end. If only he could find the right words to express how he felt. Perhaps, tonight he could speak to her before she retired for the evening?

He lifted her up to the wagon seat. Johnny's basket caught his eye, as he climbed into the seat next to Mary. "I see our care basket is nicely filled. You are a most thoughtful young lady."

Mary blushed. "Thank you."

And with a cluck and a snap of reins, they were off to the Nelsons. Charles saw Mary turn and give the back of the wagon a once-over-look. *She is a meticulous one and just what this farmer needs.*

She turned to him, "And we are off."

SITTING NEXT TO CHARLES IN THE BUCKBOARD, MARY REALIZED

this was one of the few times they were alone. It seemed Helen did not want to bother chaperoning them on this short drive. Whatever Helen's reason, Mary took the initiative and turned towards Charles. "I am very excited to learn how to can today. If I become good at this and we have an abundance of produce, maybe we can sell some of the jars at the mercantile, especially the jams and jellies."

Charles glanced in her direction. "Well, that's an excellent thought. You are just full of good ideas."

Pleased, Mary folded her hands in her lap. She was becoming more comfortable with the ride of the wagon. "I have been looking forward to enjoying Daniela's company. She has a wonderful uplifting personality."

He adjusted his large brimmed cowboy hat a little further down on his forehead. "What an appropriate description of Daniela. Couldn't have said it better myself."

Mary was comforted by his praise. Suddenly out of the corner of her eye, Mary saw a large gray rabbit leap out into the path of the wagon. It paused for a moment before deciding to spring off into the meadow. She had never seen or heard of such an odd-looking rabbit. It had long ears, and instead of hopping it was leap-ing. "Goodness. What is that?"

"Oh, that's a jackrabbit, and they are very, very fast. They even outrun coyotes. They differ greatly from Lizzie's bunnies." Charles gave a low chuckle and continued talking about their surroundings.

Charles was normally a quiet sort of man. However, this morning he was proving to be a good conversationalist. She listened to him describe more of her new home. It was obvious he loved the land.

Before long, the Nelsons' farm came into view. Spending time with cheerful Daniela would be a welcome change from seeing the occasional frowns emanating from Helen.

Stopping the wagon, he set the brake and walked around to the other side. He extended his arms to Mary. As she set her hands on his broad shoulders, he effortlessly lifted her down to the ground. Mary enjoyed the feeling of Charles hands around her. It was nice to feel small and light.

With his hands lingering on her waist, she felt her cheeks flush. "Thank you, Charles."

As fortune would have it, Daniela stepped outside. Mary wished the moment could have lasted longer.

"Good morning, you two! Mary, are you ready to try some canning?" Daniela asked with a twinkle in her eyes.

Charles promptly withdrew his hands. However, Mary observed a brief look of regret in his eyes. *Perhaps, things are looking brighter for me.*

Quickly Mary turned to face Daniela. "Why, yes I am. And, we also brought you plenty of peaches. Where should we put our goods?"

Daniela stepped forward, went up on her toes and peered into the back of the wagon. Her eyes lit up with delight. "My — MY! Please, could you put it all on the kitchen table?"

Charles and Mary emptied the buckboard of all the jars, vegetables and peaches. With the last trip finished, Mary could not believe her eyes as she looked at the kitchen table and countertops. It looked like they were going to can for the entire town. She worried they might not finish today. Slowly she turned and looked at Charles.

"How about I come back at five o'clock? I'll just find Owen and say a quick hello." Charles could be heard chuckling as he made his retreat.

Mary turned to Daniela, "How should we start?" *As Rachel says, "Life is just one big adventure!'*

Soon the ladies began the long process of canning. They washed, talked and chopped. With the two of them working hard, everything took surprisingly less time than Mary originally imagined. Daniela shared her recipe for canning tomatoes. She liked to add a healthy amount of chopped onions and herbs. She explained while some might think it excessive — the Italians did not.

The jars of tomato sauce were cooking in their bath water. Daniela fixed a cold dinner for Owen and the children. While Daniela's family ate in the dining room, the two ladies sat down at a corner of the kitchen table for a light fare.

Putting down the cheese she was eating, Daniela shifted a little in her chair. "In a way, I feel responsible for getting you together with Charles. It was my sister who wrote to me about Mrs. Turner Agency. Knowing Charles' situation, Owen and I suggested he write."

Mary finished chewing, "Yes. I do remember Charles telling me that, and I have to thank you. Charles is a wonderful man." She quickly put out of her mind, her arrival night and dinner at the hotel.

Daniela leaned forward, "How are the two of you getting along? Can I help with anything?"

Mary stopped nibbling at her slice of cheese. "I believe we are doing very well. He is most considerate." Mary paused. "I must admit to having some apprehension at times because I do not wish to remind him of the love ones he has lost." Mary's voice had dropped off to a softer and solemn tone.

Reaching out, Daniela softly touched Mary's arm. "I have found men do not talk much about what has brought them pain. You'll do just fine."

"In his letters, he described his home and the beautiful country-side. And, it certainly is wonderful to see. I did get a little bit of a surprise when I arrived — as he had forgotten to mention his mother was living at the farm. Oh, do not misunderstand, I do like Helen."

"Well, I am sure he was nervous about writing to you. Did he tell you his father homesteaded the farm?"

"No, that was not mentioned."

The ladies finished eating. Daniela cleared the plates from the table. "Now let's check on the tomatoes. I think they have cooked their required three-quarters of an hour."

Mary was amazed to see how the huge mounds of vegetables had cooked down to just twenty jars. Turning to face the many pails of peaches, she knew they would be next.

Daniela chuckled. "Now we need to separate the peaches into two groups. We will halve the pretty ones and place them into the larger jars. Then we will make a simple syrup to poured over them before sealing. At that point, they will have their turn in the water bath. The remaining group will be cut up and used to make peach preserves."

This explanation made perfect sense to Mary. "Is it like making strawberry preserves. I have done that before!" She remembered Mrs. Turner had taught all her ladies a secret in preparing preserve recipes. Mary brought out a small glass filled with lemon essence from one of her baskets. "The cook at Mrs. Turners' taught us to put a few drops of lemon essence in each jar. This allows the preserves to retain more of the fruit's original color. Shall we put in a little?"

"What a clever idea. We must add some."

As the afternoon progressed, Mary noticed the normally viva-cious Daniela was slowing down. "Daniela, why don't you sit down and rest. Perhaps you can tell me more about your children. I would enjoy hearing about them as I have cousins who are about the same ages. I'll finish taking the rest of the jars out of the bath."

Daniela slowly sat down in a kitchen chair. "Thank you, and I believe I will."

Soon the adventures and blunders of the Nelson children were regaled by their mother. Listening, Mary delighted in hearing the stories of her children's youthful exploits. Hopefully, she would have similar stories to share some day.

CHAPTER 15

Upon waking, Charles thought about all the things he had to do today. Aside from his normal duties around the farm, he had promised Mary he would show her how to deal with the everyday chores necessary to keep all the farm animals happy. Today it would be Buddy's 'turn in the barrel.' He walked downstairs and sat in his chair at the breakfast table. "Mary, why don't I teach you how to hitch and drive Buddy today? We can practice driving around the farm before I go into town later.

I understand some women do not like driving — much less learning to hitch a horse up to a wagon, but I do think it's important."

He watched Mary's face change from surprise to delight. "Charles, I would love to learn how to drive."

Rising from the table, he smiled at Mary. "Good. Come to the barn when you're done here."

Walking out to the paddock, Charles put on Buddy's halter and led the kind old horse back into the barn. There, he tied Buddy to the hitching rail in the center aisle and gave him a good brushing.

Depending on Mom's idea of a clean kitchen, Charles considered Mary should arrive any minute.

Sure enough, through the barn threshold entered Mary like a ray of sunshine. She was appropriately dressed, and her expression said business. *Um...I like this about her.*

"I am ready for my lesson. Please, just tell Buddy to be patient with me." Her eyes held a sparkle.

Charles began with explaining the many steps of haltering, harnessing and hitching. Stopping at the end of each step, he asked her to examine the placement and connections of the harness. "It's best to remember to be calm but firm and, reward the horse with patting or gentle stroking."

Smiling, she nodded. "Indeed, you can catch more flies with honey than you can with vinegar."

Charles chuckled. *She's going to get along just fine with the animals.*

Mary watched as Charles hitched the horse to the buckboard. He stepped back. "Mary, why don't you check all the connections?"

"Certainly," she replied and spent a good amount of time inspecting. Finished, she turned and looked at him. "All looks secure. Have I missed anything?"

"Not a thing." Charles lifted Mary up onto the wagon seat. Taking hold of the reins, he climbed up next to her and sat down. He nudged Buddy forward with a "cluck, cluck" and a gentle slap of the reins. The old horse walked forward, and as he did, Charles showed Mary the various driving cues.

After some driving maneuvers, he carefully handed the reins over to Mary showing her again how to hold them. A short while later, he glanced over, and saw her shoulders were stiff – but the look on her face said determination. "You're doing just fine."

Scooting over and sitting closer to her, he thought he could grab the reins if need be. The scent of lilac filled his senses. He noted she had changed her fragrances – Lavender one day, Lilac the next. *Whoa, pay attention to what's going on.* Charles then noticed the very tight hold she had on the reins. "Mary, not quite so strong a grip — a little slack will allow you to urge Buddy forward in his walk instead of crawling along. Give a little kiss to him." He paused catching a quick glance from her. "The sound will urge him to walk forward." He added a wink and watched her blush with a hint of a smile.

As they approached some bends in the back road, he promptly covered her hands with his and showed her how to make the changes in direction. In a short while, Charles noticed Mary's shoulders relax and there was a little slack in the reins.

"I am starting to get a feel for driving. Buddy is such a good boy. And I must admit, driving feels like freedom, especially for a woman."

"Well, Miss Mary, I know Montana likes its women strong."

She raised an eyebrow. "Good to know."

"Please tell me that is not the only reason you accepted my offer." *There has to be some other reason a woman of your beauty and education would settle for me.*

"Why Charles, you are making merry with me!"

Ah… my lady likes a sense of humor. Perhaps I will bring her around to loving Lizzie and me. He reached over to pull back a strand of hair that had blown across her face. Her skin felt soft.

THE NEXT AFTERNOON, MARY WAS READY FOR ANOTHER DRIVING lesson. Walking over to the front door, she grabbed her white linen duster off the wall peg. It was time to meet Charles. A crisp breeze came across her face as she opened the door. It was colder today, and the sky was filled with gray and white clouds scooting along the horizon.

Mary enjoyed learning how to harness and drive Buddy. She surprised herself as she had taken to horses quickly and with ease. Equally important to her, it appeared Charles was pleased with her progress

Entering the barn, she heard Buddy's soft neigh. Undoubtedly, he was calling for the little bits of dried apples she carried in her pockets.

Harnessing Buddy was not a simple job. She had seen some terrible carriage accidents in Philadelphia. She realized this process was a big responsibility but thought she was up to the task.

Mary walked up to Charles and Buddy. The old horse saw her and started to paw at the ground. He stopped as she reached his shoulder. Mary patted the gentle horse, "how could I forget?" After reaching in her pocket, she extended her right hand, palm up and flat. Buddy's whiskers tickled her as he gathered up the dried bits of apple with his muzzle.

"I think you will spoil him."

Charles then motioned to the wall where the harness hung, "Do your best, but remember I am here to help."

Mary finished the harnessing. Stepping back, she gave Buddy a big pat on the shoulders and then moved her hand over to give a light scratch up by his withers — where the neck meets the back. She remembered Charles had explained earlier that the mother horses nuzzled their young in that spot to comfort them. While scratching, Mary uttered soft cooing words of praise for Buddy. It was plain to see he appreciated this. *Whew! Today went a lot smoother than the other day.* With a beaming smile, she turned around.

"Goodness, Mary, I am impressed! You have done a fine job." Once more, she checked over her work.

"Now lead Buddy up to the front of the buckboard — like I showed you."

Holding onto both reins, she commanded Buddy to step back between the two long shafts, stopping at the front the wagon. Mary took a long breath and stepped back to admire her handiwork. All of a sudden, Buddy walked forward.

While laughing, she stepped forward and grabbed the reins. "Hey! Wait, a minute!! I'm not done yet."

Now Charles was laughing. "Can I help you?"

"No. I'll finish it." And she did.

⁓

STILL LAUGHING, CHARLES COULD NOT STAND STILL ANY LONGER. She had been patient through the whole process. All he wanted to do was to give her a great big kiss! But, for the moment, he restrained himself.

There she stood holding Buddy's reins for their final inspection. Charles walked around to check that everything was properly fastened. Turning to Buddy, he patted him. "It appears as if we have a quick learner here!" Seeing her pleased expression, he took off his hat and walked to Mary. He reached for her left shoulder and brought her close to him. Leaning down, he tenderly kissed her on the lips. They were soft and sweet. It felt wonderful to be holding her.

Seeing the look of surprise on Mary's face, he took a step back. *Should I have asked first?* Her look of surprise was quickly replaced with a shy smile.

"Err, I will get Mom and Lizzie, and we will head into town." He turned and walked to the house. There was going to be quite a lot of thinking about that kiss and holding her in his arms. Tonight, and certainly many other nights, he would have something nice to remember while falling asleep.

Charles entered the house. With a lift to his voice, he called out, "Mom, Lizzie, we're all going to town to get some biscuits. We need to celebrate Mary learning how to hitch Buddy to the wagon … and all by herself, too. I could also use a haircut."

"Charles, I can cut your hair," Helen eagerly offered.

Oops, I should have kept that under my hat. "No need. Joe, at the Barbershop, knows all the latest news in town. I want to acquaint myself with what's going on before the next town meeting."

With everyone settled in the buckboard, Charles handed the reins over to Mary. "You drive." He was sure his mother was fit to be tied with Mary at the reins.

~

EVERYONE WAS QUIET ON THE DRIVE INTO TOWN. MARY WAS nervous. However, with Charles sitting beside her, she felt secure. Trying to keep her mind on the task at hand, she decided to put the thought of the kiss aside. She would think about it later.

Pulling up in front of the mercantile, Mary halted the wagon. She pulled the break-handle on and wrapped the reins around it as Charles hopped out and tied Buddy to the hitching post. "Everyone hungry for biscuits? Make mine vanilla jumbles. I'll be at the Barber Shop." His eyes drifted to Mary. "It's true — I am a biscuit man," he said with a slight chuckle.

Mary laughed. "Oh, I see. Good to know."

All nodded in agreement. Within a few moments, Helen and Lizzie were already halfway to the Biscuit Box.

"Oh, Charles, I would like to make a quick run over to the mercantile." She paused and whispered, "I want to see about ordering a slate and some chalk for Lizzie."

"Excellent idea. Lizzie will be delighted. It is very thoughtful of you." Charles gave her a lingering gaze and finally turned, whistling as he walked towards the barbershop.

Thinking about the wonderful kiss he gave her earlier, she felt her heart soar with happiness. She decided she was going to like being married to Charles. The moment in the barn was such a sensual one. She had never received such a kiss before. That kiss would be one to treasure. She pivoted, and her dress whirled around her as she stepped into the mercantile.

Once inside, she was greeted by a very frustrated store owner.

"Ah, just the person I need. Miss Schulman, I seem to have a problem with reconciling the accounts in the store. Everything is in

German, or at least I believe it is German. And, I remembered our conversation on the stagecoach. You mentioned you spoke German and assisted your father with his bookkeeping service. Can you please help me? I am in desperate need." Mr. DeForest ran a hand through his hair. "I am happy to give you some items in exchange." He sent her a desperate look.

"Goodness, Mr. DeForest. I would be most happy to help."

He reached under the counter and produced three large green ledger books. "I truly can't make heads or tails of these." Turning the top one around to face Mary, he opened it.

Mary examined a few pages. "I have to admit Mr. DeForest — this book certainly looks peculiar. Please, may I look at the other two?" Mr. DeForest brought the other books over closer to her and opened them.

"As you can see Miss Schulman," and he thumbed through the second and third books, stopping to show the same writing. "This page has German on the back. However, the rest is all numbers." He looked up at her. Frustration showed on his face.

"Yes, this list here is in German. This word is potato, and this one is flour. And, over here is bacon." She pointed out the words for him. She then turned over several more pages.

"Have you ever encountered something like this?"

She studied the books for another minute before answering. "Yes, Mr. DeForest. But these ledgers have their own variation. I will need a little time to study them." She put her hand to her chin and thought for a moment. "Will you allow me to take the ledgers home? I should be able to return them in a few days."

"Yes. This is wonderful of you to help me. I know it is a lot to ask. However, the accounts are piling up and, to be truthful, I did not expect their books to be… well, different."

Mr. DeForest placed the account books in Mary's mesh bag.

"Oh, I almost forgot why I came by. I was wondering if you could order a school slate and some chalk? Lizzie will need them for her school work."

"Ah ha, I already ordered extra slate and chalk awhile back, knowing school will be starting soon. They should be arriving in the next couple of days or so."

Mary looked at the wall clock. "I'm late! I must be off to meet the family at the Biscuit Box."

CHAPTER 16

RELAXING AFTER SUPPER, MARY SAT WITH CHARLES ON THE FRONT porch bench. Both of them watched the sunset in comfortable silence. This was a new pastime for Mary as Helen seemed to have no objections to them sitting alone this evening.

Mary stole a quick glance at Charles. He was such a handsome, caring and quiet man. Recognizing she was once again going to start the conversation – she began, "the setting sun and sky never looked this beautiful in Philadelphia or Cincinnati. I now understand why people choose to watch it. I cannot remember seeing a sky filled with so many shades of reds, oranges, and yellows."

Charles gave a long appreciative sigh and turned to hold Mary's gaze. "We have some beautiful sunsets, especially this time of year. The fall seems to give us many beautiful evenings. Of course, I am gifted tonight. I am sitting beside a very pretty lady."

Mary felt her heartbeat quicken. "Thank you, Charles." She had never had any man say something this lovely to her before. A lump formed in her throat but she quickly swallowed and said the first thing that popped into her mind. "I think Lizzie is enjoying the stories. I know she will do very well in school!

The front door opened and Helen stepped out. "Oh, I do enjoy relaxing in the evening time. The sky is a wonder to look upon, and there are so many sounds to hear."

Well, so much for romance. Mary decided she would spend the rest of her evening looking over Mr. DeForest's account books. If she was successful in reconciling these, Mary knew exactly what she wanted in exchange for her task. And, it would be something for the farm. Recently she had read about a new breed of chickens, the Black Giants. This breed had a dual purpose. They were considerably larger and good layers. And, most importantly — they could tolerate the cold winters of the north. *What a surprise this would be for Charles and everyone!*

CHARLES WAS GIVING MARY A LOT OF PRACTICE TIME IN THE driving seat of the wagon. One afternoon as they drove through the outskirts of town, she noticed a white tent pitched near a partially framed wooden building. Surrounding the building were many wooden washtubs and several large steaming pots on the ground. Nearby was a sign that read — 'Laundry Done Here.' A Chinese woman holding a long wooden stick was walking through the area. The stick was a variation of the dolly back at the farm, only it had four short legs instead of three. The woman would periodically stop, dip the stick into the tub, and give it a stir. Behind the tent, sheets and other garments hung from wires strung between posts.

Just then a distinguished looking Chinese man stepped out from behind a large linen sheet. Seeing them, he made a quick bow as they passed. Mary returned his gesture with a smile and a nod of the head.

This site had popped up within a few days. Apparently, Crystal Creek was growing. She hoped they could finish the building's construction before the weather changed.

Mary bounced up and down on the seat of the wagon – almost falling off. The wagon had fallen into and out of large chuckhole in front of the livery. Charles stamped his foot on the wagon floor. "These holes are the result of horses pawing at the ground while tied up. Usually, the business owners keep the holes filled with a mixture of mud and lime as a chuckhole that large could cause an accident. I will have to bring this to everyone's attention at the next town hall meeting."

Mary stopped the wagon and secured the reins.

Charles hopped out and walked to the other side. He reached up and set Mary on the ground. She enjoyed a moment of being held and looked into his deep blue eyes. All at once, she heard an odd noise. Looking to her left, she saw an old man shuffling out of the livery. Observing his attire, she noted he wore a big pair of spurs on his boots. With each step, the man took the rowels would spin making a cycle of the jingle, jangle, and jingle sounds which echoed as he walked. He stopped when he reached Charles.

"Afternoon, Mr. Baxter."

"Greetings, Mason. We will not be too long. Just have a bit of shopping to do."

"I'll take care of Buddy here. You just let me know when you want me to hitch him back up. If you be wanting to know, Mr. Anderson is in the back working on your carriage."

"Thank you, Mason, but I won't disturb Hans." Charles turned to his family. "I'm off to the print shop. Harvest time will be approaching soon, and I want to put an ad in the Sunday bulletin. When you ladies are finished shopping, meet us at either the Print Shop or the Feed Store. Lizzie, let's go see those kittens."

Mary watched Lizzie skip down the boardwalk with obvious excitement. Charles was close behind.

Helen stepped to Mary. "I need to check with Mrs. Thompson. The ladies church group wants to establish a quilting bee. I will catch up with you shortly."

"Oh, sounds like a good idea," Mary responded, hoping for an invitation. Helen nodded. "I will catch up with you shortly." Mary sighed. "I will be in the mercantile." Mary's shoulders dropped as she watched Helen turn away and walk up the boardwalk. *Did it even occur to her, I might like to meet with Mrs. Thompson? Perhaps, she still hopes I will not be around long enough to become involved in community activities?* Either way, Mary was becoming tired of Helen's treatment of her.

Once inside the mercantile, Mary noticed two older ladies shopping in the store. She concluded it was best to wait before conferring with Mr. DeForest in private. This would ensure her work would stay a secret. So, she wandered the aisles. She knew small town gossip had long tentacles.

Finally, the ladies left. With no customers remaining in the store, Mary approached Mr. DeForest. "Good morning. I wanted to let you know I am reviewing your books during the evenings. Currently, I'm looking for a pattern to the numbers, and it is difficult to find."

Mr. DeForest frowned and looked terribly disappointed. "I do appreciate your efforts. I hope this task is not too taxing on you. You mentioned you might like something in trade for your help. What did you have in mind?"

"May I look at your poultry catalog for a moment?"

Mr. DeForest brought a set of pages up from under the counter and placed them in front of Mary.

On the second page, she found the information she needed. "I would like to have two dozen of these." She pointed to an entry near the bottom of the page.

He looked up from the page to Mary. "Black Giants. That's an odd name for a chicken. Are you sure?"

"Absolutely, they are just what the farm needs. Will this be all right?"

"Yes, of course, Miss Schulman. As I mentioned earlier, I'm in desperate need of your help on these ledgers."

"I shall also need cinnamon and currants. By the way, did the slate and chalk arrive?"

"No slate and chalk yet." He walked around and located the

other items. "I will put these on your account." He set the goods on the counter and gave her a smile.

She collected her merchandise and looked up to him. "Thank you, Mr. DeForest. Do not worry, I'll find the answer to the books." She left to meet the family at the biscuit shop. *Won't they be surprised? The bigger Black Giants will bring in much more money.*

On the drive home, Mary had another lesson with her ever-patient instructor sitting at her side.

CHAPTER 17

ALL THROUGHOUT BREAKFAST, MARY WAS AGAIN THINKING ABOUT how to reconcile Mr. DeForest's books. As if a finger snapped, her mind abruptly came back to the present when she realized Charles was talking.

"Today I need to make a run into town to attend a Grange meeting. Does anyone need anything?"

Helen stopped washing the dishes. "Oh, Charles could you please drop me off for a visit with Esther. I need to see how she and her mother are getting along."

Charles rose from his seat at the table. "I will be happy to do that."

Mary slipped another dirty dish into the wash water. "I can't think of anything I need," she softly replied.

Momentarily, a look of concern crossed Charles's face. "Mary, will you and Lizzie be all right here by yourselves for a little while?"

"Lizzie and I will be just fine. Not to worry. We can read a few stories, and I have a few chores I want to do." Some alone time without Helen looking over her shoulder or telling her to do this or that, was going to be a welcome change.

"All right then. Lizzie, keep an eye on Skippy," said Charles.

Lizzie's head popped up, and she looked at her father. "Skippy and I will listen to our stories. And then I will teach him a few tricks."

Everyone walked out into the warm and sunny courtyard to say their goodbyes. Mary watched Charles help his mother onto the wagon seat. He walked over and kissed Lizzie on the top of her head. Next, he leaned over and swiftly kissed Mary on her cheek — stepped back and gave them both a wink.

"Ah-hem, time to go. Don't want to come back late." Helen pulled her shawl tighter across her chest.

Mary watched the wagon roll down the road. Many times she had thought about that tender kiss Charles had given her after the hitching lesson. Now she had another … admittedly, this last one was on her cheek. But it still counted. Her cheek continued to tingle.

Glancing around her new home, Mary noticed an eerie quiet had fallen over the farm. The wagon had now faded into the distance. She continued to listen to her surroundings but heard nothing — not even a bird rustling in the leaves. After a moment, Mary realized she was now a little nervous. She reminded herself she was a capable and grown woman. *Besides Charles would not leave us here if he did not think it was safe. But it is true — I'm a bit of a scaredy-cat.* Mary felt Lizzie's hand slip into hers. Looking down, she saw her fidgeting with the end of the puppy's leash. Mary bent down and hugged the little girl.

Holding hands again, they walked back into the house. Mary had been thinking about having a little talk with Lizzie. They walked into the parlor, and Mary picked up their story time book. Sitting down on the settee, Mary patted the seat next to her. The little girl perched on a cushion next to her. Skippy curled up at her feet. "Sweetheart, I think this is a perfect time for a little talk." Lizzie opened her mouth but quickly shut it. Mary smiled reassuringly at her and continued. "You know, it is hard to be a part of something new. Even, a little scary. Sometimes, the experience can be exciting and scary, like the starting of school. So, I think you will understand what I am about to say. As you can imagine, I was nervous about moving out here." Mary paused seeing Lizzie nod her head. "I believe you have had a little time to get to know me. So, what I need to tell you is… I never want you to think I would like to replace your mother. I know my mother is very special to me and I would never want to have someone replace her. However, I want you to know I love you. And, I am here to care for you and help you. Does this sound good to you?" Mary felt her breath catch and her heart pound as she waited to hear Lizzie's response.

Lizzie smiled and looked up to Mary. "Yes. That's why Papa suggested I call you 'Mama,' instead. He said I have a big heart and there is always room for one more." Shyly Lizzie looked into Mary's eyes, "He's right."

Well, Mary thought her heart would melt right then and there. *I could not be luckier.* She threw her arms around Lizzie and hugged her tight. After a couple of moments, she drew back and kissed her on each cheek.

It was time to read her a story… and one story led to another. She enjoyed having this time with her soon to be daughter. Lizzie yawned. *Perhaps it was time for a nap.*

"Lizzie dear, let's keep Skippy inside the house with you for the afternoon. I'll be in the vegetable garden — weeding. If you need me, just call from the back door. AND, absolutely NO going outside alone for either of you. Understood?" Mary watched Lizzie pause and look to her.

"I understand Mama."

Mary looked at the endearing scene in front of her. Lizzie was sitting on the floor with her yellow calico dress, and white pinafore spread around her. She was holding onto one end of an old knotted sock of Charles's. Skippy held onto the other end. They were in a tug of war.

"Please let him rest when he is tired and why don't you rest as well."

"Yes, Mama. I will." Lizzie giggled as she answered … all the while continuing to play.

Mary smiled and closed the bedroom door. *Best to keep any puppy mishaps in the one room.*

For some days, Mary had wanted to weed the vegetable garden. She remembered Helen had complained the task was too difficult. It was hard on her knees and back. Hopefully, Mary could finish before everyone returned.

Putting on her bonnet and an old apron, Mary went outside and into the barn to retrieve the hoe. Entering, she called out a greeting, "Hello Daisy. Hello, May. It's just me coming in to get the hoe. You can continue eating." She chuckled as she thought, *I have never talked to animals before.* But for some reason, she knew they understood what she was saying. She picked up the hoe from amongst the other tools and carried it out to the garden.

The vegetable garden was very large as befitting a farmer. The first rows were filled with beans, onions, potatoes, tomatoes and a few herbs. Towards the back of the garden, the early winter vegetables grew. Looking at that area, she saw it was even harder to distinguish between weed and plant.

She blew out a big breath and wiped her forehead with her hand. Bending down, she pulled the larger weeds and threw them into the nearby wheelbarrow. Ridding the garden of the smaller weeds took more time. However, with a little more effort she removed them without too much difficulty.

Finished, she surveyed the results of her hard work. *How nice it looks. Surely, they will be pleased.* Looking down, Mary saw many of the herbs had wilted. She picked up the pail near the water pump and filled it. *I have only this bucket of water to give to the herbs, and then I am done.*

A horse neighed, and Mary looked up.

IN THE DISTANCE, MARY SAW A RIDER ON HORSEBACK. TRAILING behind them was a pack horse loaded with animal hides and dead birds. She stood still and listened to her heart pound loudly. *I wonder who he is? And more importantly, he seems to be heading in my direction!* She stepped a little further back and placed her pail on the ground. Charles had not mentioned that someone was coming by today. As the rider continued to approach, she noticed that he was staring at her. He was tall and had ink black hair, which was long and tied in the back. He wore a fringed buckskin jacket and had long soft-looking boots that came up to his knees. Was he an Indian? What a frightening sight! *Oh, dear! What to do? Protect Lizzie!* With her mind racing, she ran into the house.

Once inside, she bolted all the outside doors! She stopped to catch her breath. *Perhaps the rider will change course? Had he noticed she had gone into the house? Would he assume she was going for help? He couldn't know Charles wasn't here ... or could he?*

She quietly crept up to the front window and peeked out while hiding her body against the wall. The man continued to ride down from the back road to the front entrance of the barn. He stopped and dismounted from his horse. Next, he walked over and opened the barn door and led his two horses inside. Swallowing, she crept across the floor to reach the other side of the window. Once there, she rose up slightly and glanced down the road to see if Charles was coming. The small window allowed her only a tiny view of the roadway without showing herself. And, Charles was not in sight! *Dear Lord, I hope Charles will return soon!* She turned and flew up the stairs to alert Lizzie. *I must keep her from any possible harm.*

Entering Lizzie's bedroom, she walked over and stooped down to where Lizzie and Skippy were napping. She whispered into Lizzie's ear, "Sweetheart, we have to be very quiet now. There is an Indian outside." Lizzie's head popped up, and her face went white. Her eyes widened, and her lips trembled.

"Shh… darling, I am here to protect you. Do not cry. You and Skippy hide under the bed. Stay there and don't make a sound. Whatever happens, don't come out from under the bed."

"Yes, Mama," Lizzie whispered as a flood of tears streamed down her face.

"Do not worry. I will be here to protect you." Mary whispered and closed the door.

~

CHARLES LET HIS MOTHER OFF AT ESTHER'S HOUSE. BEFORE heading to the Grange meeting, he had one errand to run. Earlier in the morning, he had taken it upon himself to gather some additional food for Johnny and his family. It was time to make a quick, discreet delivery.

He climbed back onto the seat of his buckboard and drove to the edge of town. Stopping at a battered old house, he jumped down from the wagon and picked up the large basket and two gunny sacks. Walking up to the front porch, Charles saw Johnny sitting on a chair in the far corner. He was whittling on a piece of wood. The little boy glanced up as he approached. *So much for being discreet.*

"Hello, Mr. Baxter."

"Good afternoon, Johnny. How is your mother doing?"

"She is getting a little stronger, sir." The little boy looked to the door and back to Charles.

Charles smiled. "I am very happy to hear that. I have extra green beans and potatoes that I thought your mother would like. Also, my apple trees are loaded with fruit. And, there is a little-dried beef, salt pork, and eggs in the basket. Can I leave these with you?"

Johnny's eyes grew wide and round. Slowly a smile spread

across his thin face. "Gee, sir. Please and thank you. I'll go and wake Ma." The little boy got up from his chair.

"Wait, son. I think your Ma needs her rest. You set these on the table and go back to your whittling. Are you carving a horse?"

"That I am. Does it look like one to you?" Cautiously, he handed the horse to Charles.

"Johnny — it looks better than what I could do."

The little boy beamed and nodded.

Charles ruffled his hair.

"I'll check back later." Charles knew the family was looking forward to their father's return home from the long cattle drive.

THE GRANGE MEETING WAS THE SAME AS IT WAS EVERY MONTH — farmers complaining and cattlemen arguing. Everyone had a different idea of progress. At least they were in agreement about one thing. They needed a new schoolteacher and soon.

After the meeting, Charles felt sorry he had left Mary and Lizzie at home. He decided to bring them a surprise — a couple of bags of penny candy. Walking into the mercantile, Charles thought he saw regret in DeForest's eyes.

The store owner looked around. "Is Miss Schulman with you today? I have news of her order of slate and chalk. They should be here within a couple of days."

Undoubtedly, the man was disappointed because Mary had not accompanied him. *Too bad old boy.* "No. They stayed at home, but I will tell her. I would like a bag of penny candy for each of them. One of lemon drops and the other of peppermint, please."

After fetching his Mom from Esther's, they headed back home. On the drive, his mother shared what information, or rather gossip, she had gleaned. Towards the end of the wagon ride, she divulged the fact that Reverend Winterthorpe had sent word to his wife that he would return home in a week. *Of course, she mentions this towards the end of our drive.* Charles felt this news could not have come at a better time. DeForest was becoming a little too friendly with his Mary.

Driving up to the front of the barn, Charles noticed the door was open. He helped his mother down off the wagon. Stepping around, he walked into the barn. Low and behold, there was his good friend Ross. He was loading the supplies Charles had set out for him the next time he visited.

"Well hello, Ross? It has been awhile since we've seen you. How the heck, are you? Did you leave me something in the smoke-house?" Charles clapped Ross on the back.

"Yes, I left you some game meat and dried fish. And I'm fine, but some woman ran into the house like a banshee, and I haven't seen hide nor hair of her since. That is not the reaction I usually get from a woman." Ross replied with a low chuckle.

Charles felt the blood drain from his face. "Oh, no. I'll be back in a minute." Charles' voice trailed off as he ran to the house. Stopping at the door, he tried to open it. It was bolted from the inside. He knocked on the door ... then he knocked harder. Then he pounded on the old wooden door. *I hope Mary hasn't found the shotgun. She doesn't even know how to aim the thing.*

"Mary, please, it's Charles. Open the door." He yelled.

"Charles? Is that you? WATCH OUT! There is an Indian in the barn, and he has a horse stacked with dead animals!" Mary shouted through the door.

"Yes, it is me, and it is safe to open the door now." His answer was muffled.

Something brushed up against her. Mary glanced to the side at Lizzie, leaning up against her dress. She had heard her father's voice.

Mary breathed a heavy sigh of relief. All of a sudden, she heard what sounded like gales of laughter coming from the other side of the door. Confused, she very slowly opened the door. The sounds became even louder. Opening the door wider, all she could hear was boisterous laughter!

Standing directly in front of her was Charles — and yes, he was laughing. In fact, he was practically in stitches. Looking past Charles, she saw Helen was snickering into her hat. And there stood the strange-looking man Mary had seen earlier. He had an amused look on his face, but he was NOT laughing.

Within a flash, Lizzie rushed out from behind Mary's dress and threw her arms around the strange man's knees. Lizzie looked frightened. She shouted at the top of her voice, "Uncle Ross, there's an Indian in the barn. There's an Indian in the barn!"

Another round of laughter poured out from Charles and Helen. Their faces were now very red. Obviously, the stranger was not an Indian but a family friend. Mary was becoming very irritated, not to mention, extremely embarrassed.

Charles walked over and put both hands on Lizzie's shoulders. He turned her to face him. "Just a minute, Lizzie. I think Mama has mistaken Uncle Ross for an Indian. He does look a little different from most men." Charles pivoted and took a couple of steps towards the house, saying, "Mary sweetheart, Ross is not an Indian. Mr. Kincaid is an old family friend. He traps and hunts game in the mountains. Does he look like an Indian to you?" He put his hand up to cover his mouth, but Mary could see he was still smiling.

Well, this WAS embarrassing. Speechless, Mary grit her teeth. Within moments, her distress turned into infuriation. *No one mentioned this man before and that he has permission to just walk into the barn. Most importantly, a gentleman should not laugh at a lady! How was I to know, this man is a friend? That oaf! Can he not see that I'm not amused?*

Mary continued to look directly at Charles. Unable to keep her composure, she stamped her foot on the floor, turned and slammed the door shut. She was angry. She stomped upstairs to her bedroom. And for good measure, she slammed that door too. *I'll act like a lady when I am treated like one!* She threw herself on the bed and had a long cry.

~

CHARLES STOOD LIKE A STATUE ON THE FRONT PORCH. HE WAS IN shock. *Oh, No! What did I just do?* He tried to think of what he should do next? He stood looking at the closed door. *Apologize, you idiot.* Speechless, he pushed his hat to the back of his head. He turned slowly to face Ross, his mother, and Lizzie. "Err, my apologies for the lack of a proper introduction. Mary is my bride-to-be. At least, I hope she still is! I know I am in serious trouble for laughing at her mistake. And, right now I owe her a huge apology."

He turned back and opened the front door. He rushed up the stairs and with each step, he remembered how they all had laughed at Mary. He felt awful.

Desperately, he searched for the right words to say to her. He wiped the perspiration from his brow. *Is she angry enough to leave me? She probably has enough money of her own that she could ... just disappear. On top of that, we aren't even married yet — there is nothing to stop her. And of course, Mom certainly hasn't made her stay a pleasant one.* Charles frowned.

Reaching her room, he stopped. He saw her door was shut and took a deep breath. *Best to start with a BIG — I am sorry.* Slowly he brought his hand to the door and softly knocked, "Mary, I would like to apologize. May I please come in?" Charles softly pleaded. A few long moments of silence passed and his heart began to beat more rapidly. *Is she inside?* Relief flooded him when he heard footsteps approaching the door, and the doorknob turned. Haltingly, the door opened. And there stood Mary. Her face was still flushed. He felt horrible as he watched her take a step back from him.

Charles approached her. "Mary, I am so very, very sorry for my behavior. I should have told you about Ross, and I should have stopped to think you would have been truly frightened. I ... I just feel terrible. Can you please forgive me?" He looked deep into her eyes and waited. She wiped her eyes with a hankie and smoothed her hair back.

"Yes, you are forgiven." She looked down and straightened out the folds in her dress.

What a bumpkin! I need to be better about communicating with her. Then I'd have a chance to avoid a few of these mishaps.

He stepped closer to her. "Thank you. I shall try to make this up to you the best way I know how. Sometimes I forget you have only been with us a short while." Charles walked up and took Mary into his arms, tilted her face to his and kissed her tenderly on her lips. Then he bent his head down and feathered a couple of kisses on her neck while holding her tight.

While she was in his arms, he knew he did not want to let her go. He was done with the chaperoning. They would marry in a week.

MARY WAS NOW BECOMING FAMILIAR WITH THE MANY FARM chores. Helen was still her frosty self and had not warmed to her. It had been two weeks since the Reverend had left. Now Mary was feeling nervous. Matters were not helped by the fact she had not reconciled Mr. DeForest's accounts. Tonight was the third night she had excused herself from the family to work on the ledgers.

Entering her bedroom, Mary lit the lantern and closed the door. She pulled off her boots and removed her stockings. Leaning over, she rubbed her aching feet. It would be nice when her new work boots arrived.

Next, she got up and walked over to open the top dresser drawer. There she removed the ledger books. She brushed aside her feelings of weariness as she began her review. She remembered what her father had told her about such a task, 'there is no problem in bookkeeping that cannot be rectified by the proper application of arithmetic and time.' *If only, this principle could be applied to a future mothers-in-law.* She pushed her feelings to the back of her mind. She knew people were not as straightforward as mathematics.

Sighing, she then went through each line item of the accounts again. After two and a half hours, she was done for the evening. It was time to sleep. Tomorrow she would look at the problem with a clearer head.

CHAPTER 18

TODAY WAS A NEW DAY FOR MARY. AS A WAY OF AN APOLOGY FOR yesterday's misunderstanding, Charles was treating Mary to dinner at the Cattlemen's Restaurant. While they enjoyed dinner alone, Helen and Lizzie would visit with Mrs. Thompson at the boarding house in town.

While traveling to town, Mary reflected on what had happened yesterday. She always prided herself on being practical. Despite the hurt feelings of yesterday's mishap, three good things had come out of the day. The first was Charles's apology. The second was his promise to communicate better. Apologizing was a difficult act for most people. Nonetheless, it took a good person to know when to ask for forgiveness. This quality was one she could well appreciate.

The third good thing was meeting Ross. Mary was pleased she had the opportunity. She could see why he was such a close family friend. Ross had a unique perspective on life. Furthermore, he was a very likable character. He had a good sense of humor, which was key to his enjoyment of life. She could understand his respect for nature and lust for adventure. She wondered if he had a special someone in his life. *Rachel?*

She and Charles entered the restaurant. While enjoying her dinner of lamb with mint jelly, Mary remembered their first dinner there. Charles reached across the table and lightly grasped her hand.

She felt his warmth as she smiled at him.

He looked into her eyes in silence.

Her insides had turned to jelly.

At last, he spoke, "I have some exciting news to share. Reverend Winterthorpe should return in a week's time. We can be married soon."

Mary dropped her spoon, and peach cobbler fell on the table. She felt a rush of excitement. "Oh, my! This is wonderful news!" *Oh yes, we definitely need more timely communications. He must have been told about this yesterday when he was in town. All the same, maybe yesterday he was afraid to tell me — for fear I might say no. Come to think of it, it was probably a very good idea.* However, being a practical woman, she realized that some things and some people required time and training. She gazed into Charles's eyes and smiled. Her thoughts soon turned towards organizing some of her wedding preparations.

Both were feeling happy as they strolled through town after dinner. Mary let her mind wander. She recognized she had grown as a person since that day back at the church altar in Philadelphia. Soon she would be married. She looked up to her future husband. Seeing no signs of discomfort from him, she relaxed.

While walking, they approached the mercantile. Upon seeing the store, Mary had her doubts she would be able to surprise Charles with the new chickens. Her late evenings spent in search of answers to Mr. DeForest's ledgers were, so far, to no avail. Soon she would have to give him another update on her lack of progress.

She looked up to Charles, "I am hoping The General Store has received the surprise for Lizzie today." *How am I going to deliver the news about the account ledgers, especially with Charles next to me?*

"That would be nice. Why don't I leave you here while I check on the progress of the carriage? When the weather turns cold, we'll need to use it then."

Mary nodded. *What a relief.* They stopped at the mercantile door. He patted her arm and looked softly into her eyes.

"I'll be right back." Turning, he strode off to the livery.

She watched him stroll off. *At least one part went well.* Mary looked at the door in front of her. *Still, how do I tell Mr. DeForest I have no answers on the ledgers as yet?* She opened the door and walked inside. Still thinking of what to say, she turned and walked down the now familiar aisles. She looked to see if there were any new items. It was at that moment she noticed something. She paused. She could not believe it! The key to understanding the books had been here all along. She quickly moved back to the previous aisle, checking the notations on the shelves. They confirmed her suspicions.

Walking to the counter, Mary laughed and shook her head. Mr. DeForest looked at her in amusement.

"Good afternoon Miss Schulman. What do you find so amusing?"

Mary could hardly contain herself. "I did find something amusing … and much more. I found a clue to what I need to understand the ledgers. Of all things, it was on the third aisle." She knew she was speaking in riddles. However, she needed to share this information slowly.

A puzzled look appeared on Mr. DeForest's face. "I do not understand."

"Well, there is a set of numbers on the shelf directly under each item — a few numbers separated by decimal points."

Mr. DeForest cocked his head to the side. He was still confused. "Yes, but I am afraid I don't know why the numbers were put there. The writing is so small, and it just seemed unimportant because of that."

"Those are product codes the Braunsteins' made up for each of the store items. A bit like the library codes recently invented by Mr. Dewey. Those numbers correspond to the column and section headings in the ledgers you gave me. So, if you can make a list of each of the items and their codes, I can finish the ledgers for you posthaste."

"This is great news, Miss Schulman! I have been worried sick about this all week."

"I cannot come back into town for a couple of days. Why not keep the slate and chalk and deliver them tomorrow to the farm? You may hide the item list inside the package."

"Excellent idea, Miss Schulman. Oh, and I have already ordered your chickens. They are on their way here. After all the time — you have spent helping me, it is the least I could do." Mr. DeForest had a smile so broad Mary thought his face might just crack. He reached across the counter and placed his hand over hers. "I cannot thank you enough."

Just then, the doorbell jangled. Mary withdrew her hand quickly and looked to the door. It was Charles. "Done already?" she asked innocently.

Several moments passed and Charles was still standing in the middle of the doorway … JUST STARING.

CHARLES FROZE WHEN HE SAW NICOLAS DEFOREST HAD LAID HIS hand on Mary's. Standing in the middle of the doorway, he recognized his blood had started to boil. There she stood, with rosy cheeks and just a moment ago DeForest had been holding her hand. Admittedly now, his hand was no longer there. Charles blinked, thinking it might help to ease his mind of what he just observed. His mind had not calmed. And to TOP that off, Mary's question of 'Done already?' was still ringing in his ears. Silently, he counted to three. *Did that snake think he was going to steal my*

girl? What happened to ... 'I am thinking of getting a mail order bride myself?'

Coming out of the trace, Charles managed a short nod. However, he remained by the door, waiting for her. He did not trust himself near DeForest at present.

On the drive back, Charles let Mary take the reins and practice her driving. She was talking like nothing had happened. However, he could not take his mind off what he had witnessed in the store. DeForest was taking liberties with his wife-to-be. *This has to stop!*

Clearing his throat, "Ah, hem. Were you able to get the slate and chalk?"

Mary shook her head, "they were not in yet. Mr. DeForest said he would have Charley deliver them to the farm when they arrived. That's so nice of him, she replied in a sweet voice."

The next time Charles went into town by himself, he was going to settle this once and for all. That man would learn a lesson in Montana etiquette.

CHAPTER 19

MARY WAS UNABLE TO FORGET THE IMAGE OF CHARLES' FACE AS he observed her and Mr. DeForest last evening in the mercantile. That look kept popping in and out of her dreams. She woke up early but still felt exhausted. *Could Charles' reaction mean he cares for me more than just a little?* She and Mr. DeForest had done nothing wrong. *Yes, upon hearing his books would be reconciled — he had touched my hand ... but only for a moment. However, if I explain to Charles what the excitement was about, it would spoil the surprise.* Temporarily powerless to explain, she decided she might as well do the milking before breakfast.

Mary led Daisy into the milking stall and tied her up. Peeking into the hay cradle, she checked to make sure there was enough hay to keep the cow happy. Her calf Lily was in the nearby stall mouthing some oat hay.

Grabbing the milking stool, she sat down and began her task. Looking down into the partially filled pail, Mary sensed Daisy was less cantankerous this morning. Perhaps she was becoming more adept at dealing with the unruly animal, or Daisy preferred to be milked at this earlier time of day. Whatever the reason was, the task certainly went easier than on other occasions.

She looked down into the pail to judge the amount of milk. Feeling a long nudge on the backside of her dress, Mary turned to find Becky and Polly. She heard the loud rumbling of their purr as they rubbed up against her leg and dress. "Oh, so you have sought me out. I haven't seen the two of you for some time, and now you tell me you love me. Why can't your master say something similar?" Knowing she would not get an answer, she shrugged her shoulders. However, the lack of response did not deter her from continuing to talk to them. They always listened. "Well, as it happens, I have a little dish over here, and you are in for a treat."

Mary got up and carried the pail to the side of the barn. Picking up a small metal dish on the ledge near the tools, she placed it on the ground beneath Daisy. She proceeded to squirt out enough milk for the two cats. Bending over, she retrieved the dish and placed it on the ground near the grain door. Polly and Becky ran over and began to lap up their breakfast, not sparing a second glance at Mary. "Do not worry about a thank you. I will not hold it against you. And do not be a stranger." Despite the cats being good listeners, Mary still felt lonely. Since Mary had arrived almost three weeks ago, Helen had not warmed to her. If anything, it felt like the reverse. This feeling was only compounded by the fact that she was not surrounded by friends and family. Thinking about how far away her best friend was, she felt tears in her eyes. She wiped her eyes with the edge of her dress sleeve. *Rachel will miss my wedding.* Years ago, they had shared childhood ideas of them attending and fussing over each other's wedding. The memory brought forth more tears. And again she wiped her eyes.

Grasping the handle of the pail, Mary walked towards the kitchen door. She could hear a loud conversation as she climbed the small porch steps to enter the house. It sounded like an argument between Charles and his mother. It was not loud enough for her to make out the words, but it clearly was not a casual exchange.

As Mary opened the door, the conversation stopped. She felt

uncomfortable as she entered. Helen did not even look at her. *That woman definitely knows how to make a person feel unwelcome.* Mary felt her face grow warm. Quickly she placed the pail on the kitchen counter. *Just what am I doing here? It's clear Helen does not care for me. Am I to live the rest of my life with this sort of thing?*

Not sparing a look to anyone, Mary left the kitchen and went up to her bedroom. There she washed her face and hands hoping it would help to ease the hurt. After a few minutes, she composed herself and walked downstairs. Before entering the kitchen, she heard a low whisper. But again, she could not make out the words Charles had said. Seeing her, he got up from his chair and presented her with a false-hearted smile.

"Good morning, Mary. You look very nice. How was Daisy? It looks like you got a large amount of milk.

"Good morning," Mary wearily replied. "I decided to tackle Daisy before breakfast rather than after, and it went quite well. Daisy seems to prefer being milked earlier rather than later. And, even the cats were happy to see me."

Charles raised an eyebrow and then directly looked at this mother. She noticed he turned a bit red in the face.

Just then, Helen snapped her apron off the peg and marched to the stove. Mary quietly followed at a distance.

The breakfast routine was the same every morning. Mary was allowed to do the bacon — however, not the eggs. At least now, she knew how to avoid burning the bacon. The two women worked silently alongside each other.

~

CHARLES FELT THE TENSION AT THE BREAKFAST TABLE. LIZZIE HAD started the morning conversation with questions about school. His mother did not look happy. During breakfast, she didn't make eye contact with anyone, nor did she converse. *Why can't Mom see*

Mary is trying to give Lizzie a head-start in her formal education?
Lizzie should not wait another year before attending school.
Earlier this year he read an article in **The Crystal Creek Sunday**
Bulletin, which stated every family should enroll their seven-year-
olds. He discussed this idea with Mom before Mary had arrived.
He felt his mother needed to move past her stubborn notion of
delaying school. After all, this was a new age of learning. What
was acceptable for her generation was no longer acceptable now.
Sometimes I feel like I'm talking to a brick wall.

At least, he saw Mary was not responding in kind to his mother's icy manner. Instead, she responded to Helen's questions in a
cheery tone of voice. He was so proud of her.

Mary slowly turned to Lizzie. "Since, school is starting soon.
We need to get you organized. Isn't this exciting?"

Lizzie sat up in her chair. "Yes, Mama. When can we get my
books?"

"You will receive your books at the school house on your first
day. However, we can pick up other school supplies at the mercantile." Mary glanced to Charles.

He knew if this conversation continued it would further irritate
his mother. However, he decided there was nothing he could do
about it. *Mom has gotten through life quite well without very much*
schooling. But this is no reason to deny Lizzie the opportunity to do
better. He and Mary would see Lizzie receive a good education.

Helen got up from the table. "I'm going to get ready for
church." She walked out. There was no offer to help Mary with the
cleanup.

Rising from her chair, Mary started to clear away the dishes on
the kitchen table. She noticed Lizzie's discomfort and her heart
squeezed. "Lizzie, you should get ready too," she said softly.

Soon Mary and Lizzie were in the wagon, ready to go.
However, Charles decided to wait inside the house for his mother.
He was more determined not to give into his mother's unreason-
able wishes. When Helen approached the front door, he stepped

towards her and stopped. "Mother, please. You have to stop being antagonistic to Mary."

"What exactly do you mean?"

"You have done nothing but make Mary feel unwelcome since she arrived. I sent for her. And she has agreed to be my wife and Lizzie's new mother. You have to reconcile yourself to this fact."

His mother looked down and brought a hand to her chest. She glanced up to meet his eyes. "Charles, it is not too late. She is just a city girl. You can still change your mind. All these new ideas she is bringing into the family! I just don't think they are good ones. What do people from the East know about living in the Northwest?"

"Mother, her ideas have been in the church bulletin for past year. We live in a new day and age. This is what I want for Lizzie. Ever since arriving, Mary has done everything possible to accommodate you and me. And she loves Lizzie. How does anything else matter?" Charles stopped for a moment hoping his words would sink in. "She is the woman for me, and I have no intention of changing my mind."

With that, Charles paused before opening the door. "Mary has a heart of gold. I want you to treat her as well as she has treated us." He opened the door and walked out to the wagon, not waiting for his mother.

THE STRAIN BETWEEN CHARLES AND HIS MOTHER MADE THE RIDE into church seem longer than normal. It was obvious they had argued while she was milking Daisy this morning and also again before starting the drive into town. Mary could only believe these arguments concerned her. Yet, at present, there didn't seem to be any way for a satisfactory resolution to the situation. Someone had to bend and quite frankly, Mary felt she had already done more than her fair share of bending. At least, she and Charles were in agreement about one thing. It would be unfair to hold Lizzie back just to accommodate Helen's point of view. *Why couldn't Helen see the benefit of Lizzie attending school now? Why was she so dogged about almost everything?*

Mary felt she was destined to remain the cause of this friction between Charles and his mother. Continually, she had tried to please Helen, and the effort was to no avail. She was not sure if she wanted to spend the rest of her life feeling like this.

Finally, the church came into view. Near the entrance, a slight, gray-haired man broke free from a small group of ladies. He approached the Baxter family. Mary did not recognize him from any of the previous church services.

"Charles it's good to see you, young man. Might this lady be the lucky girl you told me about?"

He vigorously shook the older man's hand. "Yes, Reverend Winterthorpe. I must apologize, I had no idea you were already back." Charles placed his hand gently on Mary's shoulder. "I would like you to meet Miss Mary Schulman, formerly of Philadelphia."

"I am very pleased to meet you Reverend Winterthorpe. Charles and his mother have said so many nice things about you." Mary saw the Reverend's eyes crinkle with delight.

"Well, they are like family. I am so pleased to meet you, finally. Unlike yourself, young lady, I was fortunate to arrive last evening without the delay of a broken wheel. I am sorry that happened to you." The Reverend hesitated. "I know I said I would marry you as soon as I returned. However, I am sorry to say Mr. Furman passed away a few nights ago. I will be busy today and tomorrow with his burial. Would it be all right with the two of you if we postpone the ceremony for a couple of days? I can marry you on Wednesday. This should give you time to make the necessary preparations."

Charles looked to Mary, and she nodded.

"We waited this long, a couple more days will not matter," answered Charles.

Mary smiled politely to everyone. Glancing to Charles, she saw his disappointment. Feeling disappointed as well, she tried not to take the delay as an omen. Instead, she tried to be happy, for within a few days – they would be married. Perking up, she remembered that she would be busy with the wedding preparations.

However, her excitement soon faded. A dark cloud of unhappy memories appeared with visions of Helen's cold disdain. *How will the next several years affect me?* Mary did not want to end up a bitter woman in constant strife with her mother-in-law. How would that affect Lizzie in addition?

Charles stepped forward brushing against her dress skirts.

"And Reverend, we will confirm the new date with the Nelsons," he said with conviction.

Smiling, the Reverend nodded. "Indeed, and I will hear from you shortly." Reverend Winterthorpe slowly turned to greet more parishioners.

As they proceeded into the church, Charles anchored Mary's arm to his.

DURING THE CHURCH SERVICE, CHARLES COULD NOT HELP BUT worry about his mother's stubborn behavior. Soon he and Mary would be married. He sent up a silent prayer. *Please Lord, let us marry and have Mom accept this.*

The Reverend stepped up to the pulpit to deliver the sermon. They all sat back and listened. Soon the organ sounded out the final hymn.

Before the Reverend excused his parishioners, he stepped up to address the congregation. "To conclude this morning's service, I want to talk about a lesson which I learned a very long time ago. As most of you know, I have been away the past few weeks to see my dear mother in Cheyenne. We had feared the worst. However, with the Lord's help, she is well again. As you might imagine, we had occasions to talk, and she reminded me for the hundredth time of a lesson she taught me a long time ago."

He continued, "The Good Book tells us of the Commandments — a list of things we must not do." The Reverend paused for a few moments. "The lesson I speak of today is one we must strive to do each and every day. And, I am not talking about more praying." The last statement brought out a chuckle among the crowd, and the Reverend waited until it subsided.

"This conscientious action my mother referred to … is 'The Golden Rule — Do unto others as you would have them do unto you.' So, I ask you to go forth with kindness in your heart every day. And, freely bestow this kindness on your fellow men and women. Forgive them their past transgressions with a smile. For I truly believe we have all wished for forgiveness from others at some point in our lives."

Charles peered over to look at his mother's face. She appeared stoic. Perhaps this sermon would lead to a few days of peace. How nice it would be if his mother would heed the Reverend's advice and treat Mary with kindness.

The service came to an end. Everyone proceeded to leave the church. Charles escorted his family out and immediately found Owen and Daniela. He asked if they could be witnesses on Wednesday. Of course, they were thrilled.

Visiting time had finished, and Charles gathered up his family for the ride back home. As was their custom most Sundays, Mom would discuss the sermon. It was a pity she showed no inclination to discuss this particular one today. The drive was quiet.

CHAPTER 20

After hearing the Reverend say 'I can marry you on Wednesday,' Mary could not stop worrying. Mary spent the better part of that night tossing and turning in bed with the realization that soon she and Charles would be married. Unable to sleep, she concluded she must weigh all her options. So, she added up all the positive elements and weighed the negative ones. She was not going to sit back passively and hope all would be well. During the wee hours of the morning, a final decision was reached — she wanted very much to be Charles' wife and to be a part of his family. No longer would she sit back passively and hope all would be well. She did not want be pushed out leaving Charles and Lizzie. She acknowledged to herself that she would have to work things out with Helen. Perhaps a conversation with Helen might be in order. Maybe Charles could help Mary with this dilemma after they were married.

After the morning meal, Mary went down to the root cellar to fetch a couple of eggs from the morning's collection. She brought the eggs to the kitchen and put them in a dish. There was one more ingredient needed to bake a chocolate cake for Charles, and that was a little milk. He needed a nice surprise and, she must remember this recipe too.

Exiting the house, she saw Helen knitting on the porch, and Lizzie was playing nearby with the puppy. "Helen, I am going out to the barn to milk Daisy."

"Be careful. Daisy is rather grumpy this late in the morning," the older woman retorted.

"Thank you, and I will be careful." *Argh – always some negative quip.* A moment later an inspiration came to Mary. With her upcoming marriage, now was not the time not to allow Helen to get the better of her. She was going to be a part of this family, and Charles' mother would have to deal with it. Charles was a wonderful man, and she wanted to be his wife. *You can do this.*

Striding off to the barn, Mary was more determined to show the bovine and her future mother-in-law that she was a capable woman. Sure enough, Daisy was cooperative, and the milking went smoothly again. Perhaps it was her more experienced touch.

When she was finished, she returned the stool to its designated place. Next, she turned Daisy loose in the side pen to join her calf. Pausing, she stretched up and then placed her hand on her back. She rubbed a few spots.

With the occasional loose duck underfoot, Mary walked back across the dusty yard. She climbed the porch steps and saw Helen had fallen asleep in her rocker. She quietly opened the front door. *Lizzie must be inside.*

Mary took the milk pail into the kitchen and set it down. Eager to share the cake baking experience with Lizzie, she went in search of her. Looking in the front room, parlor, and kitchen – she could not find her anywhere. She walked upstairs and did not find her little girl in any of the bedrooms. Her heart began to pound.

Anxiously, she hurried back down the stairs rechecking all the rooms. She noted the cellar door was still latched. She opened the front door and rushed out to the porch. "Helen, where is Lizzie?"

Helen woke with a start. "What?"

"Where is Lizzie?"

"Elizabeth was just here with Skippy." Helen blinked and picked up her needles. "Did you look inside? She's probably in her room."

"She's not there." Mary's voice choked. "I … I checked everywhere." Stepping out into the courtyard, she frantically scanned the area. There was her little girl standing out in the field holding her puppy. Mary shrieked, "Oh, NO!!" And she started out at a dead run to retrieve Lizzie. Her heart was racing. One of Charles' strictest rules was — not let Lizzie out in the fields alone.

Perspiration trickled down Mary's forehead as she ran. She tripped and quickly recovered. Looking ahead, the sight before her chilled her to the bone. Mary halted. "DO NOT MOVE." Lizzie had tears streaming down her face. The puppy was struggling in her arms. A large rattlesnake was coiled several feet in front of the child. The snake's head rose to strike. She heard its rattles shaking.

Mary's heart was racing. *Dear Lord, my sweet girl!* She attempted a calm voice, so as not to provoke the snake or scare Lizzie even further. "Lizzie darling, stay very still, and everything will be all right. Do not move." Mary slowly walked closer to the frightened child. The snake was still focused on Lizzie.

Huffing and puffing Helen came walking up. "Just what are you doing out here young lady?" she hollered.

"Helen, stay back and be quiet," Mary sharply ordered.

"You will not talk that way to me," Helen huffed and narrowed her eyes. She turned to Lizzie. "Elizabeth, you get back here right now!"

The rattler's tail buzzed even louder. Helen gasped and stopped.

"Helen, be quiet and stay there," Mary commanded. Inching closer to the snake, Mary began to instruct the frightened child. "Lizzie — do not move an inch. Watch the snake and when he turns his head to look at me, back up and run to grandma. Blink if you understand me?"

Lizzie quickly blinked amongst her tears. Helen was quiet now. As Mary moved even closer, the snake shifted its attention towards her. She stopped and stared at the angry snake. "Now! Quickly back away." She ordered. Trembling, little Lizzie scooted backward. Mary jumped to the right, waving her arms. "RUN LIZZIE, RUN!" shouted Mary.

Lizzie ran towards her grandma. Helen grabbed the puppy and tightly hugged her granddaughter. They looked up at Mary.

"Helen, get her inside," Mary shrieked while she jumped away from the still angry snake. The snake's head rose higher, and Mary continued to move backward and closer to the fence line.

The snake was enraged and struck out, just missing Mary's leg. Its rattles sent up an eerie buzzing sound which echoed around them. Suddenly, it turned and slithered away towards the pen with the newborn calf.

Now, more outraged than frightened, Mary looked around for a weapon. She grabbed an old fence board that lay on the ground behind her. *Oh no! You don't get to go after something else.* Mary pursued the snake while remaining a good distance behind it. Her intention was to scare the snake away from the pen. She batted at the ground behind it with the old splintered board. The barrage finally had its intended effect, and the frightened snake slithered away towards the tree line.

CHARLES ROUNDED THE BACKSIDE OF THE BARN AND SAW MARY batting the ground furiously with an old fence board. *What is she doing?*

Charles froze when he saw his mother and Lizzie rushing towards him. It was then he saw the tears on their faces.

Stopping before him, his mother gasped for air. "Ohh, Charles! She is after a big rattler. You have to stop her."

"Papa, Papa, please help! There… there's a snake," Lizzie cried franticly.

His blood ran cold. Immediately, he ran to the barn and picked up a shovel and started off at a dead run. A rattler was not to be trifled with, and a piece of wood was not the right weapon for doing battle. It took him several long moments to reach Mary. She was moving farther and farther away from the barn. Periodically, he saw her swing the board at the ground.

Finally, he reached her. His heart was pounding, and his breathing was heavy. "Mary, get back! Get to the house and let me get rid of this nasty snake."

Mary limped toward him, and his stomach dropped.

"Did he get you?"

"I don't think so. However, it did strike near my new boot." She gently lifted her left foot up a little.

He turned back to see where the snake had gone. Within a few moments, he found it slithering towards the tree line above the barn. Charles turned back to face his soon-be-bride. "What were you thinking?" He dropped the shovel and marched up to Mary. Next, he lifted her up into his arms and ran to the house.

She turned her head to him, and he felt her labored breathing. "It was after Lizzie, and then it moved towards the calf's pen. I wanted to make certain it did not come near the house or the barn," she said half muttering in defiance.

"Quick Mom, heat some water with salt."

Helen quickly entered the house, leaving the front door open.

Tired and panting heavily, Charles stepped carefully onto the porch. With Mary in his arms, he carried her into the house. "Oh, and bring me a sharp knife and a cup from the kitchen," he shouted to his mother.

He carefully set Mary down in the parlor chair. Charles searched Mary's face. "Do we know how Lizzie got into the field?"

"I suppose she may have gone out after the puppy. I am unsure.

When I finished milking Daisy, I went in search of her. I thought she would like to help me bake. I know you said she was never to go out into the field alone. I am so sorry this happened."

Lowering his head into Mary's neck, he murmured, "Thank you, Mary, for saving my little girl." The pit in his stomach started to dissolve. *How could this have happened?* "Which foot did it strike?"

"My left foot." Mary slowly raised her left leg again. "But I do not think it got me."

He bent down on his right knee and slid up the hemline of her dress and started to unlace the boot. "Stay still," he ordered. Quickly, he worked to remove the boot and stocking. Sweat trickled down the sides of his face. He heard his daughter approach.

Lizzie crept up beside him. "Papa, I am sorry. Skippy went after a squirrel. I know I'm not supposed to go into the back. I didn't want anyone to get hurr...rt," she sobbed.

"Lizzie dear, we know this. Let me look after Mama." Charles gently wiggled the boot off. Helen hurried into the room with the knife and cup from the kitchen. "The water is heating. Is it bad? Oh, oh, this is entirely my fault. If only I had not fallen asleep." Tears rolled down her face as she rocked herself back and forth.

"Please, I need quiet now." Charles examined Mary's foot, front and back, then up her leg. Relief flooded through him. "You were lucky. I don't see any puncture marks. Are you sure this is the correct foot?" He pressed his thumbs on her puffy ankle.

"Yes. Ouch. It's a little sensitive. I tripped." Mary frowned.

"That explains why you were limping. Let me check your other foot."

"Were there any bite marks on the left leg, Charles?" Helen inquired. Charles looked up to see her face was full of anguish. She stood wringing her hands while waiting for an answer.

"No bite marks on the left foot or leg." He noted his mother continued to stand near.

He removed Mary's right boot and was relieved to see there were no punctures there either.

Charles shook his head. "What were you thinking? You cannot go after a snake, Mary. The snakes here are dangerous and very poisonous." *I could not bear it if you or Lizzie got hurt.*

Mary lifted her eyes to him. "It threatened Lizzie, and then it started towards the calf's pen. I wanted to be able to tell you where it was going."

His hand settled over hers. "You have no idea how dangerous that was. It could have gotten its fangs through your boot, or you could have stepped on another snake while you were chasing it." He sighed heavily and wiped his face with his shirtsleeve. "The livestock can be replaced. You and Lizzie cannot."

Charles stood up. "How do you feel?"

"Just fine," she said gruffly.

Cautiously, she stood up and lifted her left foot. "Ouch." Grabbing the arms of the chair, she sat back down — ever so slowly. "Actually, I think I will sit here for a while."

He turned and saw his mother was taking the bowl, cup, and knife back into the kitchen. Soon he found Lizzie quietly standing in the nearby corner watching. "Lizzie, please come here and give your Papa and Mama a big hug and kiss. I know you had a frightening day."

His little girl ran forward with her arms wide. Charles picked up his daughter and gave her a crushing hug and kiss.

He looked to both Lizzie and Mary. "You two gave me such a fright. Please do not ever do that again." Charles put Lizzie back down and watched Lizzie rush over to hug and kiss Mary.

Mary's eyes filled with tears. "Oh, Lizzie, I am so very happy you are safe. I couldn't bear it if something happened to you. No more tears sweetheart. All is well," said Mary as she continued to hug her.

Watching the two of them, Charles felt like his heart was melting. Within a couple of minutes, Skippy crawled out from behind the settee. Seeing Lizzie, the puppy whined and walked over to bump his little girl's hand. Lizzie sniffed and picked up her puppy.

Charles walked over to Mary and, without warning, he slipped his arms under her and lifted her up and out of the chair.

"Where are you taking me?" she asked.

Charles dipped his head down to kiss her gently. "To your room, of course. I have to finish cleaning the stalls. I will be back later to check on you and Lizzie. Lizzie — you need some rest too. So, it's up to your room for a nap, young lady. You'll feel better afterward."

Mary turned her head to gaze at Lizzie. "Lizzie, sweetheart, how would you and Skippy like to keep me company? We can rest together."

The little girl perked up. "Oh, yes Mama. I would like that very much." She followed closely behind her father.

"Charles, I will be just fine. I don't need to be pampered like a baby," irritation showed in Mary's voice.

He carried Mary up the stairs and set her down on her bed. Lizzie snuggled beside her. He hated to leave.

"Just rest. I will check on you later." And he closed the door as he left. Charles wondered if he should check his hair to see if it had gone gray. *I need to marry that woman and soon!*

As he returned to the parlor, his mother opened her mouth. He held up his hand.

"Please do not start Mom. City girl or not, she saved Lizzie today."

His mother looked guilty for the first time in a long while. "I did not say anything."

"I need to finish my chores." Charles grabbed his hat on the way out of the house. As he reached the barn, he looked back and saw his mother had also left the house. She was walking past the garden. The only thing in that direction was his father's grave. On one occasion, he had discreetly followed her and saw his mother talking towards the grave stone. It seemed to be a back and forth discussion. If it gave her solace, he had no intention of interfering.

~

CHARLES STILL NEEDED TO FINISH HIS WORK IN THE SMOKEHOUSE. However, first, he thought he should check on his girls. He had been frightened within an inch of his life by the thought of Mary or Lizzie being bitten by that rattler. Feeling his shirt was damp, he looked down and saw the whole front was dripping wet with perspiration.

Now he was feeling bad. He had given Mary only a meek 'thank you' for fearlessly protecting Lizzie. *And yes, she is correct. I probably would have asked which direction the snake had taken. No wonder she was a little cranky. I need to tell her how much she means to me – poetic words or not.* Later, he was certain he was going to go over the ground rules for life out here in the country!

Crossing from the smokehouse to the barn, he noticed the chickens had been put up early. The wagon was gone. He ran to the house. Entering, he found it was quiet. He checked all the rooms and came in the kitchen. Standing near the iron stove, he felt its warmth. Yet, no one was here. "Mary, Mom, Lizzie! Anyone — here?" No response. *Why had they left? And where are they now? Could I have missed a bite mark from the snake? Had they taken Mary to the doctor? I am such a fool for not having stayed longer to see if she was all right.*

Panicking, he glanced around the kitchen and saw a note on the table. He picked up the paper and saw the writing was in his mother's hand. The paper read … **Mr. DeForest sent for Mary. Taking her to him.**

A cold wave engulfed him. Charles yelled out in the empty house, "Mother, what have you done?"

DeForest was a different kind of snake. He dashed out to the barn with his heart pounding and began to saddle up Willy, his riding horse. *I've got to reach her in time.* The horse skittered away from him as he tried to throw the saddle and blanket on in one motion. He silently cursed himself. "Sorry boy, now please stand still. I'm in a hurry." Charles pulled the cinch tight. After flipping the stirrup back down, he picked up the reins and mounted the scared horse in one fluid motion. They left the barn behind in a cloud of dust. He booted Willy into a gallop and leaned forward into the wind amid the pounding of hooves. Charles urged Willy to go even faster. He prayed he would reach Mary before she got into town.

As he was galloping down the road, Charles's thoughts were racing around in his head. *DeForest was angling to steal my Mary away all the time. I should have seen it the moment they got off the stage together. He was more than attracted to her. Who would not be attracted to Mary? And to top it off, his mother made it impossible for Mary to feel appreciated around here. Well, DeForest can have her when pigs can fly!*

THE NELSONS' HOUSE APPEARED AS HE ROUNDED THE BEND. Without warning, the saddle started to slip dangerously to the right. Charles was sliding. His left leg gripped harder. Sensing he was about to fall, he lunged forward grabbing the horse's neck, holding on for all he was worth. The startled horse slowed his gallop to a trot. Charles lost his grip and fell to the ground. Willy expertly avoided stepping on him and came to a stop ten yards away. Charles saw the saddle was dangling precariously off to one side of him.

Getting to his feet, Charles spat the dust out from his mouth. He felt a sharp pain in his right hip. Examining the rest of his body, he discovered his right wrist was sore. A quick look confirmed his shirt was torn and his forearm was scraped and bloody. He had to get to his horse. "Whoa, there, boy. Easy,"

Charles pleaded in a soft low voice. He advanced slowly. His horse's breathing was heavy. As he neared Willy, he watched his horse's ears flicked back and forth for a few moments. "Easy Willy, easy."

He stopped a few feet short of the scared horse and watched Willy take a couple of steps away. No doubt, he was wondering why his master had suddenly turned into a madman. "Whoa, easy." Charles reached up and patted him. He bent down and gathered up the reins of the skittish mount. *What a greenhorn mistake!* He should have remembered to tighten the cinch on the saddle a second time. Periodically stroking the scared horse, he adjusted the saddle and tightened the cinch. He remounted and soon urged Willy into the gallop again.

What a fool I have been. Charles' stomach was churning, and his leg was throbbing. Making the last turn into town, he saw his wagon tied up across the street from The General Store. He pulled back on the reins, and Willy slid to a stop in front of the mercantile. Seeing Timmy on the bench in front, Charles spoke up. "Say, Timmy, I'll give you a nickel if you walk my horse for a while. No water for him, now."

The young boy ran over and grabbed the reins. "Sure will, Mr. Baxter."

The door opened, and his mother peeked out. "Charles, come in." She then stepped back inside.

Charles stomped over and burst into the store.

Helen smiled at her son and announced, "Mary and Mr. DeForest have some news for you."

News? Is that what he's calls it? He stalked past her. Mary and DeForest were smiling and laughing by the back counter. *I'm putting an end to this right now.*

His mother scurried after him. Ignoring her, he advanced towards Mary and DeForest. Mary looked at Charles as he approached. DeForest stood his ground and seemed to be amused.

…

"What's going on?" Charles questioned, spitting out the words. He looked for his daughter. "Lizzie, where are you?"

A faint, "here, Papa," was heard.

Again, he turned to look at DeForest. *Had Mom been encouraging this all along?*

Helen rushed forward and glanced at Mary. "I think it is time you told him."

Charles's heart was racing, and his blood was at a roaring boil. "And what would that be?" he questioned with a low growl.

Everyone followed Mary as she walked into the storage area. DeForest approached the back of a lean-two and placed his hand on the top crate. "These are for you." Lizzie stepped out from behind the crates and in her hand, was an ink black baby chick.

DeForest tilted up the first crate. "As I said, Mr. Baxter, these are for you." Inside the crate were about two dozen little black chicks. The movement of the crate had them chirping loudly.

Charles was now very confused. "What are you talking about?"

Mary smiled. "Surprise! I thought we needed to replenish the stock of chickens. These are Black Giants, and they lay more eggs than the ones you have now. Also, they grow to over ten pounds in no time. You can sell them to Mr. DeForest as fryers."

This was almost too much for Charles to take in. *SHE HAD ORDERED CHICKENS?* "So, you came to pick these up?"

"Naturally, what else did you think?" Mary raised an eyebrow. Her eyes seemed to laugh at him.

His arms fell to his sides. Charles shoved his hands in his pockets. He winced. "Ah, I just saw the note that said — he sent for you and figured…ummm." He paused and decided against finishing his sentence. "You got the chicks for our farm?"

"Of course, I did." Mary coyly smiled.

Shaking her head, Helen stepped closer. "Charles, how could you be so foolish? Mary has been helping Mr. DeForest with the ledgers the Braunsteins left him. And in exchange, he ordered these fine chickens for all her hard work."

So that explained all the time she had spent with DeForest. Now I am the fool. He was deeply touched she had applied her efforts for the benefit of their farm. Stunned, he stood still and looked at his bride-to-be.

Mary took Charles' hand and looked at Helen and Mr. DeForest. "If you do not mind, I would like to have a word in private with my future husband." She led him into the back room of the store and left the door slightly ajar. Inside, Mary stepped up to embrace him. He needed no further encouragement to take her into his arms. Bringing his hand to the back of her neck, he brought her closer and kissed her soundly. She tasted of peppermint. He nuzzled her neck, feeling embarrassed that his recent assumptions were so very wrong.

After a few moments, she pulled back and whispered into his ear, "I am touched. However, you don't need to fight for me. I love you and only you." The sound of those words melted his heart. How could he have thought otherwise? He stared into her beautiful honey brown eyes. "I shall try to be better about talking with you," he whispered.

Silencing him with a finger to his lips, she began, "I could not explain myself because I wanted this to be a surprise. I wanted you to be pleased."

She said she loves me, not sure why, but she does. His heart lifted to the sky in response. "I am so happy and lucky to have you. I just want to marry you and live the rest of my life with you."

Mary grasped his hand and started to lead him back into the store. "Now we should get these little chicks loaded and take them back home before they die of fright or the heat."

Charles pulled her back from the door. "Before we get married, I need to have a serious talk with Mom."

"Sweetheart, there is no need. Helen and I had a heartfelt talk this afternoon."

"You did?" Charles exclaimed in amazement.

"Yes. And your mother has apologized for her behavior. She

explained to me that your father's death left a deep void in her life. So, she filled it with you and Lizzie. It was very difficult for her to step aside for someone else. I told her she was not losing you but gaining a daughter. Do not worry sweetheart, your mother and I will be just fine."

Charles blinked and then shut his gaping mouth. He found he could only shake his head in wonder. A moment later he leaned down and kissed her again. She slipped her hands around him and hugged him. How long had it been since he was embraced? He could not remember.

Mary looked into his eyes and smiled lovingly. She whispered, "no more problems. Let us all go home."

CHAPTER 21

THE SUN LAY LOW ON THE HORIZON, AND THE CLOUDS TO THE south were dark and ominous. Slowly the wagon traveled back to the farm with the two crates of chicks. Mary was driving, and Helen was at her side. Lizzie was in the back, chatting to the newest additions to the farm. Charles and Willy were bringing up the rear.

Bubbling with happiness, Mary remembered all that Charles had said to her in town. His actions told her he loved her. Hopefully, he would say the words she was longing to hear in the not so distant future. She knew men often had trouble giving voice to their emotions and Charles was a quiet type. Furthermore, she was relieved and delighted about Helen's reconciliation with her. Now Mary's new life would be a happy one. She was no longer an outsider but part of a loving family. Soon she would be Mrs. Charles Baxter, wife to a wonderful man.

She leaned over. "Helen, I know it is late. However, do you think we might still have time to make your apple cobbler for Charles tonight?"

"An excellent idea. Charles still has the evening feeding to do.

If we hurry, we'll have enough time to make a delicious late supper as well."

Mary turned back towards Lizzie. She had been busy comforting the baby chicks throughout the drive. "Lizzie, would you help us make an apple cobbler when we get home?"

The little girl's eyes sparkled. "Oh yes, I can stir the apples and sugar."

Arriving at the farm, everyone crowded into the barn. Charles put Willy into his stall. Next, they all gathered around to see Charles and Helen settle the baby chicks into their new accommodations.

Helen turned to Mary and smiled. "Let's see about starting a nice supper for everyone. Come on Lizzie. You can visit the chicks tomorrow. Your Papa will take care of them tonight. Get Skippy and bring him into the house."

With Helen's help, Mary limped into the house to begin the supper preparations. It had already been a long day for everyone.

THE SUN HAD SET, AND DUSK WAS EASING INTO DARKNESS. IT HAD been a grueling day. Everyone was still excited about the new little chicks. However, it was not the new chicks that Charles was thinking about, it was Mary. This afternoon at the mercantile, she had whispered she loved him. *She loves me ... Charles Baxter!* The thought continued to resonate in his mind as he brushed and rubbed Willy down. His mother had even apologized for her behavior to Mary. Now he could picture his family sitting all cozy and happy around the evening fire.

Charles finished bringing the animals into their stalls and pens. He whistled a happy tune as he tossed the hay into feed troughs. Charles hoped he wouldn't experience anything similar to this day ever again. Finally, walking back to the house, he noticed the small raindrops were increasing in size. By the time he reached the porch steps, the rain sounded like marbles tumbling down the stairs. His dusty shirt had turned a muddy brown.

Exhaustion had set in, and Charles' hip and wrist were aching something fierce. He sighed, despite the happy ending to his day. Nonetheless, there was one more thing for him to address tonight.

Shedding his boots on the porch, he opened the kitchen door. The enticing smells reminded him he was hungry. Closing the door behind him, he heard Mary humming. She stopped and smiled at him.

"Charles, supper is hot and ready for you."

Looking at his muddy shirt and pants, he shuffled towards the stairs. "I will be there in a minute. I need to change first," he called out. "Ouch. It turns out I have a sore leg, too. Supper smells delicious! Ah, I'll be down as soon as I can." He limped up to his room. While washing up, Charles contemplated what he wanted to say to his mother about Lizzie's schooling — for the last time he hoped! It was finally time for his mother to stop objecting.

Returning downstairs, he found his mother herding Lizzie towards the supper table.

"This looks like a feast. Is that ham and scalloped potatoes I smell?"

"Yes, it is, and there is apple cobbler for dessert."

"No need to wait any longer. I'm here." Charles chuckled. And they all enjoyed the feast.

Everyone's plate was as clean as a whistle. Mary and Lizzie cleared the table.

Charles addressed his mother. "Mom, please if I could have a word with you." They walked into the Parlor, and he closed the door behind them. "Mom, I want Lizzie to go school this year."

His mother smiled brightly. "Charles, I think that is a good idea."

Dumbfounded, he slowly smiled. *Miracles do happen.* "I am very happy you agree with me. Lizzie will be overjoyed." He breathed a heavy sigh of relief.

"Now, let's sit for a moment." Helen sat down on the settee and patted the space next to her.

Charles sat down next to his mother.

"Please let me finish before you say anything. This is hard for me. However, I said it to Mary earlier today." Helen took a deep breath and continued. "I have behaved terribly for these past few weeks. Today's sermon by the Reverend was his best of the year, and it was difficult for me to sit there and listen. I talked it over with your father. Now I know you think it is silly of me to talk in front of a grave, but it has always helped me to come to my senses. My mourning for your father has clouded my judgment in many things. I have treated Mary very poorly since she arrived. I admit I was not ready for you to marry someone we did not know. Earlier this afternoon, I apologized profusely to Mary. Being the lovely person – she is, she graciously accepted. Mary has turned out to be a Godsend. And, I think she will make a fine wife for you and a wonderful mother for Elizabeth. It is time for both of us to move on with our lives."

Charles rose and took his mother's hand. He pulled her up into a hug, and he kissed both her cheeks. Tears threatened his eyes. "Mom, you never cease to amaze me. Thank you for talking with Mary and me."

Only then did Charles notice she was not wearing the small black armband that had been a constant article of clothing for her since his father's death. Now, this was the mother he remembered.

MARY, MOM, AND HIS LITTLE GIRL WERE BUSTLING AROUND THE house doing last minute alterations on their dresses, collecting flowers and baking for the upcoming wedding. Charles was excited. Finally, he would make Mary his bride. Watching everyone scurrying about, he decided to leave the ladies alone while they finished their preparations.

He saddled up Willy and took a leisurely ride into town. Upon arrival, he checked his list. First and foremost, he needed to confirm with the Reverend that all was ready for the ceremony. Second, was placing an order for additional biscuits for the wedding guests, just in case, they were needed. Lastly, he needed to get a good close shave

The first order of business was accomplished quickly. The Reverend told him all was ready and his wife was even baking a cake for the occasion. On his way to the barber shop, he placed his order for the extra biscuits at the bakery.

That done, he hurried over to Joe's Barbershop. As Charles settled down into the barber chair, Joe placed a hot towel on the lower part of Charles' face. "Bout time you made that gal of yours — ya wife before DeForest or another dude grabs her up. You know I caught that DeForest given her the eye. She's a purdy thing." Joe snapped off the towel and brushed the shaving cream on his face.

I best be quiet while he has the razor in his hand.

Sharpening the single blade on the leather strap near the chair, Joe applied the razor to Charles' face. He finished in no time. Stepping back to admire his work, he stated, "That ought to make it nice for your lady."

Glad that the shave was over, Charles could now go home to see if anyone needed his help for the big event. He headed over to where Willy stood quietly by the hitching rail at the Crazy Horse Saloon. *What a good boy you are, Willy. There'll be a treat for you when we get back.*

As Charles was approaching his horse, a man suddenly stumbled backward out of the saloon. The doors banged loudly ... back and forth. Charles looked up as Harlan went flying past him, almost knocking him off his feet.

Annoyed, Charles righted himself. "Hey! What the heck is going on here Harlan?"

Blurry eyed, the cowboy gave his head a shake. He stood still for a moment and then straightened himself. "Oh, it's you, Charles." His words were loud and slurred. "Well, itt's … Big Jake. I firred that lazy no good scoundrel, and now he's sore Sally's ahangin' around me. Thinks she's his gal. I was just complainen' to Sally while having a whiskey — er two, bout Louise goen back East to snag one of those rich does-nothin' dandies."

Just then they heard a resonating gong. Out from under the swinging doors came a large dented brass spittoon spinning over the boardwalk. From the center hole spewed a stream of thick brown tobacco juice. They watched, mesmerized as it spun like a top towards the Feed and Seed Store. It wobbled to a stop leaving a large puddle in the middle of the boardwalk.

A large dark shadow loomed over both Charles and Harlan. It was BIG Jake.

Son of a gun! Charles knew Jake was always a trouble maker. Whenever he looked at him, he felt there was something just not right about the man. *Should I leave it to Harlan?* In the past, Harlan had always been able to handle himself with any man including Big Jake. However, given his current condition, handling Big Jake was going to be a problem. It would take two men to bring him down. Charles and Harlan turned to face the giant.

Big Jake stepped forward. "I'm gonna teach you a lesson! The way I heared it, maybe you can wait and make sheep's eyes at that new school teacher your daddy's goin' make ya wet nurse. When she arrivin'? If she's a looker, maybe I'll forget about Sally and try my luck there." He roared, obviously thinking he was funny.

Charles looked at his friend. "You're the school teacher's delegate?"

Harlan's face turned scarlet red. *That's a first.* He shook his head and whispered to Harlan, "I think he swings from the right. What do you say?"

Harlan winked. "You distract him. I'll git him with a hard left."

Looking up, Charles recognized Jake had heard them talking. A huge fist was flying in his direction. He ducked and came into the man's huge pot belly. *Heck, that was the wrong spot.* Still hunched over, he looked into a smelly, dirty shirt barely covering the man's hairy and massive girth. Stepping back, Charles felt a punch connect with his face. Wobbling backward, Charles saw Harlan set up his hard-left hook. A gunshot rang out. Everyone froze. Charles turned to see Sheriff Abbott stalking up to the boardwalk while holstering his gun. "What in tarnation is goin' on here? Anyone want some jail time? Cauze my cells are empty. Charles, I don't think you want to be missin' that weddin' of yours."

She might leave me for sure. "No sheriff, just a little misunderstanding. Right men?"

All the cowboys outside the saloon, to include Big Jake, nodded and hightailed it out of the area. That left the two men alone. Charles felt the swelling beginning around his eye. He mumbled to Harlan, "See you tomorrow if I'm still gettin' married."

Harlan chuckled and said, "If she won't have you… then maybe I have a chance." Pausing, he smirked and strode off. "By the way, you had best have Mary put a steak on that eye."

Charles was not surprised. As usual, Harlan got the better part of the deal. He limped over to Willy and slowly swung himself into the saddle. *Well, I'm sure to be limping down the aisle tomorrow.*

MARY PULLED OUT THE LAST BAKING SHEET FROM THE OVEN AND set the tray down. The nutmeg jumbles smelled just like her mother's. She knew Charles would enjoy them, especially given his sweet tooth. Helen turned to smile at Mary.

"Thank you for your help cleaning the house and, I have finished making the potato salad. With the apple pies and these nutmeg jumbles you made, I think we are ready for the wedding celebration tomorrow. I am so excited for you dear. The pretty blue calico dress you made for Lizzie has her dancing around like a princess. It is the sweetest thing someone has done for her in a while. I am so blessed to be getting a daughter such as you." Helen stepped up to Mary and gave her a hug ending with a kiss on the cheek.

"I am the one who is blessed to be a part of your family." Mary's eyes grew a little misty. It felt nice to have praise from Helen, finally....

Helen stepped back and reached inside her sleeve for a hankie and then dabbed at the corner of her eye. Smiling, her soon to be mother-in-law continued, "Wait here until I return." She swung around and walked up the stairs.

As Mary watched Helen leave, she was ever thankful for her present situation. *What a change from when I first arrived. I am getting married to a man I love and happy days are ahead. Mother and Father, I know you will be so happy for me.*

Mary recounted who would be attending the wedding celebration. *Let's see – there is the Reverend Winterthorpe and his wife, the Nelson family, and the McCloud family, Ross and Mr. Holt.* The entire group had something to do with getting Charles and her together. It was going to be nice to have a houseful of guests on this joyous occasion.

Mary heard Helen coming down the stairs and turned to smile at her. In Helen's hands was a small blue velvet box. As she approached, Mary saw that Helen's eyes had grown bright with excitement. Stopping in front of her, the older woman carefully opened the box. Inside was a beautiful gold brooch designed as a pansy flower with a pearl in the center. Helen blinked and then gazed up to Mary. "My father gave this to my mother on their twentieth wedding anniversary. This brooch will someday be Lizzie's. However, I would be honored if you wore it on your wedding day — as I did on mine. My Welsh blood would wish me to say … something old for a love everlasting."

Mary felt her throat tighten and again her eyes watered. The piece was exquisite. The gold design caught the sunlight from the window. The reflection cast off by the flower seemed to wink at her. "What a beautiful brooch! I would be most delighted and pleased if you could pin it on my dress tomorrow."

Helen hugged Mary again. "Indeed, I will! And, please let me know if you need any help with your gown."

The front doorknob rattled and turned. Mary and Helen glanced towards the door. Entering the house was Charles, or at least Mary thought it was him. He limped into the front room. The two women gasped. Charles stepped closer to them. Her eyes went wide with fright.

Mary's heart raced as she hurried over to him. Questions soon poured out, "Oh my goodness. Are you, all right? What can I do for you? How did this happen?" *Ahh, I have moved into the Wild West...*

His mother shook her head. "Tsk, tsk, tsk. Let me get a damp cloth for your face, son." She hastened to the kitchen.

Hobbling into the Parlor, Charles sat down in the closest chair. The pounding of footsteps on the stairs announced another had heard his arrival. Lizzie ran into the room modeling her new dress for her father. She skidded to a stop and stared at him.

Charles cleared his throat. "Ahem. My, my, I see a most beautiful young lady in front of me. I think she is my daughter. Where did you get the pretty dress, sweetheart?" His eyes meet Mary's.

Lizzie preened. "Mama made it for me. I am going to wear it tomorrow and to the first day of school. Papa, do you feel okay?" Lizzie took a step back and surveyed her father.

The situation was looking a bit different than she first thought. She considered Helen's reaction. Mary raised an eyebrow. "Yes, Charles. How DO you feel? I believe you should answer some of the questions posed to you, dearest," she inquired.

He looked at her and then glanced at his mother, as she entered the room with a bowl of water and a wet cloth.

"The good news is that I accomplished everything on my list."

A slight moan escaped from his lips as he withdrew a slip of paper from his pocket. "I am all right, truly." His eyes softened as they held Mary's eyes.

While gazing at her son, Helen shook her head. She then handed Charles the wet cloth. "Put this on your eye."

Mary held Charles' gaze. "Here, let me do that for you. Sooo, how DID this happen?" She took the cloth and tenderly placed it on his eye.

"Ah, that feels good. Well, you see, I was on my way to where I left Willy. And suddenly, Harlan was shoved into me. Apparently, Big Jake was picking a fight with him. Harlan had been drinking and was in the saloon complaining to Sally about Louise. Anyway, he was not in any condition to take on Jake. I couldn't just leave him with Jake coming after him" he blurted out in practically one breath. He squinted at Mary and then held her gaze. "He's like my brother, what else could I do? You're still going to marry me, aren't you?"

Mary sighed and nodded. Taking off the wet cloth, she peered at his eye. The area surrounding the eye was already turning blue. "I would marry you no matter what you looked like — SILLY MAN. But from the looks of things, you will need some of those tea leaves that Ross gave us. The tea will help with aches and stiffness. Ross is in the barn. Why don't you ask him if there is something else you can do for your eye?" She walked off to the kitchen to start the tea. Smiling, Mary called over her shoulder, "maybe we should also get some of that horse poultice I saw in the barn." She heard a faint chuckle and smiled again.

CHAPTER 22

MARY PAUSED TO GAZE AT THE GOLD BAND ON HER LEFT HAND. Feeling truly blessed she wondered, *did my mother feel this way when she was first married? I hope Charles and I can be as happy as they are after twenty-seven years of marriage.* Finishing the letter to her parents and Jenny, she knew it was Rachel's turn to hear about the wedding and how she was faring. *I've got a funny story about the both of us limping down the aisle. However, that's a story for the next letter.*

She re-read Rachel's letter.

Dear Rachel,

Charles and I were wed yesterday. Our wedding was a small affair. Helen, Lizzie, and our wonderful neighbors, the Nelsons, Mr. Ross Kincaid, Mr. Holt and the McCloud family were all in attendance. The Reverend's wife baked a beautiful cake for the celebration. I cannot tell you how happy I am here in Crystal Creek. I am now a wife to Charles and a mother to a precious little girl.

You were correct in your assumption. Leaving Philadelphia was a very wise decision. If I had not departed my hometown, I would not now have the husband of my dreams.

The people here are warm, welcoming and happy to help. Speaking of friendly, I wanted to tell you about my mother-in-law. Helen has finally come to accept me. It is a long story. So, I will save it for later. However, I decided to write a brief letter now as I knew you would be most eager to hear we were finally married.

Charles is teaching me to drive the wagon and next week he promises I can ride one of the horses — astride, no less. He believes riding a horse, is much safer than driving one. And, he believes an intelligent and beautiful woman such as myself, should have no problem. Isn't that sweet?

Please thank Mrs. Turner again. Her choice of a husband for me could not have been a better one. Tell all the brides-to-be that I wish them as much happiness as I have found here with Charles. The journey will be hard. Nevertheless, it will be well worth it. Tell them their efforts and patience will be rewarded. There are many fine men on the frontier, and most have all their hair AND their teeth. I can even recommend several gentlemen in Crystal Creek. That, too, will be in my next letter. Perhaps sometime you can visit me?

Your friend forever,
Mary Baxter

Sitting at the table in their bedroom, she folded the writing paper and slipped it into the envelope. She sat back and reflected on the turn of events. Mary reached up and touched the silver good luck necklace her father had given her on her sixteenth birthday. She remembered what Rachel had said the day after the church debacle with Robert and ... she had been right. Heading out West had been the better path for her.

Mary looked out the window towards the beautiful night sky. She knew the Lord's plan for her had come true. Here in her new home, she felt she had people who loved her and who she could love back with all her heart.

Feeling special, she rose in search of the husband she had come to love.

~

EXCITEMENT FILLED THE AIR. TODAY WAS THE CRYSTAL CREEK Annual Harvest Festival. Together, Mary, Helen, and even little Lizzie cooked side dishes and baked pies to share with all the community. Helen started off by describing to Mary and Lizzie how the festival began years ago and continued to tell how it evolved into the great occasion it was now. As time moved along, Helen was now in her element sharing funny stories from last year's festival. Earlier in the morning, Charles had told Mary how the fiddle music had people dancing until their feet fell off. This she had to see!

They all piled into the buckboard and, with Charles whistling a jaunty tune in time to Buddy's trot, they were off. The new Baxter family was anxious to arrive at the celebration.

Everyone living in and near the town had lent a hand to ensure the festival's success. The McCloud ranch hands had constructed the large dance floor on a grassy area between several trees near the schoolhouse. The layout was stylish with tables set out on three sides. Colored lanterns were strung on ropes that crisscrossed over the area. They blinked and swayed in the breeze.

Mary looked at the food tables. It was evident all the members of the community had contributed. After placing her apple pies and chocolate cake on the dessert table, she stepped back and marveled at the selection of pastry and candies. Some she recognized from the family gathering of her German relatives and some from the English fare at Mrs. Turner's table.

Her husband walked up and slipped an arm around her waist and guided her to a table next to the dance floor. Ross and the Nelsons joined them. They placed their shawls and coats on the back of the chairs and Charles led the way to the food tables. The gentlemen stood back and ushered the ladies forward. Following Helen and Daniela, was Mary with the children clustered close behind. All were gawking at the delicious display of different dishes.

Charles piled his plate high. Mary was still trying to decide between the potatoes and the squash. Lizzie skipped the main courses and scampered straight for the table of pies and cakes. Mary called after her. "Lizzie, dear, you need to start over here with the dinner food." She looked at her little girl's fallen face. The Nelson children already had their plates loaded with sweets. Mary thought better and called out, "Well, since it is a holiday take whatever strikes your fancy."

Lizzie needed no more encouragement. She scurried forward and joined the Nelson children around the dessert table.

Standing near the children was Johnny. Charles had shared with Mary little Johnny's delight with the food baskets he had brought the family. Mary watched Johnny as he loaded up his dinner plate. He was dressed in his Sunday clothes and had a big grin on his face. His cheeks were rosy. Johnny glanced around the area and stopped when his eyes meet Mary's. He smiled. She returned his smile with one of her own. He then ran off to join a group of children sitting on a blanket. Near the children was a young but frail looking woman. *She must be Johnny's mother. And it looks like they are all enjoying themselves. Good.* Mary had been worried about them.

Lizzie returned to the table with a piece of ham, two slices of pie, a piece of cake and several jelly candies. Charles touched Mary's arm lightly as he leaned in and whispered in her ear. "She'll probably have a tummy ache later." Mary nodded in agreement. *Oh well, she will probably think twice the next time.*

Helen turned to Mary. "Your apple pie smells delicious. I never could make a good apple pie. I think I will get a piece before it disappears." *Now I wonder who said the daughter-in-law couldn't make a better apple pie?* Picking up her dinner plate, Helen left the newlyweds alone.

Mary glanced around. She was in awe at the large turnout. "Charles, there are so many people here. I didn't think the town was this large."

"Well, Mrs. Baxter, nobody wants to miss a big shindig."

Mary's eyes widened. "Shindig?" she asked.

"Yes, a dance party," stated Charles with a roguish look in his eyes.

A small group of men walked past the Baxter table. Mr. DeForest stopped in front of them. "Congratulations Mr. and Mrs. Baxter and many happy years ahead of you."

"Thank you, Mr. DeForest. And you will be pleased to know the baby chicks are doing well," Mary replied. *I will have to see about finding a wife for him. He has threatened to get a mail-order-bride on a few occasions. Perhaps, Charlotte would be a good match? I must remember to ask Charles about this.*

As the meal progressed, the gathering seemed to get louder, and anticipation grew for the dancing ahead. The entire crowd seemed to act like one big extended family.

About to finish the last bite of potato salad, Mary saw a large shadow cast onto her dinner plate. She lifted her head to see Harlan McCloud towering above them. He took off his Stetson and held it to his chest. "Ah, I am here to give my congratulations to the new Mr. and Mrs. Baxter. I was glad to see she still married you despite the look of that eye of yours. Ahem, Mrs. Baxter, is he still treating you well?" Harlan chuckled as he glanced back and forth between the two of them. "Now, now, settle down there, Charles. The man who introduced the two of you has the right to check-in and ask." *It seems a long time ago when he introduced us on that dusty street in front of the hotel.*

Charles stopped shifting in his chair. She saw her husband's face change from a frown to half of a smile. "Again, how gallant of you, Mr. McCloud. As a matter of fact, Charles is the best husband a woman could ever ask for. We thank you for our introduction and the good wishes." Mary glanced at her husband. His chest seemed to puff out like a rooster. He chuckled and put in his two cents worth. "Harlan, I thank you too. I can only hope someday you will be as lucky."

Mary bit her lip to keep from smiling as she watched the two of them banter back and forth. *Well, what could the rascal say to that? Serves him right and I hope I am there to see it.*

Harlan choked and stared at them for a moment and then rolled his eyes. "Well, do not hold your breath. And now I believe I will excuse myself so you may finish your dinner, Mr. Baxter." He started to walk away but stopped and turned back. Harlan held Mary's gaze. "Say, Mrs. Baxter, I'm leaving shortly to pick up the new teacher, a Miss Anne Benton. It would be nice if you would introduce yourself to her and help her get settled."

Nodding, she smiled knowing it was difficult for him to ask for a favor. "Certainly, it would be my pleasure."

Adjusting his Stetson back on his head, he stroked his mustache and strolled away.

Whooping and hollering erupted behind Mary. She turned and saw Mr. McCloud Senior had walked to the center of the dance floor. The respect the town had for this man was apparent from the sudden quiet that descended over the crowd.

"Good evening everyone. I am Alastair McCloud, and the town council wants to welcome you all to our Sixteenth Annual Harvest Festival. I hope you have enjoyed the food. The delicious ham and beef were expertly prepared by Mr. Holt of the Crystal Creek Hotel." A boisterous round of applause followed as Mr. McCloud patted his stomach. "Now it is time for the real reason we are all here, the dancing!" A lot more hooting and applause followed and after a few moments, McCloud raised his arms for quiet. "As is the custom, we reserve the first dance for recent newlyweds. I would like to introduce Charles Baxter and his lovely bride Mary."

Mary gasped. Amid a huge round of applause, Charles stood

and took her arm and led her towards the dance floor. Alastair McCloud shook Charles' hand vigorously. "Congratulations!" He leaned into Charles. "Must have been my glowing recommendation letter, which sent you this pretty little filly." Another set of whooping and hollering was heard.

Like father, like son.

Charles held Mary tightly around the waist and whispered, "I love you, Mrs.

Baxter. You are the most wonderful, giving, loving and patient woman. I am truly blessed."

He said he loves me. This quiet man declared his love to me with the eyes of the community on us. And it seems as if my perseverance and patience has proven itself. Faith. Mary smiled into Charles' eyes and whispered, "I love you too, Mr. Baxter." They took their position next to Mr. McCloud. She pinched herself to make certain this was real.

Mr. McCloud waved his hands again. "Also, let us bring out Gary Samson and his sweet bride Wendy."

A shy couple came forward amid more clapping and hollering.

"Wait, wait. We're not done yet. Let's hear it for Bertram and Sylvia Harwick," announced Mr. McCloud.

The couple shuffled out to the middle of the dance floor for their announcement. Bertram swept off his cowboy hat to hold at his heart. Sylvia was demure as she gave him a curtsey.

The music started up, and the dancing began. Mary was still blushing after hearing Charles's declaration of love. She heard the outpouring of congratulations from people as they danced near them.

The first dance had led to several more before they took a rest back at their table. Mary glanced around, and to her surprise, she saw Helen near the middle of the dance floor with the hotel owner, Mr. Holt. The smile on her face told Mary that she was not the only Baxter enjoying the moment. Continuing her glance around the dance floor, she saw Lizzie grinning from ear to ear as Ross twirled her around. The rest of the children giggled in delight as Lizzie danced past. Mary remembered very little about that first dance or the ones that followed except how it felt to have Charles' arms around her.

Sitting next to her, Mary saw the man of her dreams, strong yet gentle at the same time. His touch was intoxicating, and the music flowed over her and wiped away all of her previous fears and concerns. He loved her, and the future held only hope and promise.

THE END

RECIPES

TO MY READERS,

I hope you enjoy reading my book as much as I did writing it. As a result of my many hours of research, I realized how much history teaches us. Whether it is a base to make improvements on – such as science and medical technology developing vaccines to save future generations ... or a realization of the need to return to tried and true practices of old. When we look at today's agriculture production methods, we see the return of organic foods to the marketplace and our tables.

I am also thankful for the convenience of cooking with modern appliances and the fact they have accurate and constant temperature controls. The old methods of testing the oven's temperature for baking was never a happy thought for anyone.

Luckily, one of the things we can see repeated throughout the history of literature is the ever-present enjoyment food. Therefore, I am giving you three recipes from this Western saga of Mary and Charles.

Mary's Nutmeg Jumbles

*Preheat o*ven to 375 degrees

1 cup of butter
    ¼ brown sugar
    ¼ demerara sugar (light gold color)
    ½ cup white sugar
    2 eggs
    Beat the butter, sugar, and eggs well.
    Add 2 cups of flour, plus 2 tablespoons (I use King Arthur
Flour)
    A pinch of salt - ¼ tsp.
    1 ½ teaspoons of cinnamon
    One teaspoon of fresh grated nutmeg.

Add the flour, salt, cinnamon, and nutmeg to the beaten mixture of butter, sugar, and eggs. Mix well. Drop by tablespoons onto a lightly greased tray. (I use Air-Bake trays, no need to grease these.) Bake at 375 degrees. Baking should take approximately 10 to 12 minutes or until there is a very slight brown edge to the cookie. Remove from sheet while hot, and cool. Variations of the jumble can be made with one teaspoon of crushed caraway seeds, or 1/3 teaspoon of rose water (Nielsen-Massey Vanillas, Inc.) – it has a strong flavor, or two tablespoons of lemon juice or 1 ½ teaspoons of vanilla. Enjoy with a cup of tea, coffee or hot apple cider.

Why are these recipes a little different from the norm of today? Well, the wheat flour during the 1800's was made from a different variety of wheat. Also, the processes of milling flour and refining sugar was not the same as it is today. It is for these reasons, I use an unbleached flour and add a small amount of the demerara sugar (this is a less refined sugar). Also, demerara sugar has a slight hint of a caramel flavor – which I am sure Mary and her family liked!

Helen's Chocolate Potato Cake

Preheat oven to 350 degrees.

1 1/2 cups of white sugar
¼ cup brown sugar
¼ cup of demerara sugar
1 cup of butter, cream with sugar
4 egg yolks (keep the 4 egg whites for later)
1 cup of cold mashed Idaho potatoes (**not instant**) – creamed with only ½ cup of milk
2 cups of flour
2/3 cup of cocoa powder
2 teaspoons of baking powder
1 teaspoon of cinnamon
1 teaspoon of nutmeg
(Optional - 1 cup of walnuts broken into small pieces)
Mix all the above ingredients well.
4 egg whites (beaten stiff.) Next, gently fold the egg whites into the above mixture. Pour into a greased tube pan or cake pan. Bake for 50 to 60 minutes, until done depending on your oven and rack placement. When cool, sprinkle powdered sugar on top. You can try using a doily to create a pattern. Enjoy with a nice cup of coffee or tea.

THANK YOU

I hope you have enjoyed reading about Mary and her journey to meet Charles and Lizzie as much as I have enjoyed writing about them.

Follow Martha's newsletter and learn about her other books at WWW.MARTHALINDSAY.COM

SNEEK PEEK: THE COWBOY GETS A LESSON

Beaverton, Montana — late August 1882.

Three blasts of the steam whistle echoed up the canyon walls. The train lurched forward as it started its descent. Anne Benton woke with a start. Her book lay open on her lap ... she must have been taking a short nap. It had been hard to fall asleep lately, and when she did, she only dreamed of the last argument she had with her parents. Although she felt guilty about leaving, she had taken the only course of action left to her. Currently, all she could do was to pray Granmama's investigator would successfully complete his task. Once this was accomplished, Blinkerton Agency results would establish that Anne was correct in all her assumptions. Patience was what she needed now.

She had been traveling to the little town of Crystal Creek, Montana for approximately ten days. The train ride was long and arduous. Every two days Anne would overnight at one of the stops along the way. Granmama had finally given in to Anne's insistence on bringing her horse, Lady, out West with her. Both Anne and Lady enjoyed the much-needed breaks in travel. The layovers gave owner and horse a chance to relax and stretch their legs. Seeing the

new sights gave her a brief introduction to life in the West. Soon
Anne's long-awaited dream would come true – she would
enlighten young minds in the Western Frontier. Crystal Creek
would now have a certified school teacher.

Looking out the window, she saw the train was still passing
through the lower part of the canyon. The late afternoon sun was
already casting shadows into the crevices of the brown and
reddish-orange canyon walls. A portion of the steel-gray clouds in
the sky had seeped into the deeper cracks and seemed to dissipated
when the sun touched the edge of the walls. Layers of darkness sat
on the base of the distant purple mountains. A slight charge of
excitement ran through Anne's body as she continued to glance out
the window. She considered this dramatic change of scenery to be
breathtaking yet somewhat daunting and so very unlike her home
of New York City.

Anne checked her watch pin – it read six o'clock. It was time
to change from her traveling dress into her riding clothes. She got
up and headed to the change room with her carpetbag. With prac-
ticed efficiency, she changed into a split skirt, blouse, jacket, and
boots. It felt good to be rid of that bustle. If she had her way, she
would spend most of her time in a riding outfit. However, such
attire was simply not acceptable for a young lady when she was
living in New York City – yet another reason she was looking
forward to living in the West. She returned to her seat and settled
into the cushions to review portions of her teacher's manual.

The conductor approached from the far side of the car. Anne
leaned over and inserted the manual back into the carpetbag. Next,
she placed her coat over her arm and sat up. Lastly, she straightened her back, for she had been taught good posture said a lot
about a person. Glancing around at the people sitting nearby, she
saw no one else was getting ready to disembark. The thin elderly
conductor stopped in front of her.

"Miss, this is your stop, Beaverton, Montana. When you are
ready to have your horse unloaded, just stand in front of the cargo

car. We'll have a few men assist your handler, Mr. Hayes, with the unloading. I will also see that your trunks are brought over and placed nearby as well."

"Thank you very much, sir. You have been most helpful. I shall be ready when needed." She smiled her appreciation.

"You're quite welcome Miss, and good luck with your teaching."

"I shall do my very best and thank you again."

The conductor smiled, and with a brief tip of his hat, he continued to walk down the aisle. Anne reflected back to when she first boarded the train. It had taken some coordination and several men to assist with the loading of her mare Lady into the cargo car. However, all was well once she was settled in the expanded stall. In the end, even the men watching the loading had expressed their admiration of the good-looking bay Thoroughbred, despite her initial skittishness. Lady's reluctance to load diminished with each break in the trip.

The rumbling noise of the train changed as it slowed down. Soon Anne heard the screeching of breaks and hissing of steam as it finally came to a stop. Gathering up her carpetbag and coat, Anne walked down the narrow aisle to the platform outside of the passenger car. Pausing, she looked around hoping to see someone looking for her. The Beaverton train station was full of men with big hats, guns, spurs, and an unmeasurable amount of dust. There were no children and only a one woman in the vicinity. *Take a breath – now. You're on the Western Frontier!* Stepping down to the boardwalk, she turned and headed to the rear portion of the train to coordinate the unloading of her horse.

The sun was now beginning to set, and Anne picked up her pace … Lady would be impatient to get out of the train. While walking towards the car, she kept an eye out for the escort who was to meet her. According to Mr. Alastair McCloud's last letter – his son Harlan and some of the ranch hands would be accompanying her to Crystal Creek. She continued walking. *I'm certain I gave a good description of myself. Young woman in early twenties – a lady never tells her exact age, wearing a dark chestnut colored split skirt with matching jacket and a cream blouse trimmed with lace.* In his letter, Mr. McCloud described his son as tall, dark brown hair with a big mustache and in his late twenties. The problem was, there were many men here who fit the description. *Oh, wait ... he also said he'd be wearing a black Stetson hat – with a hole in it?*

Looking ahead, she heard a commotion near Lady's cargo car. A moment later, Anne saw the men were starting to unload her mare. *Oh, NO – you're supposed to wait for ME!* Panic set in and Anne rushed towards the car. However, as fate would have it, events had already started to unfold. The cargo door slid open. Young Mr. Hayes had Lady in hand and was trying to soothe the frantic mare. The men on the ground below were shouting for him to let the horse free. It would be better if she navigated the high-walled wooden ramp by herself. Lady let out a loud nicker. Suddenly, loud balling noises erupted from the nearby cattle pen below. Her mare spooked and surged forward, breaking free of the handler's hold. Racing down the ramp, Lady entered a paddock. Immediately, the mare cantered around investigating the sights and smells of her surroundings. As the cattle jostled around in the nearby corral, the mare snorted as a wave of dust came rolling towards her. Anne called out, "EASY, Lady, easy girl. Mr. Hayes – get the lead rope!" Just then a loud gunshot rang out from the nearby saloon. The sound echoed throughout the area! Her mare squealed, spun around and galloped towards the open gate. "SHUT the paddock gate!" Anne shouted as she ran after her horse. Changing course, Anne and the young man headed toward the open exit gate. They were too late. The mare had found her escape. With her head held high and her tail flying out behind her, Lady bolted out of the paddock.

Out of the corner of Anne's eye, a horse and rider galloped past her. She saw the cowboy's lariat swinging around over his head.

With the flip of his wrist, a loop of rope flew out of the rider's hand. A moment later, Lady's neck was caught within the rope's circle. The rider's horse slid to a stop, and Anne's horse was jerked to a halt. Another cloud of dust formed. Again, Lady called out with a squeal. Anne's heart felt as if it had stopped. Watching the sides of her mare heave in and out, Anne became infuriated. She shouted at the top of her lungs, "STOP! STOP! ... BE CAREFUL OF HER!" However, her words were engulfed by the noise of the nearby crowd. They were cheering the cowboy's quick and accurate capture of the runaway horse.

As the dust finally started to settle, the cowboy turned to her. "Miss, stop where you are! This is a wild and scared horse!!" Quickly, he turned back to the crowd. "Who owns this animal, anyway?" he shouted.

Anne slowed her running down to a walk and stepped up to her trembling horse. "Easy Lady. Easy, girl," she said in a soothing tone. She reached up and stroked her mare neck.

The cowboy quickly turned back to address her, "Miss!!...."

"Excuse me, SIR! This is MY horse!!" Anne announced. Turning, she picked up the end of the lead rope and drew the running noose off of Lady's neck. Marching over to the cowboy, she narrowed her eyes and looked up at him. He said nothing. Anne grew more irritated as she watched the brute slowly reel in his now loose rope. Finally, he looked down at her and raised an eyebrow. He swept his hat off of his head – held it to his broad chest and gave a slight bow. "Miss Anne Benton, I presume?"

Anne's jaw dropped. It was then she saw the hole in his black cowboy hat.

ACKNOWLEDGMENTS

I would like to thank my wonderful husband for his constant love and support. Many years ago, when we were at horse shows, I remember how you would bring a romance novel for me to read while I waited for my classes. As you were aware, there was always lots of time for the 'hurry up and wait' at the arena gate. You are the best of husbands, thank you for inspiring me to write. I am a lucky woman.

I would also like to thank my parents whose help was essential to this book. And, thank you for the family motto – through hard work comes achievement and enjoyment ... and telling me to always keep a sense of humor.

In addition, I would like to thank my Auntie Robin for instilling in me the valuable role of the written word, the consistent use of a good dictionary and thesaurus and most importantly your shared bits of wisdom. To my two daughters, thank you for your support as I researched my material. I have to admit, I do have a bit of a fetish with the accuracy of historical detail. Most often extensive research brings to light a deeper understanding – and, oh, do I appreciate being born in this day and age....